WHAT

Romeo and Juliet's families caused all sorts of problems, but the two lovers took that poison themselves, the idiots.

When Beth Ellingson meets Ethan Brooks, it's because her aunt and father are conspiring to steal the Birch Creek Ranch from the handsome young man. It wasn't the cutest way to meet, but just as roses grow best when fertilized with manure, sometimes beauty springs from tragedy.

Beth's father's definitely a stinker, and she wants to spare Ethan the misery of affiliating with him. But Ethan's never been afraid of a fight when the cause is just. Can these two young but beloved Birch Creek characters find their happily ever after? Or will the biggest surprise of their young lives derail all their plans and poison their future?

THE SURPRISE

B. E. BAKER

Purple
Puppy
Publishing

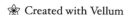

For Eli,
my inspiration for Ethan

You're a good kid.

Learn to roll with the surprises in life,
and you won't have anything else to learn from me.

❧ I ❧

BETH

Some people love school.

You read about that kind of person all the time. The poor, beleaguered little kid whose parents don't appreciate her, but who effortlessly solves sums, who reads books for fun, and who is always tutoring other people as some kind of charity effort. Sometimes the rich guy, or the athletic guy, or the handsome frat boy they're tutoring falls in love with them. Sometimes they have some major moral dilemma, because if they want to get what they need, they have to help someone else cheat.

But the heroine of every story is inevitably a brilliant student. A gifted inventor. An epic pianist or composer. Someone truly remarkable in every way. It didn't take me long to realize that I'm not the kind of person people write stories about.

School is boring.

School is long.

School is full of memorization of boring facts I will *never* use again.

I made it more than ten years before I had to learn what a *kilojoule* was, and I'm quite sure that if I live to be a hundred, I'll make it that long without ever needing to use what I learned about it.

The only exception to this rule is the girl-next-door heroine whose parents are always pressuring her to do better. Her heroic attempts to learn are never quite enough, no matter how hard she tries.

Unfortunately, that's not me either.

My dad wasn't really that interested in pursuing a formal education, and my parents never seemed too surprised or upset that I wasn't high caliber either. They kind of took it for granted that I'm not the kind of person who raises her hand to answer a question voluntarily.

The only person in my life who ever even suggested that I should go to college was my brilliant aunt, who seemed to sort of assume that I would be a genius, like her. I'm pretty sure the only reason she even suggested I apply was that she'd been living in another state for most of my life and hadn't heard much about my lackluster grades or my unenthusiastic performance at, well, at everything. Like everyone else, I just sort of assumed I'd be stuck here forever.

And it's not because I'm some kind of small-town zealot.

When I first started high school, I desperately wanted to leave Manila, population four hundred. It's one of those places where everyone knows everyone else and always has. I've memorized the outside of every house. If someone changed the color of the exterior from, say, blue, to yellow? It would be the talk of the town for weeks.

I've met the people who live in each residence down the main road, from my third grade teacher to the bus driver to the lady who runs the True Value. I even know all the ones everyone whispers about. The people who don't paint their shutters when they're peeling and who burn their trash because they can't afford to pay for pickup. Everyone talks about that stuff, even when they've already been talking about it for years.

Because there's literally nothing else to do.

Thanks to my consistently underwhelming grades for the past nine years, my parents just assumed that I wouldn't bother with the SAT, and that I wouldn't even apply to any decent colleges. So when I signed up for the SAT myself, and when my score was halfway decent, and when my grades came up enough to be acceptable, and when I told them I had applied to UCLA, they were absolutely floored. My mom always assumed that I'd do just what she did and marry someone who would take care of me. Even though Dad's been a big disappointment, for some reason she still thought I'd put all my eggs in some guy's basket and hope for the best.

When Dad heard I applied for UCLA, he assumed it was because some guy I liked was going there. When I told him I meant to study photography and apply to work at National Geographic, or maybe become a photographer for an online magazine or publication, he laughed in my face.

So when our principal told us there was a college class we could take on exchange through a local online university that would transfer for credit, my hand was the first one to shoot up. Maybe if I took a college class and still managed to get a decent grade,

3

my parents would finally believe that I could handle this. Which is how I wound up signing up for a psychology class.

About a week into courses, I learned something that seemed bizarre. It was a principle called the illusory truth effect, and it's a psychological phenomenon that explains that humans are more likely to believe something, even something untrue, if they've heard it over and over. Even if it's something the subjects knew was false at the outset, if they heard it enough, they'd change their beliefs.

It sounded wrong at first, frankly, but once I looked into the experiments behind it, it blew my mind. Apparently the conditioned response that changes a lie to truth in the human mind is just as effective with adults as it is with kids.

For instance, even if someone grew up in a cattle ranching town, and they have known their entire life that a baby cow's called a calf, but they heard over and over for a few weeks that a baby *horse* was called a calf instead, when they were tested, they'd either be unsure which was right, or they'd have changed their mind to believe the horse definition.

I couldn't help thinking about how that would impact children whose parents had nothing good to say about them.

If a girl's parents acted, for her entire life, like she was a worthless piece of trash, she would eventually believe it. And then, even if someone else told her she was great, even if they told her several times, that girl probably wouldn't be convinced. That actual truth would need a *lot* of oomph to dislodge the illusory truth.

And when people think they're worthless?

4

That's also how they act.

Often those people who are dealing with situations like this, who believe they aren't worth much, spend their entire lives looking for someone who thinks they're special. They'll cling to the person who tells them that, as if that person is the only person on earth who can save them.

Because they know it's not true, but they wish terribly that it was.

Even kicked dogs want someone to pat their head. Even losers with bad grades and a difficult time focusing want a bright future. Deep down inside, we all want to be worthwhile.

We all want to be loved.

If only I'd known that I *was* lovable before it was too late.

ETHAN

College is where you go when, instead of learning about life, you want to learn the things people *write* about life in books.

Sadly, I've never liked to learn that way.

When I was younger, my mom and dad would sit and read for hours sometimes. I'd come into the family room, ready to talk about my day, but they'd both have their noses tucked into books. I'd ask a few questions and they'd answer them, doing their best not to look annoyed, but I knew that I was keeping them from learning and experiencing the world in the very way they liked to do it.

I was more of a walk-around-and-pick-flowers-and-dig-holes kind of kid. I wanted to learn about the sunshine by feeling it on my face. I wanted to learn about stinging nettle by letting it bite into the skin of my palms. And I wanted to find out about chemical reactions by watching them happen in a beaker instead of reading about the results in a textbook.

So when I was facing the great high school question head on—what are you doing when you graduate?—I wanted to close my eyes and hide. Or run away. But then a slow-talking lawyer called and offered me a golden ticket. I happened to overhear a conversation between the lawyer and my mom, where he explained that my great-uncle Jed had died, and he had left us kids a massive cattle ranch. . .if we moved out here and worked it for a year.

I knew Mom would never agree to doing something like that instead of attending a four-year college. Desk jobs like hers are more transferrable in the storms of life, as evidenced by her ability to work remotely, to support her family by tapping along on her computer in the middle of nowhere. She basically turns her thoughts into money.

Of course she wants that same kind of stability for her kids.

But by some crazy miracle, she listened to me, and we're here, and it feels like I can breathe again. Kevin and Jeff are the nicest guys, and for months now, they've been showing me how to do everything patiently and calmly.

Repeatedly, too, for a lot of things.

Honestly though, lots of ranch tasks have come easily to me. Driving a tractor isn't that different from driving a car. Fixing a fence is pretty much basic common sense, once you know how to use wire cutters, a level, and a post hole digger. I learned a lot of the things I needed to know about equipment repairs from working part time for my friend Alex in high school. He fixed up four wheelers and dirt bikes in his dad's shop after hours, and I helped.

It may be wishful thinking on my part, but it feels like even my mom's happier here. Actually, *freer* might be a better word. She always looked drained back home. But here, she's stuck going outside every day for some task or other, from collecting eggs and refilling animal feed, to helping me trim cow hooves. She may not like a lot of the things we do, but she comes back with sun on her face, wind-blown hair, and a calmer attitude. She's often covered in mud, too, but some people say that's good for your skin, right?

My one complaint is that even my mom has made more friends than I have. Manila doesn't exactly boast a happening night life, and since the two college classes I'm taking are online, there's no way to meet kids my age who live close.

Somehow my mom has still met tons of people, and tonight she's hosting a dinner party. I'm not annoyed by the dinner—it's nice she has friends— but I wish I had someone to invite over.

We all know the second that people start to arrive.

Roscoe, our border collie, loses his mind. He's actually a pretty cool dog. He's busy, and he's a little emotional, but it's nice to have a big, shaggy bouncer around to alert us of intruders. On a place this big, without some kind of alarm, people could be here for an hour before I even knew they'd arrived.

I consider hiding in my room until Mom calls us for dinner. I'm supposed to write a paper on Shake-speare's *Romeo and Juliet,* and I wonder whether I could use that as an excuse.

So far, I've only written one line.

Romeo and Juliet's parents were a problem, but the real idiots were the lovers themselves. At the end of the day, they're the ones who drank poison instead of facing the future with bravery and strength.

⚜

I wonder whether it's too obvious if I write about my dad's death and how my mom, who loved him dearly, kept going for her kids as well as for herself. It feels like a much braver move, and frankly, a much nicer love letter to my dad than rolling over and giving up. But before I can write another single word, I hear an unfamiliar voice. A girl's voice.

A *teenage*-sounding voice.

My heart beats a little faster in my chest and my breaths come quicker. Is there a girl here? Who is she? I hop to my feet and walk through my door without even thinking. Gabe and a little kid I've never seen before shoot past me and duck into the room I've just vacated, not even seeming to notice that I'm standing here. I'm pretty sure they're about to blow up the room like a bomb went off, but for once, maybe I don't care.

"I've heard good things, young lady," my mom says.

"I'm Beth."

Beth.

The name rolls around in my head like a marble —cold, hard, and shiny.

I start to walk through the doorway, but then I pause. Maybe I should listen to her for a moment before I charge into the room like a bull. Then I could form an impression of her before seeing her face.

"You're a little older than my Izzy," Mom says.

That's promising.

"But I hope you'll keep an eye out for her, and for Amanda's two daughters as well." Mom acts like they're headed for inner city Chicago instead of a tiny town where their biggest threat is a bully taking their Cheetos. I guess you can take the mom out of Houston, but you can't take the Houston out of the mom.

"Sure," Beth says. "I'm sure they won't need help finding anything. Manila High School's not exactly large."

Ha. She had the same thought as me.

"I could hardly believe it when I found out they had the six upper-level grades at the same school," Mom says. "But Izzy's happy that she and Emery will be at the same place with Whitney joining them next year."

"You have three kids?" Beth asks. "Is that right?"

Three kids? This feels like an auspicious time to make my entrance. I stroll through the doorway. "Four." I finally see the face that matches the voice I've been listening to like a dehydrated castaway on a desert island.

I can't decide whether she's really as beautiful as she looks, or whether I'm just starved for teenage attention.

Her hair's just a little bit curly, right at the ends, and it frames a heart shaped face with huge, almost anime-like eyes. They're a dark, soft brown, and the blonde tips of her hair make them look even warmer, like the summer sunshine on a hay field.

Oh, no. I'm worried my brain's shutting down. I need to say something quickly, or she'll think I'm a half-wit.

"I'm Ethan," I say. Good. My name. I remembered my own name. It's a start. "I'm the black sheep of my family."

Black sheep? Can I only speak in farm cliches, now? And why black? Where did that come from? I'm not a bad boy. Although, I did fight with Mom over attending her version of college. Maybe that's what my brain meant.

"More like a black ox," Mom says.

Ah, she's saying I'm big. That makes me look good. Girls like big guys, right? And now I'm preening like an idiot. I need to make a joke. "But I know what noise a sheep makes," I say. Then I baa. Like I think I'm Old MacDonald. My utter lack of social interaction with people my age has broken my brain. "What sound would an ox make?"

Beth should be cringing.

She should be looking at me with a scrunched nose and a dangling mouth, wondering how stupid this new kid really is.

Only, she's not, and I realize something.

She's stuck on the same desert as me.

There can't be many teenage guys here, and that means I'm a tall glass of water in the middle of nothing. That's the only explanation for her expression. She's giggling.

"Oxen complain about everything and break stuff all the time," Izzy says from the kitchen. "And they don't go to college like they should."

"Hey." Sisters suck. Why would she out me like that, seconds after I meet someone new? "I'm taking online classes."

"We all know. You haven't gone a single day without whining about them," Mom says.

It's like they've all had meetings where they planned to make me look idiotic the second a teenage girl shows up.

"I can't wait for college," Beth says. "Like, I'm literally counting down the days."

"You don't say." Mom's beaming now. "Well, come right in, Beth. How do you feel about handsome oxen?"

Oh, no. I'm going to kill her. My very own mother—I can practically see my face splashed across the front of the local paper. **Big City Boy Snaps and Murders Lawyer Mom.**

Except, Beth giggles again. "Can't say that I've met an ox before now." She just agreed that I'm handsome. I love my mother. She's brilliant. "Mostly here, we just grow pigs."

And now I'm laughing.

"Pigs aren't as bad as I thought they were," I say. "Our next door neighbor, Miss Saddler, has a pretty cute one."

Beth arches one eyebrow. "The ones at school are not housebroken. They love mud, and they eat anything, and it shows."

And I'm laughing again. Mom gives me that look that means she'd like some adult time, and I'm old enough to know that doesn't really include me. Not yet, anyway. I follow the other kids into the living room. Gabe and his friend are still in my room, making a huge mess, I'm sure. Normally, I'd head in there so I could get credit for keeping an eye on them, but not today. Not with Beth here.

"So you're in high school?" Beth asks, looking at the girls she was tasked to keep an eye on.

Izzy shakes her head. "Not yet. Well, I wouldn't be at home, anyway. I'm in eighth grade."

"I'm in high school," Maren says. "Starting my sophomore year."

"I'm about to start my senior year," Beth says.

That seems to annoy Maren, for some reason. Maybe she's not keen on being replaced as queen bee. Like in Victorian England, maybe being older is somehow better?

"So you're seventeen?" Izzy asks.

"I'll be eighteen in January."

"You're almost the same age as Ethan," Emery says.

Beth looks a little confused. "So you're a senior too?"

"My birthday was two days ago," I say. "I barely made the cut off for kindergarten—graduated from high school a few months ago."

"But you're basically the same," Emery says.

Beth blushes, for some reason.

"Maybe everyone should introduce themselves," I say. "It's a lot of kids to meet all at once."

"I'm Ethan's little sister," Izzy says, always quick to jump in and boss people around. "I'm next oldest in the family. And I ride horses a lot."

"Okay," Beth says.

"That's my little sister, Whitney." Izzy looks like an English teacher when she straightens up, her shoulders square, and points. "She's still at the

13

elementary school, but only for another two years. She's in fifth grade."

"You met Gabe already," I say. "Or at least, you saw him."

"He and Aiden went to play?" Beth asks.

I nod. "That's the fourth kid in our family. He's going into second grade. He's seven."

"And you two are. . .cousins?" Beth asks.

Emery nods. "Our dads were brothers. I'm Emery, and I'm in seventh grade." She looks down at her feet. "It's weird that I'll be at the same school as Maren."

Poor Emery. She always looks either elated or depressed. I guess we've switched to depressed for now. Sometimes it's hard to keep up.

"I'm Maren." She sighs heavily, as if everything around her is a huge imposition. "I'm a cheerleader."

"Wait, already?" Beth asks.

Maren rolls her eyes. "The school told my mom that tryouts will be next week. I can't imagine I won't make it out here."

Beth blinks, clearly unsure what to do with such a snotty reply.

Maren has that effect on people, but it's not like I can explain with her standing right here.

"Who wants to play Twister?" Whitney yanks the box off the shelf and pulls the mat out. It's her favorite game right now, and she begs people to play most days. Usually she's stuck playing with just Emery, who never seems to be able to say no, even though she always loses.

It's kind of funny watching them try to spin the round dial and play at the same time. Yesterday, Emery fell over while trying to spin the dial, knocking Whitney over in the process. Whitney berated her for a full five minutes.

And then they started over.

Because for Emery, the only thing scarier than being yelled at by Whitney is letting her down. Our family's interesting.

"Sure," Beth says. "I'll play."

"Me too," I say.

Whitney's jaw dangles and her eyes widen. "Wait. Ethan?"

I'm going to kill her. "I play sometimes."

"Never. You play never," Izzy says.

Apparently, I'm going to be sisterless soon. Will that be sad? Or will it be a community service? I grit my teeth. "I played last month. Remember?"

"Can you play with this many people?" Beth asks.

"You can," Whitney says. "We get all set up, and then we all get individual colors picked for us."

"Who runs the spinner?" Beth asks.

"Me," Maren says. "Because there's no way I'm going to get all tangled up with you guys. Especially if Ethan's playing. He's so big that if he falls, he'll smoosh you all into jelly."

Do all my siblings and my cousins really hate me? Or are they just so naturally obnoxious that they can't help it?

"Okay, let's go." Whitney shoves the spinner at Maren and smooths the board. "I'll go first."

Maren's the worst possible person to have spin. She doesn't really spin it randomly. She'll look at the board and come up with strange colors that are impossible and flick it to land on those.

She's one-third demon, I'm sure of it.

"Alright, yellow." Maren purses her lips. "Who's next?"

"Me," Emery says.

Maren doesn't even bother spinning. "Red."

"Hey," Izzy says. "You didn't even spin it."

"It's a waste of time at the beginning. You just need to get on the mat."

Izzy rolls her eyes. The only thing she hates more than being bossed around is being bossed around by Maren. "Fine. Me next."

"Blue." Maren looks like she's planning something. That's never good.

Emery's standing on the far side, with Whitney facing her on the front of the mat. Izzy steps onto the blue dot on the far end, making them into a weird kind of isosceles triangle.

"You next," Maren says, glaring at me. "Green."

"I think you should start spinning it now," Beth says.

All of us freeze. No one tells Queen Maren what to do. We expect her to rip Beth a new one or freak out and storm off.

But all Maren does is glare, look down at the spinner and flick it, shake it until it stops on green, and then say, drolly, "Green."

Beth laughs.

Not a *you're so stupid* laugh. But an *alright, you got me* laugh.

And wonder of wonders, Maren laughs with her. Beth tamed the beast.

I take a step and drop my right foot on the far corner on a green circle. "Alright."

"Beth," Maren says. She flicks the spinner. "Yellow."

Beth, being polite, carefully picks the dot that's one away from Whitney, and one away from me. Even so, she's facing me, with her foot poked inward to the second row in the mat.

For the first time in weeks, I actually like Maren. There's no way she didn't plan that.

"My turn again," Whitney says.

"Blue," Maren says. She definitely didn't spin it that time.

Whitney frowns, but doesn't argue, dropping her free foot on the blue, facing inward. She's a Twister pro, and she knows not to get your feet crossed at the beginning.

"Emery," Maren says. "Blue."

"Hey," Emery says. "You have to spin."

Maren's smile is devilish as she flicks the spinner and it lands on blue. It's not too hard to manipulate a plastic spike in a piece of cardboard, as it turns out. "Blue."

Emery huffs, but she pivots at an angle, both her feet at a diagonal to one another.

"Izzy," Maren says, "you're yellow."

Izzy rolls her eyes, but steps onto the yellow.

"Ethan, blue."

I'm starting to regret letting Maren pilot this. "Fine." I stretch a bit, but my foot slides past Izzy and finds the second blue dot. I'm straddling the yellow line, but it's fine.

"Beth, blue." Maren's grinning like an insane person. No one should have that much fun telling other people what to do.

"I think after this you have to spin it," Beth says. "And I mean, really spin it."

"Agreed," Izzy says. "No more puppet master crap."

Sometimes my sister sounds so much like my mom that it's almost painful.

"Fine." Maren says.

But Beth turns, sliding her free foot onto the middle blue dot—the only one left. Our legs brush, and even through the pants leg, I swear something electric shoots up my spine.

I drag in a breath as quietly as I can, hoping no one notices.

"What's wrong with you?" Izzy asks. "We're not even to the fun part yet."

With sisters, there is literally no time when something you hope won't be noticed goes unnoticed. Never.

If you pick your nose, expect everyone to be alerted. If you toot, just admit it to the whole room. One of them will rat you out for sure. If you drop something and make a mess, they'll trumpet it to the world. Or snap a photo and send it to the group chat with a joke about oxen breaking things.

"Nothing's wrong," I say. "Mind your business."

"Mind your *own* business," Izzy says. "*Mind your business* makes you sound idiotic."

"I say that," Beth says.

I stifle my laugh. Izzy hates being laughed at— actually, most people probably hate it, but for Izzy, it's like trapping a black cat firecracker in a bottle. The insides explode, the glass fills with smoke, and then everything turns black.

It's bad all around.

"It needs that extra word." Izzy lifts her chin and her eyes slew sideways. "But whatever."

"Whitney, red." Maren looks practically angelic.

Whitney bends over and drops a hand next to Emery's on a red dot. That was ridiculously easy. Maybe Maren really is spinning it.

"Emery, blue."

Maren's little sister sticks her foot between both of Whitney's to touch a blue dot. Pretty painless, still.

"Why didn't they just move their feet?" Beth's understandably confused. With families as big as ours, we gave up on traditional Twister rules years ago.

"You have to keep three things down at all times," I say. "So now it's about to get much more interesting. We have to hit the right color, but we can only lift one thing in favor of something else."

"And you can have more than one person on the same dot," Whitney says. "But if either of you falls off the color, or if your elbows or knees touch the mat, or if you fall, you're out."

Beth's brow furrows.

"Izzy, green."

"Are you actually spinning these?" Izzy asks. "Because—"

"I saw her," Emery says.

No one questions Emery, because she and Maren don't often agree.

Izzy compresses her lips and crouches down, sliding her arm past my leg to reach the green dot between Beth and me.

"You better be careful," I say.

"Or what?" Izzy bumps me, shoving me up closer to Beth.

My heart races, and I can't remember why I was threatening her.

"Ethan, green."

"But he's already on green," Beth says.

"I have to find another green dot," I say, already crouching down like Spiderman, looking for a way to snake my arm past Izzy and Beth to reach a green dot. It puts my face right next to Beth's hip, but I manage it.

And I'm thinking nice thoughts about Maren, for once.

Beth has a very nice hip, and I could stare down the length of her thigh all day. It's nice to have an excuse.

"Stop drooling," Maren says, "or I'll kick you out."

And now equilibrium is restored. I hate her again.

"Beth," Maren says nonchalantly, as if she didn't just attack me and make me feel like an idiot, "red."

There's no way she's spinning this.

No.

Way.

Beth cringes a bit, shoving her face right next to my shoulder, and reaching as well as she can, but as she stretches, she bumps me hard, and I shove Izzy, unintentionally, but she falls forward, knocking me forward, right into Beth.

I would totally have smashed her flat, but years of push-ups finally pay off. I manage to hit the floor with the heels of my hands, hovering over Beth by a mere inch. Her eyes are on mine, her breath short and shallow. She licks her lips, and my eyes drop to her mouth.

"Whoa," Izzy says in my ear. "I had no idea you were so strong. Can you do a push-up with me on your back?"

All my excitement, all my glee at how impressive I look, deflates. It's hardly like a moment from a movie, where the guy and the girl lock eyes and feel a zing.

I have a twelve-year-old, pain-in-the-neck sister on my back, and there's another one staring at me with a look of triumph. But when I look down at Beth, she's wide-eyed and I can feel her breath on my face.

I forget all about the girls and their drama. This is awesome.

❦ 3 ❧
BETH

I've been asked out three times in my life.

The first time, it was the guy who used to bite everyone in kindergarten. He stopped biting people, thankfully, but his face was always covered with acne. We had both just turned fifteen, and he and I bumped into each other in the lunch line.

"Wanna go see a movie some time?" He had mumbled the words while looking down, his skin flushing even redder than usual.

"Huh?" I had asked.

"Never mind," he had mumbled, just before sprinting toward the other end of the lunch room.

It had taken me about ten seconds to review the interaction in my mind and realize that he'd asked me out.

The second time, I had just come out of the girls' bathroom—also at school—and a bunch of people were laughing. This time, the guy asking was pretty cute.

Only, I'm a fairly tall girl.

And this guy was a solid four inches shorter than me.

"Hey, Beth." He had shoved his hands in his pockets and forced a pained smile. "I hear you're not dating anyone. Wanna change that?"

I wasn't sure what to say. Was he asking me on a date? Or to be his girlfriend? He was in my math class, my history class, and my computer class, and I'd never even had a conversation about anything other than the pencil sharpener in the eight years I'd known Rylan.

"Why aren't you answering? What's wrong with me?" he had asked. "You think you can do better?"

I shook my head.

"You're a ho anyway."

"I like hoes," I muttered. "They keep me from crouching over when I'm working in the garden."

The crowd of boys had burst out laughing.

Rylan never met my eyes again, but I'm pretty sure he tripped me a week later in PE.

The third time was a year ago, and it wasn't at school. I'd gone back to Seattle to visit my grandparents, and they'd had some friends over. Their friends had their grandson with them, and he was two years older than me.

Jackson.

He was tall. He had dark, dark brown hair and bright green eyes. He had walked onto the back porch and gestured for me to follow him. It was such a smooth, confident move that I went without even thinking about it.

"You're better looking than I thought you'd be," he had said.

I frowned at that. He thought I'd be ugly?

"My dorm's getting fumigated, so I came home for the weekend, but Mom and Dad went out of town and sicced my grandparents on me, like they think I need a babysitter."

"You're in college?" I asked.

His smile was cocky. "Just started at the University of Washington."

It's a good school—or so my grandparents had said. "What year?"

"Freshman," he said. "But I have some AP credit, so really, I'm like a sophomore."

"That's cool."

"Alright," he said. "You can come with me."

"Huh?" I asked.

"I'm about to bail on this." He threw his thumb over his shoulder at the dinner my grandparents were preparing inside. "And I'll take you with me." He hopped over the porch rail and started for his car.

"Wait."

He turned back and tilted his head. "What? You afraid your parents'll get mad?"

I was, yeah, but also, I didn't even know him. Where was he going? What would we be doing? I felt like he ought to at least tell me that much.

He shrugged. "Doesn't want to go on a date with a college boy." He snorted. "Strange kid after all."

I wasn't totally clear that I had been asked out, but he did say a date.

That word—date—made my stomach flip. Jackson looked *nothing* like the teens I was used to seeing. He was tall, he had broad shoulders, and his hair was long and shaggy and kept falling across his eyes. Plus, for some reason I couldn't pinpoint, I

24

hated that he called me *kid*, and I wanted to show him that I wasn't one. "I'll come."

I hopped the balcony too, twisting my ankle as I landed, and gritting my teeth so it wouldn't show. "Where are we going?"

"You'll see."

It wound up being a really irritating party thrown by a few of his obnoxious friends. Other than me, there were only two other girls, compared to about six guys. I spent the first hour saying 'no' to everything the teens there offered me. And then I wound up calling my grandma and asking her to come pick me up.

Basically, until now, my love life has been pretty disappointing. In fact, if you asked me about it, I'd tell you that. Romance in a small town is practically nonexistent. What there is of it is lousy.

But now?

With Ethan's gorgeous face hovering over mine, his breath warming my face, his muscles taut and trembling above me. . . Who cares how sad things were before? His lips are only a few inches away and I can't help staring at them.

He notices, and his eyes drop to my mouth.

"All three of you are out now," Whitney says. "Get off the mat."

"Thank gosh," Izzy says. "I'm sick of this stupid game." She climbs off his back, jostling him, and Ethan compensates by rolling to the outside, freeing me.

Sadly.

And moments after the game ends, with Whitney and Emery duking it out until the bitter end, it's time to eat.

Growing up, my family almost never ate together. Mom would order takeout, or sometimes she'd cook something, and then Dad would eat when he came in from outside. Mom rarely ate much dinner, preferring to hide in her room, usually drunk, and I'd eat alone.

In front of the television.

The few times we ate together, usually when someone like Aunt Donna came back home for some reason, it was always awkward. I felt like I had to make sure someone was talking, so I'd ramble on, only to have Mom snap at me to stop saying dumb things. Nothing I said was clever, and no one pretended otherwise.

I'm sure there are some great things about being an only child, but sitting here, surrounded by the noise and chaos of all these siblings and cousins, I can't think of a single one.

I've seen scenes in movies where someone crowd surfed at a concert. They'd fall off the stage and an ocean of hands would hold them up, while they bounced and traveled around, lifted by a sea of people. That's how I feel at dinner. Like here, no matter what you say or do, someone will lift you up, carrying the conversation along boisterously.

Four girls, three boys including Aiden, and a bevy of adults. All of them chattering, making jokes, and smiling. No one even seems to notice that I'm not talking, and it's warm in a way I don't recall ever experiencing.

"You were tripped?" Ethan says. "Or you wore those new purple converse you've been dying to wear that are still too big, and you stumbled over your own feet?"

Izzy scowls. "They aren't too big."

"They aren't? Ugh, that's even worse. Are you telling me you really do have clown feet?" He's grinning ear to ear.

Izzy's scowling, but you can tell she's not *really* mad. "It's good to have career options," Izzy says. "Unlike some people, I have a bright future."

Ethan rolls his eyes, and then Whitney takes up the charge, telling him that cowboys stopped being cool at least a hundred years ago. But even when they poke fun at him, you can tell they love him. And he loves them, too.

"Beth, are there any teachers my girls need to watch out for?" Abigail asks. "You're the only person here with any inside information." She's smiling, so I can tell she's at least half-kidding.

"Mrs. Abbott is pretty nice," I say. "She teaches English. But Mrs. Fisher is really, really strict. I hated her class freshman year."

"It sounds like there may not be any other options," Abigail says. "Is that right?"

I nod. "That's the bad thing about a tiny school, I guess. Not many chances to change classes."

Abigail sighs. "Well, if you survived her, hopefully they can, too."

"I'm sure your girls are much smarter than me," I say. "They'll probably be her favorite students."

"Oh, I don't know about that," Ethan says. "You look really smart, and Izzy here had trouble last night tying her shoelaces."

"I had trouble changing the laces out, because Gabe put a knot in them." Izzy kicks Ethan. "I can tie them just fine."

27

"Ow," Ethan says. "They say the truth hurts, so I'll let you decide who to believe, Beth."

I'm laughing now, too. "I always thought I was missing out, not having a brother." I twist my lips. "Now I'm thinking maybe not."

Izzy and Whitney clap and jeer.

Ethan cocks one eyebrow at me. "Just when I thought she was nice and sweet."

"Nice and sweet are overrated traits," Whitney says. "Get some spiky-toed boots and join the rest of us." Her smirk is half terrifying, half inspiring.

"My mom has ruined them," Ethan says. "She's raising two little man-eating lion cubs."

"Ruined?" Abigail arches one eyebrow. "In what way are lionesses bad?"

"They kill most of the meals to feed the entire pack," Steve says. "I think that lionesses are probably the most under-celebrated of all animals."

Ethan rolls his eyes. "Dude. Really?"

Steve chuckles. "I could say the same to you."

"My friend's dog had puppies last year," Izzy says. "Her lab had fourteen puppies." She looks around the room, daring anyone to argue with her. "Anyway, when I went to visit, the puppies were all six weeks old, and a few of the puppies kept attacking their mom."

"Attacking?" Abigail asks.

Izzy nods. "Biting, snapping, growling. Attacking. Anyway, they did it to get the mom's attention." She smirks. "Just like Ethan does." She turns toward me. "Don't worry. He loves lionesses as much as anyone. He just likes to growl about it to get some attention."

"Attention's hard to come by around here," Ethan

says. "I have to fight for it any way I can." He tilts his head, and I can't help noticing how handsome he is in an effortless way. Unkempt blonde hair. Expressive face. Eyes that almost disappear when he smiles because they squint up so much. "Imagine how nice it is to be an only child. No snapping and biting and attacking at all."

I open my mouth to say that it's not that great.

But Gabe jabs Ethan's upper arm just below his shoulder with a fork before I can.

"Hey." Ethan yanks the fork out of his hand and chucks it at his little brother's head.

Now Gabe's crying and turning toward his mother to make Ethan look even more villainous.

So maybe things aren't *quite* perfect.

Still, I'd take this mostly well-intentioned chaos over my miserable silence any day. And twice on Saturdays.

"These rolls are amazing," Aunt Donna says.

Amanda reaches into the basket in the center of the table and feels around. "Looks like they're all gone."

"There are more on the pan." Abigail starts to stand.

"I'll get them." I grab the basket and hop up, racing toward the oven. It's hard to be helpful in this group. Everyone's so quick to do things. Since I didn't make the meal, refilling the roll basket feels like the least I can do.

While I'm busy, the conversation gallops off in another direction. It's such a startling contrast to my usual dinner, eaten alone in front of the television, that I can't help myself.

Abigail, Ethan, Emery, Izzy, and Gabe are all on

one side of the table. I know Whitney's technically their other sibling and not Emery, but it's close enough. I pull out my phone and frame up a photo—the light from the front windows makes the whole room glow. Everyone's smiling—Izzy and Abigail are laughing, their heads thrown back. Ethan's smirking, and Gabe has a look of righteous indignation on his face. Emery looks pleasantly involved, like the Mona Lisa of the scene.

I snap a photo, like an outsider looking into a Norman Rockwell painting, and slide my phone back into my pocket.

"Where are those rolls?" Amanda asks. "Please tell me there really are more."

She doesn't look like someone who usually eats rolls, but I can see why she'd make an exception for these.

Excess roll demands notwithstanding, dinner's pretty much over. Abigail starts pointing and her children hop up to start cleaning with just a little grumbling. Even when my aunt Donna tries to load the dishwasher for them, they refuse her help and do it themselves. They're moving around me so quickly with such a sense of purpose that I feel pretty out of place.

"So how's school?" Maren asks me when I sit again.

"Huh?" I ask. "Oh, it's fine."

"Be honest. Are the guys hot?"

I can't help curling my lip.

"No?" Maren blinks. "Because I've met a lot of adults who seem pretty good-looking for their age."

"Who?" I can't help the shock in my tone.

Maren lowers her voice. "That vet, the doctor."

I laugh. "Dr. Dutton and Dr. Archer." I'm careful to keep my voice low, but I can't help noticing that Maren's mom and Ethan's mom kind of scooped up the most eligible bachelors in town within minutes of arrival. I shake my head. "Neither of them have children. The guys at our school are. . .disappointing."

"So, like, would Ethan be considered hot?"

As if he's a dog who just heard the word 'treat,' Ethan's head perks up and turns toward me. He smiles.

So, of course, I lie. "Probably not."

His face falls a little.

"What college do you want to go to?" Maren asks.

"Huh?"

"You said you can't wait to go to school." She sighs. "Mom's pressing me to get some plan together, and I just don't want to deal with it. Maybe I can just tell her that I want to go wherever you want to go."

Why did I say I can't wait to go to college? Probably because saying that I like living in a small town —limited dating options excluded—sounds like I'm a hick. I wanted to sound fancy, but now I'm already being called out. I don't even know that many colleges, and with my grades, I can't think of any I'd get into.

"Maybe the University of Washington. My ex goes there."

Maren's eyes light up. "Your ex is in college?"

I shrug like my little lie is no big deal. I mean, we *did* go to a party together. Which was kind of a date, so it's not a huge lie. "Yeah, but I don't think he likes it much. He said the dorms were super gross, too."

Or at least, any place that needs to be fumigated can't be too nice, right? After that, I kind of retreat a little. The last thing I need to do is say something else that's stupid. It's like being around these people makes me feel like my real life isn't good enough, and that makes me even dumber than usual.

Just then, Abigail places a plate of cookies on the coffee table. Everyone dives in, half the plate disappearing in seconds.

"Aunt Abby's cowboy cookies are so good," Maren says. "You should grab one before they're gone."

I'm just grabbing one when I notice the Brooks children all ducking out the front door.

"Don't worry," Abigail says. "Aiden and Gabe are back in his room, breaking more of Ethan's Pokémon figurine collection, so we can actually pretend to be real adults for a minute."

My Aunt Donna looks kind of ill. "Breaking? Oh, no. I'll go see—"

Ethan's headed out the door, but he turns back. "I pretend to care, since Gabe feels like he's getting away with something, but really?" He shrugs. "I'd have just given them to him. Don't worry about it."

My Aunt Donna doesn't look charmed.

She looks sick.

Which means she feels guilty.

Her face is pale when she says, "If you're sure."

"Don't give it another thought." Ethan's smile is beautiful, and when he grins, his eyes squint up a little bit.

It's disgustingly cute.

"I'm just glad he's got a friend. It's hard in a new place." Ethan cares about his annoying little brother? He's kind *and* considerate of his siblings? I'm swimming in equal parts jealousy and admiration. It's a weird feeling, which distracts me for a moment. "You coming? Or would you rather stay inside?"

Ah, so they're doing more chores, which they don't want to force me into. But if I stay, I'll be the only kid left in a room full of old people.

Pass.

I dart to my feet, and before Ethan's even had time to close the door, I shoot through it. "What animals are you feeding?"

"Well, this is for the household animals and horses mostly," he says. "So in theory, I'm just monitoring the girls to make sure they do it right." He looks. . .confident. Cocky, even, like he thinks I'm following him because I want to spend more time with him.

"I'm a girl, so I can help." I force a smile, even though I'm a little annoyed. Does he think any country girl would obviously like him?

He's right.

But it still bothers me, for some reason.

"Are you a fan of horses?" Ethan asks as we walk toward the barn.

"Are people fans of horses?" I can't help raising one eyebrow.

Ethan smirks. "You must not spend much time on Instagram. It's all my sisters do—scroll through horse videos—or you know, it's all they *did*, before we convinced Mom to come here. Now they get to spend time with real horses more than just once a week for an hour—they used to take lessons, but it was pretty limited."

"Yeah, I mean, I guess they're fine."

"If you think they're fine, you're not a fan." Ethan leans against the side of the barn, his eyes shifting to see what his siblings are doing. "Another load of shavings was dumped in the corner this morning," he says. "We need to—"

Izzy hisses. "Don't stand there acting like you're a god or something. Get over here and help." She tosses a rake his way.

Luckily, Ethan has good hand-eye coordination —better than Izzy's, anyway. The rake totally would have hit me in the face, but his hand snaps out and catches it before it can.

Moments later, Whitney's explaining how to do basic barn tasks, like mucking stalls, separating flakes of hay, and refilling chicken feeders, like I grew up in the city. I should really have told Ethan from the start that I grew up riding, that we have chickens of our own, and that I've helped grow and cut hay since I was five. In fact, I once got caught in a grain silo and almost died under a million pounds of grain.

But it feels like it's too late to correct them, so I let them school me, as if I've lived in Manila on a working ranch my whole life and yet know nothing. Eventually, though, my Aunt Donna starts honking and it's time to go.

"It was nice to meet you," Ethan says. "My cell doesn't have the best reception up here, but I'd still love to get your number."

My heart races a bit, and then doubles down yet again when he smiles his crooked smile.

34

"Oh. Sure," I say. I rattle off the numbers and he puts them in.

"I want it too," Maren says.

Ethan waves at her absently. "Yeah, yeah. I'll text it to you." He's still staring right at me, and I know I'll be thinking of that exact face when I go to sleep tonight.

The whole drive home, his crooked, dimpled smile keeps popping back into my mind, and I wonder if I looked like a dope in that moment. Is it terribly obvious that I like him?

"Did you have fun?" We're pulling up our long drive, and I realize that little Aiden's sleeping. I've been silent the whole way home, not that it's too far.

I can't bring myself to look at my aunt or she'll immediately know. She's a pretty smart lady—maybe she already noticed that I like Ethan. "It was fine," I lie.

"What did you think about Maren?"

"She's snobby." I shouldn't have said that probably, but I'm only capable of hiding one thing at a time, clearly.

"Izzy?"

"She acts even younger than she is." And she's so stinking cute, it bugs me. I wish I'd been that sweet or bossily well-intentioned at any point in my life.

"So none of the Brooks children met with your approval?" She sounds like she's feeling me out for an arranged marriage or something—and then I feel a little panicky. Did she already figure me out?

"My approval?" I need to get back to casual fast. "Uh. Sure."

"Well, I won't be likely to be invited over again, but even if I am, I promise not to drag you along."

Drag me along? Did I take this faking thing too far? I want to be dragged back. Especially if he doesn't actually text me. "I mean, I'd go over again."

It hits me then. What if this whole thing wasn't about welcoming new people at all? What if. . . Could we have gone there for something *she* wants? I think about that guilty look she made when Aiden was in Ethan's room.

"Wait. Did you say we wouldn't be likely to be invited over again?" My baloney alarm's ringing. "Why not? It looked like Aiden loved that cute little guy. What was his name?" I'm pretending that I didn't fall in love with and memorize the name of every family member so she won't realize how pathetically starved for attention I am. "Abe?" As if anyone would name their kid that. . .

"Aiden and Gabe got along, but. . ." Aunt Donna sighs. "It's just a hunch, that's all."

A hunch? She has a *hunch* that after a lovely dinner and a few hours with a bunch of smiling kids, her son, who has no friends, will never be invited back? That does not compute. And now the whole thing feels. . .off. "Nothing in this family's a hunch." I can't help myself. I squeeze the armrest and start thinking about possible reasons she'd want to go over there if she didn't want to be friends. None of them are good. "Don't lie."

"Look, I didn't mean anything. It's just that people in this town aren't always welcoming to outsiders and—"

"That's because there aren't any outsiders." Is she kidding right now? How stupid does she think I am? "When's the last time someone new moved here?"

"Aiden and I—"

"Someone who didn't grow up here," I snap. "You know what I mean. Manila's usually the land that time forgot."

Aunt Donna cringes. "Look, I've got to get Aiden in bed, and it's past time for you to be—"

"It's nine-forty-one on a Saturday night." I can't help scoffing. "I'm seventeen, not *seven*."

"Well, the Aiden stuff is still true."

Her already sleeping son needs to go to bed, so she can't tell me things now? Or she needs more time to come up with a lie to cover for what she's really doing? She really does think I'm an idiot. "Whatever. You're as bad as Dad."

Looks like that insult landed. Aunt Donna looks ill. "Look, that ranch has been in the Brooks family for a long time."

Huh? "What does that have to do with us?"

"When Jed died, he left the ranch to them," she says.

"I know." I'd heard that much.

"Except he had a stipulation, probably because they're outsiders. He said that it had to be worked by them for a year before they could inherit it."

"Right, Ethan mentioned it." Why did I say his name? Why didn't I say the kids told me?

"Well, anyway, I'm not sure they'll really want to hang out with us, since they're not from here."

"Nice try." She had a hunch. That means there's more than a general guess. "What aren't you telling me?"

Aunt Donna looks like her foot's caught in a rat trap. "Here's the deal. As part of my divorce settlement, I'll be coming into quite a bit of money, but that money's coming from the sale of real estate, and

I'll have to buy more real estate with it as part of the terms of the deal. It's called a 1031 exchange."

"I still don't get—"

"I'd like to stay here, close to family, and the obvious place for me to buy is—"

Oh. She wants to buy the ranch, which means they'll be leaving. So she doesn't want me to get my hopes up that we'll be great friends, because she thinks they'll be gone soon. "Jedediah Brooks' ranch. Which means, they'd need to not keep it."

I can't believe that someone finally moves here, someone her kid likes, too, someone who she seemed to like, and she wants them to sell up and leave, just like that. "You want them to sell to you? But Ethan wants to stay. He wants to keep the ranch."

"Something like that." Why does Aunt Donna look so sick about it? Maybe she feels guilty about buying out the new people, too.

"I hate this crap." I fold my arms. "You took me over there, knowing you wanted to kick them out." I can't keep sitting in this car with her. I'm too mad.

Ethan's mother isn't too happy he's working as a rancher. She wants to go back home. That much is completely clear. I imagine that, as soon as they get a decent offer, they'll be gone. I might slam the door a bit too hard when I exit, but as I run up the path to my house, I just keep thinking about Ethan and I get more and more upset.

He's the first guy I've really liked. . .maybe ever. Which is pathetic, but nevertheless true. And the only thing worse than losing someone you like is losing someone you *love*.

That's why, when he texts me the next day and

calls me the same night, I blow him off. In fact, every time he texts me for the next week, I either ignore his text or I respond with something noncommittal. If I like him this much after one single family dinner? How bad will it be when he blames me for losing the ranch and leaves forever?

But I can't help looking at the shiny, warm photo I took of their family every night before I go to sleep and wishing I had a life like that instead of the one I have.

4

ETHAN

I need a car.

After my dad died, Mom let me drive his, and that was pretty cool. It was a four-door BMW—a few years old, but really nice. I mean, it was an older guy's car, but I didn't complain.

But when we moved out here, she understandably felt that it wasn't really a "ranch" car, and she sold it.

Now we share her Tahoe, and it's pretty annoying, to be honest.

Mom's all into the "earn your own way" thing, and I don't mind. I've seen lots of my friends get into trouble by having their parents hand them everything, but I'm running a ranch right now so I can't really pick up part-time work. And unfortunately, it's pretty unclear where the money from the cattle will go when all is said and done. Mom probably knows what the will says, but when I try to read it, it's like my French final exam.

Unintelligible.

Which means in addition to not having a car, I

have no plan to get a car in the foreseeable future. So when I tell Mom I need the Tahoe to grab some supplies for fence repairs, she hands me a shopping list and tells me to stop at the True Value to pick up groceries.

Of course, at the top of the list is toilet paper.

I mean, it's hardly a shock. With eight people in the house, we go through toilet paper at an alarming rate, even with only two bathrooms. The worst part is that it fills the cart, leaving very little room for everything else. And some of the other stuff is a little annoying, too. I mean, I don't mind buying the girls tampons, but should I really know that one of them has a yeast infection?

I mean, what even *is* that?

Ugh.

I'm just tossing the athlete's foot cream—I'm guessing Whitney's the one who needs that, because Mom made her throw out her barn boots—on the pile when I bump into Beth.

As in, I literally bump into her with the front of my cart, knocking two cans of refried beans out of her hands and onto the tile floor.

"Oh, I'm sorry," I say.

When she looks up at me, her eyes fly wide. She looks. . .guilty. Embarrassed.

She should.

She's been avoiding my calls and texts for over a week. It's not like I'm a predator. I may have liked her, sure, but mostly I was just happy to have a friend who's almost my age in town. I did finally give up, but she could've just been honest and said she didn't want to share her number in the first place.

"It's fine." She swallows and bends over to pick

up her dropped cans. That's when I notice what else she's holding. Industrial-sized black trash bags.

"Whoa, disposing of a body?" I can't help my smirk.

"At least I'm not a boy who's menstruating." She eyes the two different boxes of tampons in my cart pointedly and then meets my eye questioningly.

"I live with six women," I say. "Did you really think I'd refuse to buy them tampons?" I shrug. "Never been a big deal to me."

Beth frowns.

Did I say the wrong thing? Thanks to my mom and sisters, girls aren't the enigma to me that they are to most guys.

Except for this one, apparently.

"Well, I better go check out before my cream turns into cottage cheese." I look pointedly ahead of me.

"I'm sorry I didn't text you back," Beth says. "It's just that. . ."

I wait, but she doesn't elaborate. "Oh. Well, that explains it. Now I'm not offended at all."

"Offended?" She blinks. "Why would you be offended?"

"When someone gives me her number voluntarily, then doesn't reply in any real way to a single call or text?" I shrug. "I don't know. It's not like I feel like a creepy stalker or anything."

Her face drains of color. "It's not like that," she says. "Things with my family are just. . ."

"I get it," I say. "I mean, things with my family are also. . ." I nod my head. "Actually, wait. I don't get it, because again, you didn't say anything. Things are. . .busy? Things are tense? They're stressful?

Those are all the kinds of adjectives you might use to tell me why you blew me off. If you cared." I shrug again. "But whatever. I got the message."

She grabs my cart, dropping the already dented bean can again. "No, it's not like that." She looks at her feet.

"Then I should keep messaging you? They felt a little like messages in glass bottles thrown out to sea, but if you say I should keep sending them. . ." An idea hits me. "Or, maybe you prefer that. Maybe I should save our glass bottles and scribble little notes. Then I can fling one at your house whenever I drive past."

Beth's smiling. "My parents would *not* like that." As if mention of her parents somehow triggers her, her whole face shuts down again. "The thing is, you're really nice, but I just don't think we should be friends."

"That's fine." I take her bean can and her trash bags and throw them on the cart. "I didn't want to be your friend."

Her head snaps up again, her eyes searching mine. "What?"

"I wanted to ask you on a date." I realize that I'm doing that thing my mom does, where I enunciate really well, making my words super crisp. It always makes me think she's mocking me, so I make sure I sound normal again when I continue. "Because I thought you were cute, last week when you just showed up at my house for dinner."

Beth's blinking repeatedly. Then her mouth opens, but she doesn't speak.

"How about this?" I ask. "How about if, instead of being my friend, you let me take you out?" I can't help glancing at the can of refried beans. "I'm sure those are great, but I could drive you into Green River and we could get some real tacos." I smile my widest smile. "I know that the food options here aren't really that amazing, but I'm pretty sure I can beat a dented can of refried beans."

Beth inhales sharply, her nostrils widening.

Even so, she looks awfully cute. She's wearing baggy jeans and a really cute little fitted top with bunchy floral fabric. Her hair's pulled into a messy knot on the top of her head with a weird gold headband tightly in place, keeping the unruly bits away from her face. She's also wearing clunky Doc Martins that are electric blue. Somehow, it all works.

"So, is that a no?" I twist my lips and scrunch my nose, expressing my disappointment in her poor decision-making. "Because if you haven't tried Taco Time, you may not know that they have both soft burritos *and* crispy burritos, and they have these little fried rolls with cherry filling." I nod. "It's pretty amazing."

Beth laughs.

"Say you'll go."

There's that inhale again. And the nostril flare. "I can't, Ethan."

"You're secretly married?" I shake my head slowly. "I knew it."

"I'm not married." Her lip is twitching.

"You've been engaged since birth to a man your dad owed a favor to." I whistle. "That must be tough."

She rolls her eyes.

"You have gonorrhea from sitting on a public toilet, and you've decided to stay away from boys

44

from now on as a community service? Because I know a doctor who could write you a prescription for that." I drop my voice to a hissing whisper. "If left untreated, I hear it can make you blind."

She shakes her head. "You're an idiot."

"Wait, is that the reason you're blowing me off?" I ask. "Because I've been holding back my magnificence, so as not to scare you. In fact, I'm smarter than Steve Jobs. Smarter even than that weird Tesla guy. What's his name? Musk." I lean against the handle of the cart. "Now that I know you value my intelligence, I'll tell you that I can perform complex equations in my head."

"You can?" Beth frowns. "Then why did you want to work a ranch instead of going to college?"

"Would Picasso attend art school?" I shrug. "It would be a waste of time. That's just my level. I'm trying to give those other kids who need to learn things a chance, is all."

"How generous of you," Beth says. "But even knowing you're smart, I can't go with you to Taco Time."

"Are you playing hard to get? Because that only works if at some point, you let me get you." I lean closer and widen my eyes as if in alarm. "Or, if that's not it. . ." I drop my voice to a whisper. "I could bring some Imodium, if that would help. I know it's kind of a long drive home."

Beth's face crumples. "Ew, what's wrong with you?"

"I'm hilarious. I think you must have misspoken."

"Ethan."

"I'm doing in person what I did with the texts?

45

Pushing too hard?" Maybe I did go too far, but she's laughing. She seems to really like me. After living in the middle of a social desert for a few months, my social meter must be way off. "Alright, I get it. I'll just leave you and go pay for my tampons."

She snorts that time.

I swear, it really *feels like* she likes me. She said she *can't* date me. "Do you have a boyfriend? Is that it?"

Beth freezes.

"You could've just said that. It's not like I'd rat you out to your aunt or something, if he's someone you're not supposed to be dating."

"I don't have a boyfriend," she says. "What I have is a miserable family."

Now I can't help frowning. "What does that have to—"

"Ethan, trust me. We should not go out, okay?" She snatches her trash bags and her cans, and then she pushes past me, beating me to the register. But when she gets there, she shoves a twenty on the counter and darts out the door.

"Wow, honey," the checker says. "She was in a real rush to get away from you."

She really didn't need to tell me that. I'd already noticed. I just wish I understood *why*.

✿ 5 ✿

BETH

I f you look at the balance sheet, it's a complete runaway slam-dunk of a decision. We, as a country, should totally eliminate alcohol.

At every single level, drinking is bad. People become dependent on liquor easily. I did a paper on it for health class and was horrified to learn that one in eight Americans, according to the *Washington Post*, is an alcoholic, or deals with an alcohol use disorder.

One in eight.

It causes accidents that kill innocent people.

It destroys the human liver.

In addition to liver disease, it also causes high blood pressure, heart disease, stroke, and digestive problems. It contributes to cancer of the mouth, breast, throat, esophagus, voice box, liver, colon, and rectum. It weakens the immune system and causes cognitive and memory problems. It even harms unborn children if the mother continues to drink while pregnant, which one in eight do. That doesn't even begin to address the mental health complications and risks, or the litany of experiences people will willingly offer up about the times it has made them do and say embarrassing or terrible things.

Plus, hangovers.

And in exchange, there's one single reason that people keep using it, one reason that its prohibition was a miserable failure.

It makes people temporarily feel good.

Never having drunk a single drop of alcohol, I can't really speak to that. I suppose that's why I hate it as much as I do. When your mother has been an alcoholic from the very moment you were born, when she disappears at regular intervals because of it, when she gets checked into rehab programs that never work, I suppose it's natural to hate it.

But I'm also curious.

I always have been. I'm equal parts scared of alcohol. . .and curious about what makes it such a compelling poison that humans simply can't give it up, in spite of the horrifying and undeniable costs on the balance sheet. How good does it make humans feel? Why are we willing to risk all that damage just to keep it at our side?

Of course, my mom's example has been quite effective in keeping fear at the forefront and helping me remember not to even risk trying it.

The past few weeks have been good ones, though. Mom got out of a new rehab program at the end of August. Aunt Donna came home, so we don't have Grandpa living with us anymore. Even with a live-in nurse, it was still pretty awful to have him yelling half the day and most of the night. And Dad seems excited for some reason. I'd almost think *he* was buying the stupid ranch and not Donna, with as happy as he seems to be lately.

Last night, he straight up *gave me* a hundred bucks. Not because I asked for it. Not because I said I needed lunch money. He just called me to the family room, said I ought to go shopping, and then handed me a hundred-dollar bill.

Today, when I walk into the kitchen, he's doing the dishes.

I can't remember the last time Dad did dishes. He usually just lets them pile up until either Mom or I swerve in our usual game of Dishes Chicken.

"You seem happy lately."

He turns around, slinging soapy water all over the floor. Mom's not going to love that if he doesn't wipe it up quick. He smiles, then. Full-on smiles, not just a little grin. "Sure, I guess I am."

"Well, that's good," I say. "I'm happy to see you happy."

"Your mom's doing great, and business is, for once, going really well."

I shouldn't say anything. I know that. But he seems so happy that I guess I drop my guard. "Do you think you could talk to Aunt Donna about something?"

Dad frowns. That's the expression I'm used to seeing. "Did your grandpa do or say something? Because—"

"No," I say. "Nothing like that. It's just that this really nice family moved here recently, and I know their kids from school." I'm not stupid enough to admit that I want to date one of them. "But apparently Aunt Donna wants to buy their ranch, and the thing is—"

"Are you talking about the Brooks families?"

I freeze.

49

"Because if you are, you should know that I fully support your aunt in buying that ranch."

"Why?" I ask. "You know everyone around here. Surely there's someone else whose property she could buy. Or she could keep living here and use the money to buy, like, an apartment complex or something. That would be easier to run and it would provide income for her and Aiden."

"Beth." Dad's not just frowning now. He's scowling. "Did you mention that to your aunt?"

"I mean, not specifically, but she knows that I like the Brooks family, and I wish they wouldn't leave."

"Do not breathe a word of any of that nonsense to Aunt Donna. Are we clear?"

Now it's my turn to frown. "Why shouldn't I mention it to her? She's the one—"

Dad drops the cup he was holding and it clatters across the floor. Luckily it doesn't break, but I brace myself. A noise that loud is sure to attract Mom's attention, and she's going to lecture us both for sure. Only, she doesn't make a peep. She must be sleeping or something. Maybe she was up late binging a show or shopping online.

"You will not mention it to your aunt, and you will not bring it up to me again either." Dad doesn't pick up the cup. He doesn't wipe up the second splash of water that he created either. He just turns back to the sink and starts washing again.

Does he really think that's a good enough answer? I'm not four years old. That's not a reason. It's a command. "Is it because you want her to stay here and watch Grandpa forever?" I can't really blame him for not wanting Grandpa back, but it's not really fair to Donna that she has to care for him alone. She doesn't even have a live-in nurse to help. "That house she's in is really small, and there's no way she's going to want to—"

This time, Dad doesn't drop a cup.

He throws it.

It smashes against the wall.

No matter how deeply Mom's sleeping, she'll for sure wake up to that noise and come in here. And I hope she does, because when Dad gets this mad, he really scares me. "You will not ask about the Brooks family again. You're not a Brooks. You're an Ellingson, and don't forget that. Are we clear?"

If Mom was gone, I'd slither away to my room to hide. When she's gone, I escape any way I can, but I know Mom will be here any minute, and that makes me brave. "But why does it have to be *that* ranch? Why can't she just buy another ranch? I'm not betraying our family to ask why a totally new family can't keep their family farm."

Dad's hands are balled into fists at his side and he's trembling as he walks toward me.

"Mom," I say. "Mom!"

But he doesn't stop. "It's not your aunt who's buying that ranch, you idiot. She'll buy it, sure, but then I'll buy it from her with the life insurance proceeds from Grandpa when he dies. That way she gets the cash she wants, and I get the ranch I want, all of it tax free."

"I don't understand," I say.

And that's true—I don't comprehend the reasons they're doing it that way or the motivations behind it. But I've known Dad for long enough to get the gist. He's doing something shady, and he's using other people to do it.

"Their ranch joins our property across the back," Dad says. "I've wanted it for years."

"But—"

Dad lifts his hand, his face red, the muscles in his arm taut.

My heart hammers in my chest.

But he extends one single finger, and he shakes it at me. "Do not ask me about this again, and do not talk to anyone about it, especially any of those Brooks kids. Am I being clear?"

I nod tightly.

As I'm walking stiffly back toward my room, it occurs to me to wonder why Mom didn't show up after Dad shattered that mug. Did she go somewhere? Her car was in the garage when I got home, but maybe someone picked her up. I reroute and turn toward my parents' room, tiptoeing as quietly as I can. When I peek my head through the door, I see my mother immediately.

She's passed out, her eyes closed, her mouth open, her fingers clutched around something.

A white pill bottle.

My heart sinks.

She was doing so well. She was better. The rehab worked this time. I was sure of it. So what happened? Why's she like this again?

Where did she even get the pills?

I jog across the room and snatch the bottle out of her hand, checking with one hand to make sure she's still breathing as a reflex. Her color's good, but it never hurts to check. Her breath is warm and steady on my fingers.

Which makes me itch to slap her awake.

I'm not a violent person, but I get angry about this. Why is such a smart, sophisticated woman enslaved? Why can't she kick this habit? I check the bottle and see words I should have expected, I suppose.

Vernon Ellingson.

She must have paid a visit to check on Grandpa and swiped them.

I could kick Aunt Donna for not keeping a better eye out, but I guess it's not really her fault. She's not Mom's keeper. Actually, I don't think she even knows about Mom's issues. Dad tries to keep it quiet, and so does Mom when she's not jonesing for more pills.

I already know what Dad will say.

"Well, I guess this means she hasn't hit bottom yet."

I think that's, like, a phrase they teach you in rehab or something. As if there is definitely a point in time when Mom will finally change. Something inside of her will snap, when she hits this magical bottom, and then she'll change who she is and how she functions.

I decided years ago that this is just how my mom is. Some people's moms sing. Some of them sew. Some of them bake cookies. My mom is funny and smart and loving. . .when she's sober. And I just can't count on her being sober.

I'm rummaging through her drawers when Dad storms into the room.

"What are you doing?"

I turn around and chuck the bottle at him. "You knew, didn't you?"

He turns away, looking at his own nightstand.

"How could you be in there, all happy, knowing Mom's using again?"

"Listen," he says. "It's been a rough week for her with her parents, and—"

"You knew, and you left the bottle in here?"

"It was empty already when I came inside," he says. "She got agitated when I tried to take it."

Dad loves Mom.

In fact, she may be the one thing in this world he truly loves.

I've always known that.

But sometimes I think that he's not very good for her. He never gets angry with her. He never does anything to stop her, other than taking her to rehab and following their instructions. If he ever got angry, or yelled at her like he yells at me and Aunt Donna, or if he monitored her activity or behavior, some of that might help her change.

Which is why, after Dad kicks me out of the room and gives me a tongue lashing, I do what I know he hasn't.

I search the house.

It takes me almost an hour. I don't find any more pills, but I do find a six-pack of beer. I might have thought it was my dad's, because if your wife's an addict, you might hide your beer, but I found it inside a baby bassinet, covered with a blanket, in Mom's photography prop cabinet. There's no way Dad would put it there.

The fact that Mom bought beer and hid it under a baby blanket makes me even angrier than usual. I have a crush on a handsome, kind boy, a kid who buys tampons for his sisters and mom, and who has the brightest, shiniest family ever, and I can't go on a date with him, because I know that once he gets to know my family, he'll hate me just for my last name.

And my parents don't even know because they just don't care about my life at all.

My mom only cares about being high, and my dad only cares about my mom. And making money. I think about how he threw that mug a foot away from my head, and how he stood in front of me with his fists clenched, shaking, and I pick up the six pack, and I walk down the hall and out the front door.

I'm not thinking.

I'm just moving.

And that's when I realize I'm walking toward the Brooks' ranch.

Which is exactly where I can't go, especially holding a six pack of beer. I mean, what am I thinking? I pull an about face and turn around, heading the other direction. At first, I'm fueled by my rage, my feelings of disgust, and my general unhappiness.

But the six pack is stinking heavy.

And it keeps hitting the side of my leg as I walk.

Also, my fingers kind of hurt from carrying it.

I haven't gone very far—I'm on the edge of Dr. Archer's property when I sit down. I'm not ready to go home, but I can't keep carrying this stupid wad of cans. The ground is hard, and this late at night, it's actually a little chilly. A few feet away, I notice a fallen log, but not, like, from a tree that just fell down.

Dr. Archer's property's too nice for that.

It's a log that, after clearing away the tree, they left, cut at an angle to make a rough-hewn bench.

What kind of person has a rough log bench on

the edge of their property, just sitting in the middle of a grove of trees? And that's when I notice the little stream.

It runs behind our house, so I should have thought about it. It's Birch Creek, and this little bench is here, presumably, so you can sit next to it and hear the burble of the water or something equally cute.

Steve's parents didn't steal from people or get high all the time, I bet. Maybe they were like Abigail and her husband before Ethan's dad died.

Steve's mom died, too.

I wonder if we're only allowed a certain amount of happiness in this life, and once we've reached it, *bam*. I suppose the good thing about that is, I'll have a lot of happy time banked up for the future. My husband should thank me. He won't get offed at forty. Surely my crappy childhood and lousy parents will have earned him a long, happy life.

I drag the stupid, secret cans along the ground, coating them with dirt and detritus until I'm in front of the bench, and then I plop down a little too hard. It hurts my tailbone, honestly.

What's wrong with me? Did I expect a wooden bench to be soft?

I'm an idiot.

Why did I carry these cans all the way here, anyway? I should've just emptied them right off. I pop the top on the first one and start to pour it out, watching as the yeasty, smelly golden contents, barely visible in the moonlight, trickle down, past the side of the bench, and disappear into the earth just a few inches before joining the creek.

It makes me sad, for some reason.

What did that beer do wrong, to just be absorbed into the ground? I mean, I know it's not alive. I know it does bad things to people, but does it deserve to just disappear like that? For some reason, it makes me think of myself. I didn't hurt anyone, and I don't want people to hate me. I can't control who my parents are or what they do, but I can't date Ethan because of it.

I keep pouring for a moment, and then I yank my hand back up. The can's probably half-full, still. I lean toward it and take a whiff. It's as foul as I remember it. It smells like something that's just gone *off*.

Why do people drink it at all?

What exactly is the point? I mean, it reeks. It's expensive. It's bad for you. And it makes good people do horrible things. So why do people make it, buy it, and drink it so much that whole stores are dedicated to it? Why am I stuck, digging through my own home and stealing my mom's stash?

Suddenly, I can't be one of those idiots who doesn't understand for one more moment. I take the nasty can, and I bring it to my mouth.

And I take a swallow.

For some reason, it felt like it should be momentous or something. Instead, it's just gross. It's warm, it's as yeasty as it smelled, and it tastes *sour*. I hate it.

But for some reason, I keep on drinking.

Maybe because I want to know what it does. I want to understand, finally, why my mom and other people *hide* it so that they can have some. And maybe, just a little bit, I want it not to hurt so badly that my family sucks so much, by comparison to, well, to everyone else's that I know.

I mean, I have a home.

I have my own car.

I have a cell phone.

I usually have food to eat.

It's not like I have the *worst* life.

But something being livable isn't the same as it being good, and it feels like everywhere I look, people have *good* lives. It makes mine feel pretty shabby.

As I finish the can, a warmth spreads through me, which is kind of nice, given how chilly it's gotten. Also, something that felt like a tight knot in my chest feels. . .better.

Looser.

I'm not happy, but I'm less sad. So I drink the second can.

And the third.

I'm halfway through the fourth one when I realize that I'm drunk. Like, well and truly drunk.

It should horrify me.

I mean, I hate when my mom gets drunk. I hate that my dad doesn't even care that she's drunk. I hate that she has to leave for months at a time and we have to pretend she's not gone, or that she's on a girls' trip, or that she's visiting my grandparents.

All because of this.

Well, not really this. Usually my mom wants pills. That's her drug of choice. But when she can't get them, she'll take alcohol. And for the first time ever, I might know why.

I've just popped the top on my fifth can when I realize that I need to take a pee. Like, really bad. I stand up, stumble over the log that seems like it moved, and crouch behind it.

I'm pretty sure I got some pee on my pants, but it's not like anyone is going to notice. I'm in the middle of *nowhere*, and it's the middle of the night.

Wait. Is it? I think it is.

I check my phone.

It's nine-thirty-six. So, close enough.

I'm washing my hands in the Birch Creek, which is probably really clean because it's ridiculously cold, and that means it's snow fed, right? That's when I'm startled by a frog. I lurch sideways, shouting, and run onto the road.

Which is how an SUV almost crashes into me, the brakes squealing, the tires skidding. It stops just in time, the door bursting open, a man jumping out.

A really beautiful, really large, really shiny man.

"What the heck—" Ethan Brooks is even more gorgeous than I remembered. He's well-muscled, and his wind-tousled blonde hair's blowing across his forehead. He freezes when he recognizes me, his mouth gaping open, his eyes wide. "*Beth?*"

6

ETHAN

My dad was sick for a long time before he died. I mean, I've met people whose dad or mom was sick for *years,* so I suppose it's relative, but the time we spent in the hospital dragged. It felt like a really long time.

Until he was gone.

And then it didn't feel like we'd had nearly long enough.

I had always liked superhero movies, but after that, I kind of hated them. I mean, when I was a kid, I liked them because I loved the idea of having magical powers. If I could fly, or run fast, or lift heavy things, think of the good I could do. Think of how many people would be amazed by me.

Everyone wants to be special, and I was no different.

But as I got older, I liked other things about them. I loved the line in the original Tobey Maguire *Spiderman*, where his uncle says, "With great power comes great responsibility."

It's a little corny, of course, but it's also true. So

many of the superhero movies out there have good themes. The superheroes want to change the world, or heal the world, or protect the world, and I think that's a good thing. I've certainly met plenty of people who don't try to do anything to better the world. I've never wanted to be like that.

But after Dad died, I didn't want to watch those movies any more.

At first, I thought the doctors were heroes. I thought they could save my dad from the cancer that was replacing his organs with junk cells. I thought they would be the real-life superheroes.

Only, they failed.

He died.

That's when I realized—I mean, I knew it before, but I hadn't *really* accepted the truth of it— that superheroes don't exist. There are no magical powers. There's no special pill that changes you, no miracle cure that fixes things. No one can leap small or large buildings. We're all mortal, and we're all subject to the whims of fate.

All my hopes that I might better the world died with Dad. But forget being a superhero, I was almost a super villain tonight. I almost struck someone with my car.

Only, once I hop out, my heart pounding, adrenaline spiking in my system, I realize it's not just anyone.

It's someone I know.

"*Beth?*"

"Ethan?" It's Beth, alright. She's wearing jeans, wet to her mid-calf on one leg, like she stepped in a lake or a huge puddle, and her hair is loose around her shoulders. Her eyes look dazed and a little lost.

"What in the world are you doing, running out into the road?" My heart rate's coming down, but I'm still shocked. I barely pulled my mom's Tahoe onto the side of the road in time to miss her. "Why are you out here?" I glance around. "Isn't that the horse doc's place?"

Beth nods.

And that's when I notice what she's holding—a beer.

I step closer and take a good sniff. I've never had any alcohol—my mom's got strong opinions about waiting until it's legal, and she never drinks anyway —but when I might have had some at a party, I was busy dealing with a dying dad. The year after that, I didn't really feel up to partying.

And now I'm here. The tiny town without a local bar, where I could definitely *not* get a fake ID, even if I wanted one. So where did Beth get beer?

Her parents, probably.

A lot of adults are way cooler than my mom about it. "You're drinking." I state the obvious, because I'm not sure what else to say.

"Beer," Beth says, "is just as gross as it smells." She laughs then, and stumbles away from the road.

I catch her before she can fall and belatedly realize she wasn't falling. She was trying to sit on a weird bench that's facing some trees.

It's in front of a little stream.

The wet ankle makes more sense, at least.

"Why are you out here, drinking alone?"

"Why not?" Beth asks.

That makes no sense, but it doesn't seem like she's about to explain it to me. I glance back at where my car's still running, barely off the road. "I should move my car."

"You should get home before your milk turns into cream." She laughs again, too loudly.

I can't help joining her this time. Even drunk, her memory's not too bad. "It was before my cream turns into cottage cheese," I say. "But no fear of that. I was actually picking up chicken feed, so there's nothing in my car that can spoil." Before she can stop me, I hop in the SUV, pull it further off the road, and cut the engine.

It's not like she invited me to join her, but she's stumbling in front of cars on the road, so I'd say she's not really safe to leave alone.

"So, Beth," I say.

"Nope." She holds up one finger, tipping the can in her other hand sideways, beer sloshing out. "You and I can *not* go on a date."

"I wasn't going to—"

"Because my mom is a pain-pill-popper, and my dad's, like, an evil villain who steals stuff."

"What?" I sit down next to her, barely containing my smile. Drunk Beth is entertaining.

"Yep." She tries to set the beer down, but it falls over, beer sloshing all over the ground. "Oh, rats." She watches, tilting her head sideways, as all of it just pours and pours and pours out onto the dirt.

"Did you want that?" I ask.

She shrugs. "Not really. I'm not my mom."

I'm struggling to keep up. "You stole your mom's beer?"

She leans closer, her eyes intent. "Pills," she says, "didn't you hear me? That's what she likes. Piiiiills."

"Okay," I say.

"But when she can't steal those from someone, she'll drink." She lunges forward, her hand knocking over another can of beer, this one unopened.

"You still thirsty?" I ask. "Because I feel like maybe you've had enough."

"I didn't want any to begin with, but my mom can't have it. It's bad for her. So I'm helping."

"Helping?" I stifle a laugh. I'm not sure Beth's really helping anyone. "Did you walk here?"

She straightens up, forgetting about the can, which she promptly drops in the dirt. "I sure did. I'm an excellent walker."

I had no idea drunk people were so funny. "I'm sure that you are."

"I'm also very, very good at making my dad mad." She shakes her head. "He threw a cup at the wall earlier." Then she covers her mouth. "Can you pretend I didn't tell you that?"

He threw a cup? That doesn't sound very good. I can't think of a time my mom or dad threw, well, anything. At anyone. Not even at the wall. "Um, sure."

"Oh, good. I knew you were really a good guy." She bobs her head then, but not just once. She bobs it, and then she keeps on going, like she's turned into bobblehead Beth.

I press one finger to her forehead. "That's probably going to make your head hurt. Maybe try to hold your head still."

She leans more heavily against my finger, her chin jutting forward. "You're so hot."

"Oh." I can't help smiling. "Thanks."

"And your family is so shiny." She bites her lip, and then she leans even closer. "Like the *sun*!"

The sun? What's she saying?

"I have this photo I took of you guys, and sometimes when I'm really depressed, I look at it. No, that's not right. I *stare* at it."

"You have a—what?"

"Here." She tries to pull her phone out of her pocket, but her fingers are fumbly, and she manages to pull and pull and then wham. Her phone flies outward, hitting me in the nose.

It feels like someone punched me, which I know isn't very manly, but that phone's hard and it hurts. "Ow," I say, my hand covering my nose. I really hope my nose isn't bleeding. If I were Izzy, I'd be a goner. Her nose bleeds when the weather turns. Or when she sneezes. Or if she blows her nose too hard.

Luckily, mine's fine.

"Here." Beth waggles her finger at me, and it's clear she managed to pick up her weaponized phone from the ground. "I look at this because I'm like a big dark stain, but your family's like a shiny sunshine that's on your face and warm. If you look at this, you'll feel all better. Ready?" She turns her phone around and shows me a photo.

She must have taken it the other day at dinner. It's just me and Izzy, Mom and Emery, and Gabe. It looks like Izzy made some kind of joke. I'm making kind of a weird face, like I just heard something mildly funny, but I'm too cool to admit it.

I reach for her phone. "Here, that's not a good photo. Let me delete it for you."

Beth gasps, ripping her phone away from me. "No. I would hate you forever if you took it away."

Hate me forever? "I think that's a little melodramatic."

"It's my Normal Rockwell."

"*Norman* Rockwell?"

"Yes." She shakes her head up and down, but after a few bobs, she stops on her own this time. "You can't have it. It's shiny for me."

Shiny for her.

I think drunk Beth is adorable, but she's not the clearest. "Okay. I won't delete it, but here." I snatch the phone before she can object and take a quick selfie, my fingers throwing up the peace sign.

"You took a picture?" she asks. "That's so good. Now I have my Normal Rockwell *and* the hottest guy who ever asked me out."

"Why would you tell me no?" I ask. "If I'm the hottest guy?"

She slumps forward then and drops her chin on her palm. "Because I can't marry the shiny prince. I have to find a villain's kid or something."

"A villain's. . .what?"

"My dad's making your mom sell the ranch so she can go back home."

What on earth is she talking about? Drunk Beth is adorable, but she makes no sense at all. "Okay," I say, my voice high and squeaky. "I'm cutting you off, villain-spawn."

"You should." She sighs slowly. "You should cut me off, and then you should kick me to the curb, and then you should—"

"Beth." I grab her shoulders and turn her toward me. "You are really drunk. I'm going to drive you home, and then—"

"No way," she says. "You can't drive me home. My dad will see you, and the villain always tries to

66

kill the prince, only you don't have your sword. So he might win."

"My sword?" I chuckle. "You're right. I left that at home. My mom doesn't like me driving with it."

"You need to have your sword, or the dragon can eat you."

"Is your dad a dragon?"

"Well, no, but if he were in a cartoon, maybe."

I wish I was recording this. There's no way she's going to believe any of it tomorrow. "Here, hand me your phone again."

"Okay."

"I'm texting you a message."

"From my phone?" She frowns. "That makes no sense."

"Watch." I open up a text to herself. It's an open string, and I can't help seeing what else she's texted herself.

PICKLES
PECANS
PURPLE GRAPES
PIMENTOS
MILK

"Wow," I say. "It's too bad milk isn't spelled with a P, or that shopping list would be way cooler."

"Huh?"

"Never mind," I say. "But look." I type her a message that hopefully she'll get tomorrow.

DEAR BETH. I'M JUST REMINDING YOU THAT WHEN YOU WAKE UP TOMORROW, YOU SHOULD TEXT ETHAN. YOU MAY NOT REMEMBER THIS, BUT YOU GOT DRUNK LAST NIGHT. THEN YOU STUMBLED IN FRONT OF HIS CAR. HE NOT ONLY DIDN'T

HIT YOU, HE SAVED YOU. AND THEN HE WALKED YOU HOME SO YOUR DAD WOULDN'T KNOW. YOU OWE HIM. SO LET HIM TAKE YOU OUT FOR ICE CREAM. HE'S A GOOD GUY, AND YOU ALREADY TOLD HIM HE'S HOT AND THAT HIS FAMILY IS SHINY. CHECK YOUR PHOTOS AND MAYBE YOU'LL REMEMBER.

"Oh, you shouldn't send that," Beth says. "I already know all that. I'm right here."

"I haven't been drunk before," I say, "but from what I hear, people may not remember everything super clearly when they wake up the next day."

"I guess," Beth says.

"Better safe than sorry, don't you think?"

She shrugs.

I hand her the phone and then I swoop my arms under her armpits and lift her to her feet. We've gone about four steps when she flails like she's about to walk off the edge of a cliff.

"Wait!" Her eyes are wide, her mouth open, her breathing sharp. "Wait, Ethan."

"I'm waiting," I say. "I haven't moved."

"Okay." She nods. "Good." She nods again. "Very good, even."

"Okay," I say. "What did you want?"

"There's still one can of beer left," she says.

"I'm good," I say, "and I really don't think you should have any more."

"But we can't just leave it there," she says. "My mom will find it."

"On the edge of Dr. Archer's property? I doubt it."

"She will," Beth says. "She's like a blood dog."

68

"A blood *hound?*"

"Yes." She stumbles back toward the bench, falling to her knees in front of the last can of beer. "And this one." She upends the mostly empty can, spilling the last few swallows on the ground, and then she opens the last one very carefully, staring intently at the lid.

"This stuff is very bad. It should be illegal."

"Since you're seventeen, it *is* illegal."

"Wait, are you twenty-one?" She turns toward me, wide-eyed.

"I just turned eighteen," I say. "It's illegal for me, too."

"Phew," she says. "No one can drink it, then." She dumps it over, watching as the liquid splashes out, some of it hitting her pants. I try not to cringe. For some reason this is therapeutic for her.

Hopefully her parents won't kill her when they realize she's taken it.

I help her get back to her feet, and I'm about to walk her home when I hear a voice.

"Ethan Brooks."

I close my eyes, hoping for a moment that I hallucinated his voice.

"What on earth are you doing out here this late?"

I turn around slowly, one arm still keeping Beth upright. "Hey, Dr. Archer."

His eyes scan over me, Beth, and then the cans we're leaving. Finally, he turns toward my car. "You drove over here, and now you're drinking?"

I open my mouth to tell him about Beth, how she almost got hit, how I found her, and then I remember what she said about her dad being a dragon. And about how she's villain-spawn. What will happen to her if I rat her out? I thought I'd given up on being a superhero. I thought that dream was long dead.

But looking at Beth, some relic of that desire stirs inside of me.

"I'm sorry," I say. "It was irresponsible."

Dr. Archer swears under his breath. "Your mom's got a lot on her plate. Rumor is, Donna Ellingson filed an affidavit today."

Beth coughs.

"She's testifying that your family was gone too long, and the alien folks are demanding the ranch go to them instead."

I can't even speak—and then I realize that Beth must have known something about it. The villain-dragon thing makes more sense. She can't date me because her dad's a villain.

Oh, good grief.

It should make me angry.

I should toss her right under the Dr. Archer-shaped bus.

But for some reason, the news does the opposite. She thinks I'm hot. She thinks my family's shiny. She's upset with her dad, who threw a cup at the wall. Did he do it because she was upset? Did she defend us? Either way, I want to help her get home.

And there's no way I'm going to risk getting her into more trouble.

"I need to get her home," I say. "I think that alcohol hit her way worse than me."

"Clearly," Dr. Archer says. "Do you think you *can* walk her home?"

I nod.

"Give me your keys."

"But I'm—"

Dr. Archer scowls.

I hand them over.

"When you get her home, I'll be waiting on the street with your car. I'll drive you home."

"But then, how will you get home?" I ask.

"I have legs, boy."

"Oh."

Thankfully, Beth says nothing on the way home, at least, not until I get her within a dozen yards of the front porch. I kind of expect an attack dog to run out, barking and foaming at the mouth. Or her dad to be sitting on the porch, cleaning his gun. Or brandishing it.

The lights aren't even on.

Do her parents even realize she's not home?

I hand her phone back. "Can you get inside?"

"For sure," she says. "I can definitely walk."

She doesn't sound as confused, and I wonder how long it takes for someone who's drunk to not be drunk. "Alright, well, go inside. Be safe."

"Stay shiny." She waits for a moment, for what I don't know, and then she starts walking toward her front door. I watch as she opens it, waves, and then disappears inside. I really hope no one gets mad at her. It sounds like she was trying to get rid of the beer to keep her mom from drinking it, but why wouldn't her dragon-father do that instead?

There are too many things I don't really understand.

But now I'm even more interested than before.

Beth may think that she's villain-spawn, but she's shiny to me. My mom's an actual dragon, with her words, anyway. She's out there, spitting fire at all the bad people in the world, defending her lair and baby dragons, and she's turned her daughters into miniature dragons, too. It's almost exhausting to talk to them, because they're sure to argue about most everything.

Not Beth.

Drunk or sober, she makes me laugh. She calls us shiny and me hot. She's cute, and kind, and bright, and she's *easy* in a way none of the girls in my family are.

She's what I didn't realize I wanted until I saw it.

I'm still thinking about that as I turn toward the road. True to his word, Dr. Archer's already there, the Tahoe window rolled down, his arm hanging out. "Let's go."

I don't know what to say when I get in the passenger side, so I settle for, "Thanks."

"Don't thank me."

"Why not?" I ask.

"Because I've been thinking this whole time about what to do. Your mom doesn't need anything else to worry about, but I don't want to just let you off. You can't just wander around, getting drunk with girls." He levels a very serious stare at me.

I consider telling him the truth.

"You're going to have to work this off." He nods. "Yes, that's what we'll do. You'll come over to my house a time or two a week, and you'll help me do things around the barn."

"But—"

"Or I can tell your mom about this, and she can decide how to punish you for such irresponsible, *illegal*, and disappointing behavior."

He's trying to spare my mom and teach me the

evils of drinking underage. I suppose I can't fault him for that. It's either help him replace fence posts, or tell Mom about how I found Beth.

And I like Beth.

If I tell Mom, she'll hate her for sure. Mom's amazing. She's smart, she's funny, she's kind, she's loyal, and she's terrifying—in the best way.

But she's also pretty black and white.

I like Beth enough to be willing to do some manual labor to keep Mom from thinking badly of her from the get-go.

"Your mom's got a meeting—I overheard. Come over tomorrow, at four o'clock. Alright?"

I just nod. Because what else am I going to do?

7

BETH

I've always loved superhero movies. I loved the cartoon ones, like *Teen Titans, Big Hero Six,* and the *Spider-verse* when I was young, and as I got older, Marvel became my go-to brand. Even so, my dad thought it was really weird that of all the different films I saw over years and years, after I'd left all the other cartoons behind, *Megamind* remained my favorite movie to watch. I couldn't explain it to him, because he'd definitely take offense to my reasons.

I mean, it's a little on the nose—a little blue alien who *chose* to be the bad guy?

It's kind of been my brand, to be honest, but not by my choice.

When I was six, my dad bought new computers for the school. And then he used that purchase to force the school into some kind of shady deal to buy our cattle for the ground meat in the school lunches. I only found out because I overheard the principal complaining to one of the trustees.

Then when I was nine, he got into some huge

fight with the car repair shop, refused to pay them, and we started having to drive into Green River every time our car needed something.

I was eleven the first time I overheard him blackmailing someone at a PTA meeting. It didn't make a lot of sense to me, but I was smart enough to understand that my dad was threatening the guy at the Division of Water Rights. The guy wasn't pleased.

And I was twelve the first time I saw my dad shoot and butcher one of Jedediah Brooks' cows—the brand was plain as day.

"Dad, that's not our cow," I said.

He rolled his eyes. "Don't be such a goody two-shoes," he said. "Do you have any idea how many of our cows Old Jed has kept over the years?"

"Didn't he call yesterday to tell you he had three of them that just came down off the mountain?"

"He lives right at the base," he said. "So all the neighbors' cows wind up at his place if they get lost. Do you really think he always calls?"

He called us about two or three times a year, and it felt like it was probably a hassle for him to catch our cows, call us, and coordinate pickup. If he didn't do it, how would we ever even know?

But he did do it. Regularly.

"Why'd you steal his cow?"

Dad gritted his teeth. "I didn't steal it. It accidentally wound up with ours after the drive home, and I didn't bother calling him to tell him that he lost it."

That's when I noticed another cow he was about to butcher had a different brand, one I didn't immediately recognize. I knew it before, deep, deep down, but that was the moment when I realized that my dad may not have blue skin, but he really was a villain.

Worse, it probably meant that I was doomed to be a villain too.

When I wake up the morning after my beer walk with a splitting headache, the events of the night before streaming back in fits and starts, I bolt up in bed and cradle my pounding head. Did Dad really throw a mug at the wall? Did he yell at me because I was upset about what he and Aunt Donna are doing to the Brooks family?

Did I really steal that beer I found and *drink* it instead of dumping it all out?

And most importantly of all . . .did Ethan Brooks really almost hit me with a car and then walk me home? I cringe inside. I remember myself as being really cute and funny, but was I? I've seen my mom when she's drunk, and she does not look cute. She's definitely not funny.

I do remember Ethan laughing a lot, but there's a big difference between laughing *at* someone and laughing *with* them. I'm terribly afraid any laughing he did was the former.

I groan audibly as I force myself to the edge of my bed so I can search for my phone. When I find it, the battery's at four percent, and I have a text message unread. My heart leaps into my throat, but thankfully it's not from Ethan.

It's from me.

I do that sometimes, if I'm worried I'll forget something. It's easier than trying to open up a note and leave myself a message there, and it'll remind me too, because I leave the text unread.

But as I start to read my reminder to myself, I want to curl up in the corner and die. Because it really doesn't look like something I typed to myself. It reads more like something *Ethan* would have typed.

DEAR BETH. I'M JUST REMINDING YOU THAT WHEN YOU WAKE UP TOMORROW, YOU SHOULD TEXT ETHAN. YOU MAY NOT REMEMBER THIS, BUT YOU GOT DRUNK LAST NIGHT. THEN YOU STUMBLED IN FRONT OF HIS CAR. HE NOT ONLY DIDN'T HIT YOU, HE SAVED YOU. AND THEN HE WALKED YOU HOME SO YOUR DAD WOULDN'T KNOW. YOU OWE HIM. SO LET HIM TAKE YOU OUT FOR ICE CREAM. HE'S A GOOD GUY, AND YOU ALREADY TOLD HIM HE'S HOT AND THAT HIS FAMILY IS SHINY. CHECK YOUR PHOTOS AND MAYBE YOU'LL REMEMBER.

My photos? My heart races. What's in my photos?

I swipe and see Ethan's smiling face, washed out horribly because of the flash of the camera in the pitch dark night.

That was definitely a message from Ethan, and he says I told him he was hot. Also, that his family's shiny.

I wonder what else I told him. If I mentioned something about my dad and aunt, my dad's going to *kill* me. That smashed mug will be like a fond memory of a happier time, I know it.

I wrack my brain, but can't recall anything I might have said about the ranch. Hopefully that's because I didn't say a word about it. But I definitely can't go for ice cream with him now. You do *not* try to come back from something like almost getting killed while stumbling drunk into the street in front of some guy, or having him walk you home so your parents won't find out what an idiot you are.

Shiny, beautiful boys should run very far and very fast when they see someone like me coming.

So why did he text me to tell me I had to go on a date with him? Does he pity me now? Or does he want to laugh at me? It makes no sense. If I were him, I'd want to forget that I even know Beth Ellingson. Or at least, once I found out her dad and aunt were trying to kick me off of my family ranch, I definitely would. Clearly he has no idea about any of that yet.

I spare him any of the stress or awkwardness that would surely follow any future interactions we would have, and I don't text or call. In fact, I plug my phone in and walk away, determined to put a nice, healthy breakfast between last night and this shining, bright Saturday in early fall.

Only, my stomach has other plans.

Apparently it hates food and wants to see me die.

Also, I hate the bright Saturday morning. It's also evil. I should name it Patrick.

"Drink this." My mom plonks a weird-looking shake in front of me. "I made it for myself, but it's also good for colds, and you look pretty sick, hon." She drops her head against the cool countertop and groans.

I realize that I look just like her, but since she has no idea I stole her hidden beer, she doesn't realize I'm suffering from a hangover, not a cold.

"It's okay," I say, shoving her shake thing back toward her. "You drink it."

She grimaces and shakes her head tightly. "I did something bad last night." Her whispered words still sting.

"I know." My voice is small—embarrassingly small. I clear my throat. "I saw you."

A single tear rolls down her cheek. "I'm sorry. I had to go over there—a nurse had to leave early and your aunt wasn't back yet. I sat with your grandfather for a few moments, and I saw them, and. . ."

I know this story.

Mom does alright when she has no temptation, but we live in a world full of pills and alcohol. It's literally everywhere, so when she's feeling vulnerable and it's just *there*. . .

"What will you do when Aunt Donna notices—"

"Your dad already put the bottle back, and he left it open and next to the toilet. I'm sure she'll think he dumped it out or flushed them."

Great. Another thing for my Aunt Donna to fight with doctors about or beat herself up over. At least we know Grandpa's going to be fine, but Aunt Donna doesn't.

And that's the worst part of all this—the cost to the people around an addict is steep. Their behavior is so compulsive and so damaging that it inevitably falls out on everyone else to deal with the consequences.

But it's my mom.

I can hardly lecture her about how horrible she is, so I say nothing. It's become a habit after all these years. I wish I had the guts to tell Dad that Mom will never hit bottom with him always cleaning up after her like this. She's an addict with her own personal cleaning crew.

"Listen," Mom says.

But then the doorbell rings.

Mom looks down at her fuzzy pink bathrobe and fluffy slippers and her lip curls. "Um."

"It's fine. I'll get it."

Mom shuffles away as quickly as she can, but she does pause to point. "Drink that before it gets warm."

I nod as if I'm going to listen, and then I jog to the front door, each step sending a pounding pain through my skull. *Why do people drink if it wrecks your body so badly?* I swing the door open. "Hello?"

I am *not* expecting Ethan's gorgeous, smiling face.

It hits me like an open-handed slap.

"Hey. Just wanted to make sure you were alive."

I shush him as quietly as I can. "Did you really think that coming here at the crack of—"

"It's ten-twenty-six," he says. "I've been up for almost five hours."

I roll my eyes. "But not all of us have cows to feed."

"Your family does, though, right?" He quirks one eyebrow.

"I mean, we do, but that's my dad. And the people he hires to help do it."

Ethan shakes his head. "I know what we have to pay Jeff and Kevin. I have no idea how your dad can do very well, paying people to help out. The profit margin on cattle ranching isn't as high as I hoped."

"It's definitely more of a lifestyle," I say, parroting the phrase my dad always uses. "But look, you can't be here. My mom will hear you and come out any time, and—"

Ethan reaches toward me.

I try to close the door, but his hand grasps the frame, blocking me. "You didn't call or text." His voice is hurt. "You could have said you wouldn't go to ice cream, but you should have at least told me you were alright."

He's right. He almost killed me last night—my fault—and he didn't just leave me there. He kept me company, helped me not drink that last beer—it's all coming back much more clearly—and then walked me home.

He was basically a saint.

"I'm sorry," I say. "That was rude of me. Even ruder than leaping in front of your car last night."

"It was more of a stumble than a leap." His lips are twitching.

"Hey." I frown.

"But listen." He thrusts a bag at me.

"What's that?" I ask.

"It's not anything big," he says. "But if you're still on the fence about letting me take you out for ice cream, I thought this might help." The tops of his ears turn just a little pink, and I wonder what in the world he brought me.

When I take the bag, the tips of our fingers brush and a thrill races all the way up my arm. I try to suppress the shiver. It would be awful if he knew I thought he was hot *and* he noticed my reaction to touching him. "Okay, well, thanks."

"I get it, I'll go." He leans against the door like leaving is the furthest thing from his mind. "But Beth."

"Yeah?" I try to force a scowl.

"You better call me once you open that, or at least text me, or I may have to come back to confirm that you're fine."

I hate how badly I want to hear from him and how happy it makes me that he's planning to follow up. Again. "Yeah, sure," I lie. "For sure I will."

After he leaves, I practically race to my room so my mom won't see the bag. Two minutes later, she's tapping on my door. "Beth?"

I shove the bag under my bed and turn around so I'm looking at her when she opens the door.

"Who was it?"

"Wanted to wash our windows," I choke out.

"Huh?"

I clear my throat and think calm thoughts. "Just some guy who wanted to give us a quote to wash our windows."

Mom blinks. "How much did he want to be paid for it?"

I was not expecting that. "What?"

"What did he say he'd charge? Did you get his card?"

I shake my head. "I—he said—I told him we weren't interested."

"You were talking up there for a long time," she says. "You told him you weren't interested and then he wouldn't leave?" She doesn't look suspicious, just confused, but I wish she'd just drop it.

"Mom, did you really want to pay someone to wash our perfectly fine windows?"

My mom tilts her head. "Have you *looked* out the window lately?"

And that's how I wind up spending my formerly

free Saturday washing windows. For fifty dollars. When she kept pressing, why did I name that amount? I should have said *five hundred* dollars. Then maybe she'd have dropped it.

Since my phone's charging, I have an excuse for not noticing if Ethan calls again, and that's something.

But when I go back inside, no one has called, and no one has texted. I live in Manila, Utah, so it's hardly surprising that no one called me.

It still bums me out.

It's one of the hardest things I've ever done, to wait until after I eat, after I shower, and after I talk to my mom again about the windows to open the present.

I hide in my closet to open it, just in case.

Although, it occurs to me to wonder why I'm so nervous that my mom or dad might see me opening a gift. What exactly do I think it would be? It's not like Ethan would give me something risqué, right? After a few agonizing minutes of dithering, I finally upend the bag, dumping the contents on the carpeted floor of my closet.

Pink tissue paper.

White tissue paper.

And a pink fabric. . .something.

I unfold it and realize that Ethan gave me a hot pink baby doll t-shirt with a huge heart on the front of it. The entire heart's made of bright, sparkly silver sequins.

What on earth?

I had every intention of ignoring him. After all, I can't encourage this kind of thing. Dropping by and giving me gifts, albeit weird ones, can't be encouraged. But I'm so confused that I can't help myself.

WHAT ON EARTH DID YOU BUY ME A PINK SHIRT FOR?

I don't know what Ethan usually does on a Saturday, but this Saturday he's waiting by his phone to text me, apparently, because he replies within ten seconds. IT'S *SHINY*.

WHAT IS THAT SUPPOSED TO MEAN?

IF YOU WEAR IT, YOU'LL BE SHINY, TOO.

HUH? Is he crazy? What's he talking about?

YOU SAID YOU'RE A STAIN, BUT IF YOU PUT THAT ON, YOU'LL BE SHINY LIKE US.

Oh, no. What exactly did I say?

WEAR THAT ON OUR ICE CREAM DATE.

I CAN'T GO ON A DATE WITH YOU, ETHAN.

I KNOW ABOUT THE RANCH. I DON'T CARE.

The bottom drops out of my stomach. He knows? How could he not care about *that*? My dad's trying to send his family packing so he can take the land they should inherit and *he doesn't care*?

YOU AREN'T YOUR DAD.

OBVIOUSLY.

WHY CAN'T YOU GO GET ICE CREAM?

ETHAN.

BETH.

He is too much. LOOK. YOU MAY BE FINE WITH IT NOW, BUT WAIT UNTIL THE RANCH GETS TAKEN.

MY MOM WON'T LET THAT HAPPEN.

He's so sure, but only because he doesn't know

84

my dad. I once saw him punch a guy at a Saturday morning basketball game. No one else was watching and when the guy complained, my dad laughed and said he was lying. He said it was an *accident*, but I knew it wasn't. I'm pretty sure the guy he hit knew, too. Ethan's mom's amazing, but there's no way she can beat my dad.

It's not going to be a fair game.

It never is, not with my dad. He'll do whatever it takes to win.

And winning means sending Ethan and his family packing. I suddenly feel like I want to cry and like I want to puke at the same time.

HOW ABOUT THIS? I text. IF YOUR MOM WINS AND YOU KEEP THE RANCH, WE'LL GET ICE CREAM TOGETHER TO CELEBRATE.

He doesn't reply.

MY TREAT.

Of course it would be my treat—only, I know there's no way I'll ever be paying for that ice cream.

Or wearing the adorable, sweet shirt he bought me. Unlike the Brooks family, nothing about me is shiny, and even a blinged-up shirt from Target can't change that. I'm a blue-skinned alien with a big head, and I always will be.

8

ETHAN

When I was growing up, Monday night was ice cream night. Sure, sometimes I had a basketball game, or there was some kind of school project that got in the way, but probably forty-five Mondays a year, our whole family went out for ice cream.

For a while, we were obsessed with Baskin-Robbins. It was kind of the gold standard, right? But then we discovered Marble Slab, and that was a whole new level. Right before Dad died, Mom discovered this strange kind of ice cream from Korea, called bingsu.

She loved it!

Every Monday, we'd drive all the way into China-town to get shaved, sugary milk stuff that often had fruit or breakfast cereal toppings.

Then Dad got diagnosed with cancer.

We never talked about it, but those ice cream Mondays, that family activity that I always took for granted. . .it died before he did.

And it's never been revived.

I shouldn't have asked Beth to ice cream, probably. No one has even breathed a word about going to ice cream since Dad passed. Not even clueless Gabe. Maybe he forgot about it. Kids don't have the best memory. But I think it's more likely that he remembers them, but like the rest of us, he's afraid of how Mom would react if he suggested going for ice cream.

Without Dad.

He was the big ice cream fan, long before Mom's obsession with bingsu. He was the one who would taste five different flavors every time we went, talking to each kid about what he should choose *this time*. Even thinking about that makes me a little emotional. Which is stupid. I should be happy about memories of things that used to make us smile.

So why did I ask Beth to ice cream?

Maybe it's because I want to feel that joy again. I want to be able to go grab ice cream like it's no big deal. It's just frozen sugar and cream. It's not this happy memory we can never recapture. No, it's just a thing that people do to have something delicious or enjoy some time together.

But when Beth texts me and says, WE'LL GET ICE CREAM TO CELEBRATE. MY TREAT, my throat closes off. My eyes well up with tears.

It's stupid.

He's been gone for almost two years. Like, get over it, Ethan.

I haven't replied and it's been way too long, for a text. She's going to think I'm mad or something, so I need to say *something*. Anything is fine, probably.

I CAN'T LET YOU PAY. There. That's suitably flirty and easy breezy.

CAN AND WILL.

That makes me smile. Now she's the one telling me we should go out, which is definitely forward progress. WHAT DO YOU LIKE ON YOUR ICE CREAM?

ON IT? She sends a scrunched up face. NOTHING.

MIX INS, I MEAN.

JUST PLAIN CHOCOLATE FOR ME. I'M NOT FANCY.

I'M NOT FANCY EITHER, BUT ICE CREAM'S BETTER WITH MIX INS.

I DON'T EVEN KNOW WHAT YOU'RE SAYING, BUT IF WE GET LUCKY, CHILL GRILL, OVER IN GREEN RIVER, MIGHT HAVE HUCKLEBERRY.

IS THAT A JOKE? I ask.

NO JOKE. IT'S A REAL FLAVOR, AND IT'S SEASONAL, AND IT'S AMAZING.

Once I learn to keep things innocuous, I manage to keep her responding for over an hour. And the next day, I do even better. We may be enemies, and it does seem to be the case that her family is trying to oust us from the ranch, but once my mom quells that mess, I'll be ready to swoop in.

In the meantime, I'm working my best Romeo vibes via text.

I KNOW WE SAID AFTER THE TRIAL WE'D GET TOGETHER, BUT YOU TOTALLY IGNORED MY BIRTHDAY.

I DIDN'T IGNORE IT. I *MISSED* IT. THAT'S NOT THE SAME.

YOU SHOULD AT LEAST TAKE ME OUT FOR A BURGER.

WHAT ABOUT *MY* BIRTHDAY? YOU MISSED THAT, TOO.

GREAT! THAT'S EVEN MORE REASON FOR US TO GO OUT. WE CAN CELEBRATE BOTH OUR BIRTHDAYS, I text.

YOU'RE RIDICULOUS.

BUT YOU DIDN'T SAY I'M WRONG. BIRTHDAYS MUST BE CELEBRATED.

OH FINE, she texts. ICE CREAM AFTER THE TRIAL, *IF* YOUR MOM WINS.

SHE WILL. I'M SURE. SO WHY BOTHER WAITING?

STOP BEING GREEDY.

DO YOU REALLY BLAME ME? I text. IF YOU WERE ME, YOU'D BE GREEDY TOO.

WHAT?

YOU'RE THE FIRST PRETTY, SMART GIRL I'VE MET SINCE MOVING HERE.

I'M NOT PRETTY SMART. I'M PRETTY STUPID.

I MEANT THAT YOU'RE BEAUTIFUL *AND* SMART.

YOU MUST NOT GET OUT MUCH. She's funny.

SADLY, THAT'S TRUE.

GO OUT AND MEET SOME NEW PEOPLE.

WHAT IF I DON'T WANT TO MEET NEW PEOPLE? WHAT IF I ALREADY MET THE ONLY PERSON I WANT TO MEET?

I went too far, apparently, because she doesn't reply after that. I tossed and turned half the night, which is why I was late getting the cows fed that morning. It didn't help that Mom had an early meeting, but the combination meant that the kids missed the bus. Aunt Amanda took her girls early to do something at that store she's starting, which is such a stupid idea that I don't even know where to start, so I'm kind of stuck.

I'm groaning as I wave them all into the Tahoe. The last thing I wanted to do was interrupt my ranch tasks by driving three kids to school in Manila, but I try not to complain too much.

"Ethan," Gabe says.

"Yeah?" I sound a little terse, so I add the word, "Buddy." Then I sigh. "What's up?"

"Do you think Dad's watching us from heaven?"

I glance sideways at Izzy, who's sitting in the passenger's seat. "Uh."

"Yes," Izzy says. "He is. Mom says so."

Gabe nods. "Then do you think he knows where I hide my candy?"

Izzy snorts. "Uh, yeah, probably."

Our little brother's shoulders slump and he looks at his feet. "Will he tell Mom, do you think?"

Izzy laughs louder than me or Whitney.

"Why is that funny?" Gabe asks. "Aunt Amanda bought me gummy bears last time we went to the store, and they're my favorite. I need to know if I should eat them all today, or if I can eat just a few every day."

"I think a few a day should be safe," Izzy says.

"Roscoe's more likely to rat you out than Dad is," Whitney says.

Gabe nods slowly, like that makes sense. "Roscoe doesn't even like them, though, so I think it's fine."

"You gave some to Roscoe?" I can't help cringing.

"He eats anything," Gabe says. "He ate my salad last night. Except not gummy bears. He spit those out, and I didn't want Mom to see, so I had to eat them, and they were all slimy."

I cringe. "Oh, Gabe."

"What?"

I'm the one who gets stuck cleaning it up when Roscoe has an upset stomach, so aside from the obvious ick factor of Gabe eating after a dog, I'm not really happy to hear that Gabe's the one causing all the diarrhea. "No more salad and no more candy for Roscoe, okay? They're not good for him."

"But I've seen Emery feed him her broccoli." Gabe's voice always sounds so innocent, even when he's saying horrible things.

"Gah, don't let her do that either," I say. "Dogs aren't supposed to eat that stuff."

"Actually," Whitney says, "I read that dogs can eat a variety of things, including vegetables, as long as they don't eat chocolate or grapes."

"They aren't supposed to eat cooked bones either," Izzy says.

"Or pecans," Gabe says.

"But I think your gummy bears are safe," Izzy says. "So don't worry."

We're finally at the school, and I'm in the process of dropping the kids off when I notice a girl in a bright pink t-shirt climbing out of a car in the parking lot. Her hair's pulled back into a ponytail so it's harder to tell, but it looks like Beth. It might be a little creepy, but once the kids are all out and halfway to their respective school doors, I shoot forward, blocking her path. When she looks up, I can't help smiling.

It's her.

And underneath her jacket, she's wearing the shirt I gave her.

Her eyes widen first, and then she inhales, her mouth opening, her jaw dangling. And then, as if things are running slowly for her this early in the morning, she glances down, a look of horror on her face.

She got caught wearing the shirt I gave her.

I roll down my window. "My, you look quite sparkly today, Elizabeth."

She swallows.

"I was annoyed I had to drop the kids off, but. . ." I tilt my head a bit and stare at her shirt. "Now? Not nearly as much."

Her face is adorably close to the color of her shirt. It's not quite as pink as the shirt, but closer than I thought it could get.

I can't help beaming. "How do you feel about grabbing that burger?"

She shakes her head. "No way."

"But you look so *shiny* today. I feel like people should see this new you." I should stop smiling so much. She might think I'm gloating.

"I need to do laundry," she says. "Don't read into it."

"So you're saying I should bring you some more clothes?" I shrug. "Message received."

"Ethan." She arches one super cute eyebrow, but after seeing my mom do the same move a million times, it's like being hit with a Nerf gun after training to withstand an AR-15 attack.

"Beth, you're a lightweight. It's good that I like lightweights."

"I have a school project," she says. "I can't go to dinner."

"I'll bring it to you," I say. "How about we meet at that old bench in front of Steve's." I have work to do there this afternoon anyway. "I'll even bring a cupcake."

"What? Why?"

I roll my eyes. "So you can sing happy birthday to me, of course."

"Seven-thirty?" I ask. "Sun should just have set." I drive off before she can tell me no.

She probably won't come, but I grab some sandwiches and a cupcake from the True Value before heading back home just in case. Sure, they're not the best food, but I can stick them in Steve's fridge and grab them before I leave, and if she doesn't show, I can eat them both.

One of the perks of being a teenage boy.

Assuming Steve doesn't notice the cupcake.

Actually, even that's not super strange for me. I'm like a vacuum cleaner for food. The rest of the day crawls by. Steve sets me to work breaking up poop in his pastures, which isn't hard work, but it's so boring. Every time I check my watch, it's been even less time than the last time I checked.

But finally, *finally*, it's seven fifteen. Steve's on a horse, so I flip the arena lights on for him.

"Headed home?"

I nod.

"Alright, drive safe."

I'm using the four-wheeler, since I don't want Mom to know I'm here, or to ask *why* I'm coming to Steve's. "I'm going to grab some food I left in your fridge," I say. "I hope that was okay."

He shrugs.

I peel the now-soggy lettuce and tomatoes off the sandwiches and then I wrap them back up. I stuff them in my bag and head out, my heart hammering so loudly I can hear it in the back of my ears.

Why do I get so excited? What do I like so much about Beth? If my mom asked me that, I don't know what I'd say.

She's cute, sure. She's kind. She's funny. There aren't a lot of options around here, but I don't think that's it. I've met a few other girls, some through Izzy and Maren and a few through Jeff and Kevin, but none of them so much as made me smile.

Beth is. . .well, to use a word she already used. . .she's shiny.

Her dad may be a villain and her aunt may be shady, but she's not like that. She's like sunshine and birds singing and a cool, fresh breeze when I'm sweaty and gross.

Maybe I don't tell her those exact words.

I check my watch for the eighty-ninth time. It's seven-forty-three.

She's thirteen minutes later than I said to come. It's not like she's coming to eat amazing food, so maybe it's for the best. But still, I got my hopes up.

By seven-fifty-one, my nerves are frayed.

My heart's a little disappointed too, because I knew she wouldn't come, but I really hoped I was wrong. She wore the shirt. Was she really behind on her laundry? Is that all it was? But then the bushes rustle. A twig snaps.

And a deer bounds into the clearing.

I drop the sandwiches. Both of them roll out of

94

the paper and into the dirt, because I didn't re-wrap them very well.

"That sucks," Beth says.

My head snaps up.

The deer bounds away.

"I prefer my dinner without dirt and sticks." She jogs toward me and crouches in front of them. "Maybe I should have explained that."

I want to laugh.

I want to cry.

I want to hug her.

I just stand here, like a lump.

She looks up at me. "Are you alright?"

"You came," I say, like a dope.

"I was promised burgers." She pokes one of them. "I wonder how sick I'd get if I ate this, which is not burgers."

"I had to get it early in the morning, or I'd have had to explain to my mom why I needed the car. Sandwiches seemed like a safer choice." I pull the cupcake out of my bag. It's a little smooshed, in spite of its plastic box, but it's mostly fine. "I did bring a cupcake, though."

"But then what will you eat?" Beth stands up.

I shove the cupcake closer, and she finally accepts it. "I've got two sandwiches." Before she can argue or even squawk, I bend over and grab one of them. I brush it off and take a huge bite.

Beth bursts out laughing. "Gross."

"Since you've never had a brother, I imagine you have a lot of gross things to look forward to in our future." I beam, sure that bits of turkey are showing in my teeth.

"Wow."

I take another bite, speaking around the food. "You've been missing out."

I smile again, turkey mouth and all, and this time, Beth smiles back. It's definitely progress. I sit on the bench and pat the spot next to me.

"No beer this time?" I can't help asking.

She covers her face with her free hand. "Don't bring that up."

"Why not?" I crane my head around so I can see every part of her face that she's not covering. "You were really cute drunk."

She groans.

"I mean it," I say. "I've never drunk myself—my mom's a lunatic about that stuff—but I've had lots of friends who acted way stupider when they did."

Beth shakes her head, dropping her hand. "Way stupider?" She sighs. "What a great recommendation."

"It could have been worse," I say. "You didn't puke on me."

She straightens. "That's the bar?"

I shrug. "Drunk teens usually do, but you can hold your alcohol, apparently, so bravo."

"I don't want to hold it," she practically explodes. "I'm—I shouldn't have—the whole thing was—"

I drop a hand on her forearm. "Whoa, calm down." I haven't even mentioned that I'm doing work for Steve because we got caught. I wonder whether she remembers seeing him.

"It's just that, my mom is—" She cuts off. "Never mind. Look, I don't drink, okay? It was just a bad night, and—"

"It's fine," I say. "I won't mention it again."

Her shoulders droop and her face falls and her eyes drop. "My mom's a mess," she says, her voice terribly small. "I don't want to be like that."

"Then you won't be," I say. "I'm sure of it."

"I'm afraid I will be," she whispers. "It's probably my biggest fear."

"Meanwhile, everyone wishes I would be *more* like either of my parents." I can't help my dry chuckle. "Instead, I'm this reject who doesn't want to sit in classrooms or type words on a computer."

"My Aunt Donna's some kind of super genius, and my dad kind of hated her for it. School isn't always the answer."

"Preaching to the choir," I say. "I know plenty of people who went to great schools and they don't seem very happy."

"Is your mom happy?" Beth glances down at the cupcake, like she forgot she had it.

I stuff the rest of the sandwich in my mouth and lean forward to grab the other one. It's attracted a half dozen ants at this point, but I'm obviously not picky. Plus, I'm bigger than them. I start flicking them off. Unlike the Houston ants, I doubt they'll rally their friends and come to Gulliver my Travels.

Beth pokes at the frosting, peeling off the pink rose and eating it. "She seems happy."

"I mean, it's hard to tell since my dad died," I say. "She used to be really happy."

"Does she work more now?" Beth drags a finger through the fluffy white part of the cupcake frosting.

"So much more," I say. "She used to work a day or two a week, and then she did all the other stuff, like school meetings, house stuff, grocery shopping, cooking, meeting friends. But then Dad got sick and that stuff fell apart, and then when he died. . ." I shrug.

"I bet that's hard."

"She's kind of like superwoman," I say. "I'm sure she doesn't sleep enough, and I bet she's not very happy most of the time, but she never really complains, and she just keeps going, no matter what happens, no matter what goes wrong."

"I meant hard," Beth says, her voice somehow even smaller, "for *you*."

"Oh." For me? No one really asks about me. "I mean, I'm fine."

"Saying you're fine doesn't actually make it true," she says.

I roll my eyes. "But, like, I am. I work, I sleep, I eat." I take a big, mostly-ant-free bite of my second sandwich. "See?"

"And are you happy?"

I think about it, since she seems to really be asking, not as a courtesy. "I'm not sure I was happy back in Houston. After Dad died, when I wasn't watching the kids or taking them somewhere, I went four-wheeling with my friends almost every weekend, and I watched television, and I worked out, and I didn't really think about my dad being gone."

"That doesn't sound so bad, other than the 'dad being gone' part."

I guess she's right. "I mean, the thing is, I had an amazing dad. Not everyone can say that, but mine was. . .he was as good as my mom. I mean that as a really big compliment."

Beth doesn't say anything. She just licks the frosting off her finger and watches me, expectantly.

It stresses me out, talking about Dad, and I haven't really done it, not since Mom stopped making me go to that therapist. "So thinking about him being gone, well, it made me sad. I guess that made me just stop thinking about him at all. So that's why I did all the other stuff."

Beth cringes.

"I know. It's not the best solution, but it worked. I wasn't like, depressed, or anything. Only, every time I tried to think about college, I'd think about him, and. . ." I frown. "I wonder if that's why Mom was so worried about me not going. I bet she thought it was something like this. College made me think about Dad, and that made me sad, and so I didn't want to deal with it."

"Your mom sounds smart."

I shake my head. "I mean, she is smart, but that's not why I didn't want to go. I never wanted to go, even before. My dad knew that, but my mom didn't. And when I heard about this ranch, something inside of me wanted to *die,* thinking that some random people might get the ranch where my dad spent his summers, where my grandpa grew up."

"Your dad would have hated losing it too, probably."

"I'm not sure. See, my dad really only cared about one thing, other than us."

Beth lifts her eyebrows.

"My mom. We never came back here, because she was a city girl, through and through. It never occurred to him she might like it here, so I think he'd have been fine with not having the ranch if he thought it would keep her happy." I stuff the end of the ham sandwich in my mouth, and then I realize there's a chunk of twig in it, and I fish that out.

Beth's laughing when I chuck it on the ground. "You're kinda gross."

"Hey, it's your fault for running that deer through here."

"I spooked it, and it scared me too," she says. "Do you think I'm some kind of deer whisperer?"

I laugh. "Probably not. You look almost as city as my mom."

"I'm offended," Beth says. "I can rope a calf like any decent Manila native."

"Can you really?" I cannot imagine her, with her gracefully sloping arms, and her carefully combed hair, and her strappy sandals, roping anything, much less a muddy, recalcitrant calf.

"Of course. My dad's a rancher. Geez."

I shake myself a bit. "That's a new side of Beth I'd really like to see."

She giggles.

This is going better than I expected. "You asked if I'm happy. I have been happier here than I was back in Houston, and right now? I'm the happiest I've been since losing Dad."

Her face shuts down like an inn that's closed for business.

"Whoa, what was wrong about that?"

She shakes her head.

"Listen, I know I'm coming on strong, but I like you."

"I'm not super smart," she says. "And I'm not tough like your mom. No one would call me super, not even my own mother. And my dad really is a jerk, just like I said, and—"

I take her hand, expecting her to pull away.

But she doesn't.

A warmth spreads through me that I've never felt before. "Beth."

She looks up at me. "What?"

"I have a mother and two sisters who are total spitfires, and I love them to the ends of the earth."

"I can tell you do."

"But that's not what I want."

Her eyes widen and she swallows, her fingers tightening on mine. "It's not?"

"I like how calm you are. How. . .serene. That's the word I'd use. I like that you're more reserved and that you don't reach out and snatch any bit of energy and attention that's in a room."

"It did feel a little like the middle of a cattle drive at dinner."

My mouth dangles open. "Yes. That's how it feels being around my family. And the energy is fun, and it's all I know, but I want something a little more. . ."

"Calm?" She smiles. "But Ethan, I'm pretty sure exactly no one else I know would call me serene."

I laugh. "Fair enough. I still don't know you that well. But I want to get to know you better."

"Even if this is all going to end with a sharp drop off a high cliff?"

"Even then," I say. "And if it does, I'll call you Juliet, and you can call me Romeo, and we'll figure it out."

"I hated how they died at the end."

"Me too." I can't help smiling. "I mean, what idiots were they?"

"So stupid."

I stare at her face, and I realize that the more time I spend with her, the more I like it. "You may say you aren't smart, but we're smarter than they are. We wouldn't take poison, because neither of us are quitters. I'd do whatever it took, and I think you would, too."

9

BETH

I asked for a dog for Christmas every year from the time I turned three until I started high school.

It's not like having a dog on a ranch is difficult. Literally everyone I know has one. But my dad's mantra is that extra things like that, pets kept for emotional reasons, are always a bad idea. I knew my mom didn't care, but my dad's point was that he would be the one who had to do everything for it, which was true. Mom's always been utterly unreliable.

Christmas Day came and went, and still no wagging tail. No lolling pink tongue. No shaking puppy body. When I didn't get one that year either, I decided to just give up.

I'd have taken an old, decrepit one, really, but instead, I got yet another stuffed animal. This time, a beagle. I threw it on the pile of them in my rocking chair and pulled on my coat to go sulk in the barn.

It's not like I had nothing.

I had a horse I loved.

I knew that, for most city people, a horse was every little girl's dream. I liked my horse. Her name's Nedra, and she's a dun, and she's really sweet. She toted me around like a champ for trail rides, cattle drives, and any other time I needed to ride. But horses are a lot of work, and I'm not the only one who rode her. Dad's always had a handful of cattle hands, and she was used most days for real work on the ranch.

Even so, after tromping through the foot of snow on the ground to reach the barn, and ducking inside to circle the stalls until I reach hers, petting her nose made me feel a little better. She whuffled my hand for a moment, but once she realized I didn't have a carrot, she did what she always did, circling around so I could scratch her butt.

It wasn't quite the face lick or the hand bump I had hoped for, but it was better than nothing.

That's when I heard the whining sound for the first time.

My ears perked up like a hound on the scent of a fox, and I circled the barn, listening. When it came again, I was closer. It took me nearly an hour and a lot of quiet patience, but I finally found the source of the intermittent whines.

A small coyote—a pup—was pawing at a tiny hole on the corner of Dad's barn, trying to widen the opening enough to slip inside. Its nose would appear, one eye visible, and it would whine. Then it would disappear and its paws would once again dig and dig and dig. After any significant noise, it would disappear, but a moment or two later, it came back.

I clapped my hands twice, startling it, and then I

grabbed a hoe and used the sharp end to widen the opening. After waiting a bit, my patience paid off.

It returned, and this time, it squeezed through.

That pup was even cuter than I thought at first. I knew it was a coyote, because I'd seen plenty of dead ones in the past. In fact, this one was probably looking for a decent spot to weather this massive snowstorm because his mother was missing. It wouldn't surprise me if I found out his mother had been killed by my dad.

It's what he did.

Ranchers kill coyotes, always, without fail. It's a rancher thing.

Except this one looked just like the pet I wanted so badly, and it was *right here*, and if I didn't let it in, it would clearly die of cold. So I decided to take care of it. My parents had no idea why I kept darting outside and spending all day every day of my Christmas break in the barn, but they didn't really care.

I left them alone, which was a welcome break.

And if some of our choicest kitchen scraps didn't make it to the chickens, and if I asked for a lot more beef-based meals than usual, well, they didn't care about that either. I was happy—Nippy was the cutest pet ever, and he loved me. My parents were happy—I wasn't complaining about anything, and I was spending more time outside. Everything was fine.

Until Dad caught me feeding Nippy the scraps I'd swiped out of the trash and lost his mind.

He shot him five minutes later.

When I wouldn't stop crying, when I refused to speak to him, when I ran into my room and slammed the door, he didn't yell. He didn't bang on the door. He didn't even apologize. He simply stood outside my door and said, "You can't have a pet coyote. They're killers. It would've eaten our chickens and been a drain on our resources." In that moment, I wondered whether he saw me as a drain on his resources. But then he went one step further. "You've always been too soft."

I wondered whether he thought Mom was too soft, and that's why she couldn't stop with the pills and the drinking.

That night was the first time my dad played the villain in *my* story, and I still haven't forgiven him for it. Even now, when I close my eyes, I can see it. He glared at me, tilted his head and then shook it, walked across the barn—Nippy trotting along trustingly at his heels—opened his safe and pulled out a gun, and then shot him in the head.

Right in front of me.

He made me clean up the mess, including burying Nippy's body. I still can't think about it without shaking. When I told my mom, she was clearly on some kind of binge, because she patted my back, said, 'there there' and ordered me a bunch of clothes I didn't want.

"You'll feel better when those arrive." Her smile had been a little dull, and I realized later that she was totally high when we'd talked.

When I called Ethan shiny, I'm not sure he knew what I meant. I doubt someone like him can really understand what I mean when I say I'm *not* shiny. He's right, though, that I can't really know what he'll think about me unless I let him get to know me. But that's the scariest part.

He likes me right now.

A very large part of me wants to keep it that way.

Messed up people can only end up with messed up people, right? There's some kind of rule, I'm sure. Anyone who's as bright and shiny as Ethan will surely run when he starts to see the truth of who my family really is. Knowing that someone like him likes the idea of me—that's enough.

But I'm greedy at heart, just like my mother. As much as I want to say *no* to more time with Ethan to preserve his impression of me, I can't quite bring myself to do it. After the day I watched him eat two ground-sandwiches to spend time with me, he just texted me more. And every single text made me smile. Not a normal, lips-curling-upward kind of smile, either.

No, his texts made me *beam*.

And I started looking at things a little differently.

I've always been in charge of photos for the year-book, ever since my freshman year. My mom's a photographer, and at first, I just tagged along when she had seminars. Then, around eight or nine, I started paying attention. Sometime after that, I realized that for my mom, the seminars were often a cover. Dad would relax when she was 'working' and he might not notice that she was high. Plus, in a new place, there were new doctors, and when she met with a new doctor, he would often write her a prescription for pills.

But even if Mom wasn't paying attention to what was being taught, I was.

At first, not much of it made any sense, but over time, phrases like the rule of thirds, fill the frame, the rule of space, the golden ratio, they started to gel. And then other things, like apertures, aspect ratios, and shutter speed also started to swirl around in my brain. By the time I was in high school, I was teaching my art teacher basic photographic principles. . .and she assigned me to take photos for the school.

But after meeting Ethan, my photography changed.

Instead of snapping clean, classic images, or focusing on the individual in front of me, my point of view shifted. I still took the photos I had to take, but I noticed small details, like the sky's brilliant color shading when I focused on the dimension of the gravel on the ground. I started to notice the shiny, beautifully unique things that were all around me in sleepy, old Manila.

Brownings, with its metal moose on the side and unique metal walls. The aging school building with stunning mountains in the background. The flaming gorge I've driven past nine million times stood out in a new way.

Isn't it strange how your feelings about the world you've always known can change when your feelings about yourself and your own value in it shift, just a hair?

And that's what happens to me when Ethan starts flirting.

For the first time in my life, I start to wonder whether I might have been wrong about myself. Maybe I'm not trash. Would someone like Ethan like someone who was garbage? I find it extremely hard to believe.

Could I be worth more than I ever believed possible?

TONIGHT, EIGHT O'CLOCK.

There's a blizzard coming, so I know I won't see him for a while. It's exciting, meeting at the corner where our property meets Steve Archer's. First, there's the danger that the horse doc may catch us again, though as long as we aren't drinking, hopefully he won't get angry about it. But secondly, it feels like we're snatching moments together, and that makes them seem more special, somehow. Like seeing glimpses of a beautiful vista as you peer around the cracks in a fence. Because it's not *yours,* because it's not *easy,* it feels more worth the effort.

So with trembling hands, I text him back. WEAR A HEAVY COAT, CITY BOY.

He sends me a freezing cartoon emoji with icicles hanging off by way of response.

The moments crawl until it's time for me to sneak out. It should be easy—Mom's at rehab again. It's just me and Dad, and he never cares what I'm doing as long as I don't ask him for anything. It's sort of like being an emancipated teen with a credit card. I'm easing the cake I bought at the True Value out of the fridge when he speaks.

"What's that for?"

I drop it.

Of course I do.

I'm not very good at lying, and hiding things is like lying's younger brother—not quite as impressive, but still related. I'm obviously equally bad at it.

"Oh, man," I say. "Now it's ruined."

"Why did you buy a whole cake?" Dad shakes his head. "What a waste."

I think about Ethan, brushing ants and dirt and sticks off those two soggy sandwiches and eating them anyway. It makes me laugh.

"Why is this funny?" Dad glares. "You're cleaning it up."

"I could probably salvage the top," I say in a fit of generosity. "Want some?"

Dad rolls his eyes in disgust and leaves.

Thankfully, he isn't around to notice that I *do* salvage the top, and I shove the cake box under my arm when I slide out the back door. I'm stuck racing across the dark and hard-to-navigate ground, praying half-heartedly that I won't twist an ankle. I'm late, but Ethan's waiting patiently when I arrive.

"You came."

"You were worried?"

He shrugs. "I think I'm always worried until I see you."

I can't help my grin. "Me, too."

"My Juliet."

I shake my head. "No, that had a terrible ending, remember?"

"But we decided that we'll do better."

"Why don't we pick a different story?"

Ethan moves closer. "Everyone in the world knows that one—their love story is epic." He bites his lip. "Did you ever watch *Little Women* as a kid?"

I shrug. "I think so. Isn't that the one where the sister is just awful and throws her older sister's book on a fire?"

He nods.

"And then someone cuts her hair," I say. "And then the awful sister gets the guy?"

Ethan laughs a little too loud. "My sisters hated it, too."

"Shh," I say. "What if Dr. Archer hears you?"

"Oh yes," he says. "We'd be in real trouble if he heard us standing here, laughing, while holding. . ." He squints. "What is that? A mashed ball of. . ." He lifts his eyebrows. "Yogurt?"

I thrust it at him. "It's floor cake. I figured if you'd eat ground sandwiches, you wouldn't turn your nose up at floor cake."

He snatches it so fast it practically makes my head spin. "Never."

"But what made you laugh so loud?"

"My sisters rewrote the ending," Ethan says. "And they made me perform it as a play."

"They what?" I can see it now, Ethan as his sister's boyfriend. "Which one played the writer?"

"Izzy, of course," he says.

"And who played the guy the horrible sister ends up with?"

"She didn't get the guy, and that was clearly Gabe."

That makes *me* laugh. "Then who—"

"The point is that we can rewrite the ending." Ethan's eyes are intent, and I can't look away.

"But the ending from the *Romeo and Juliet* movie is epic and well-known," I say.

"The movie?" Ethan's eyebrows shoot up.

"Yes."

"It's not a movie."

"Um, I hate to disagree with you, but I think Claire Danes would say otherwise."

"That's like saying *The Lord of the Rings* was a movie," Ethan says. "I mean, it was turned into a movie, but it was a book first. And *Romeo and Juliet* was most definitely a play before it was anything else."

With anyone else, I'd be embarrassed, but not with Ethan. He's made it clear that he thinks I'm great, so him mocking me feels like. . .like it felt to watch him tease Izzy and Whitney.

It feels like I'm family.

Like I belong.

It feels nice.

"Fine, *fine*," I say. "But don't call me Juliet anymore."

"What if, in our version, Juliet and Romeo win their families over, and they get married and live happily ever after?"

"It feels unlikely." I can't help worrying. It's like we're standing on train tracks, watching the huge machine chug along toward us.

"Well, first, your aunt will decide she doesn't want our ranch." Ethan plops down on the bench, shivering just a bit.

"I told you to wear a heavy coat."

"I wasn't cold earlier," he says. "But that front is starting to roll in."

I sigh. "You probably weren't cold because you were working at Steve's." I unwind my thick blue scarf and wrap it around his neck. "Here. This will keep all that heat from escaping around your neck and head." I'm almost done wrapping it when his eyes catch mine. He shines like the sun, even in the moonlight.

"Yes, this little wad of yarn will fix everything." The corner of his mouth turns upward, but his eyes drop to my mouth. "Actually, I can think of something that would warm me up."

My heart leaps in my chest and then it takes off at a gallop. "Wha-what did you have in mind?"

Ethan's twitching lip transforms into an evil grin. "I think you know." He leans closer, and I know what he's going to do.

I want him to do it, but I'm also scared. I throw my finger up, pressing it to his mouth. "This could still end really badly. We haven't written that part yet."

"We both see our families' weaknesses," Ethan says, leaning closer. He has just a tiny smudge of frosting on the corner of his mouth. I can't seem to look away from it.

"I definitely see mine," I say. "But your family's great."

"How about this. I vow to be too smart to take poison, and if your family pushes you over the edge, I promise to call Dr. Archer to pump your stomach." He smiles his cocky grin.

"Maybe." His lip is so close. I want to reach out and lick the frosting off.

Ethan's eyes follow mine, and his voice is barely a murmur. "The bad news is that we're about to be stuck in our respective homes, thanks to a blizzard."

I think about all the time I'm about to spend with *just my dad,* and I want to cry. I can't stop looking at that delicious smudge on his very delicious looking mouth. Without really thinking about it, I lean closer, my eyes still intent.

"I really, *really* want to kiss you," Ethan says. "But my family has some kind of terrible stomach bug." He sighs melodramatically. "I wouldn't be a very good boyfriend if I exposed you to it." He scoots over about four inches, his exhalation dramatic.

Boyfriend.

The word explodes through my heart, and I practically shudder.

I've never wanted anything as much as I want that word to be true.

"I'm willing to risk it," I whisper.

Ethan's grayish blue eyes stare into mine intently, and then he slides back over, his head dropping, his mouth closing over mine. He's not fumbly or unsure, and my body curves toward him instinctively, one of my hands lifting and sliding into his thick blond hair.

He makes a little sound then—a little sigh—and for the first time in my entire life, I *swoon*.

Sitting down.

I never understood that word until this very moment, but now? I get it. It's not about passing out, or falling over, or even being caught by the guy. No, it's when the very soul in your body moves toward another person and a little thrill of joy runs through you from head to toe all at the same time. It's when your yearning meets his and they curl against one another, perfectly fitting together.

I shift upward, pressing closer against Ethan, who's quite warm up close, and he shifts too, pressing his hand against my cheek.

But then there's a big crash.

And I realize the stupid cake has, once again, hit the floor. Only, this time, it's face down on a big muddy spot.

"Well, that's too bad," Ethan says.

"Are you really that hungry?"

His grin shifts back to fiendish. "Not for cake." He snorts. "But that white frosting's going to be pretty hard to clean up."

"Blizzard," I say. "If we just scoop up what we can and toss that plastic container in the trash, no one will ever notice."

"I'm liking this terrible northern weather more and more." Ethan leans forward again, but instead of kissing my mouth again, he presses a kiss to the end of my nose. "It gave me a good reason to kiss you, too. And now, maybe you'll miss me over the next few days."

"I was already going to miss you," I confess, the words so small that a part of me hopes he didn't hear them.

"I miss you now," he says, "just thinking about the next few days."

I lean against him, my face pressed against his chest for a moment, until a strong wind gust hits us both, and we shiver in unison. "You better get back," he says. "I've got to get home before my mom leaves."

"Go," I say. "But whenever you do have cell reception." I hold up my phone.

"I'll text you, sweet Juliet." He grins.

I still don't love the comparison, but maybe, just maybe, we can rewrite the ending. I don't hate that idea at all.

❧ 10 ❧

BETH

I was never much for Shakespeare. In fact, I never even read it. I'm more of a Cliff's Notes kind of girl. But over the next few weeks, I actually break out the play.

I don't ever read it, but I do watch the movie several times.

And I meet Ethan even more often. We have cake. We drop more cake. We make out. All of it's fun, even though the weather in Daggett County is not doing us any favors.

He wears my scarf every single time.

I wear the shirt he gave me, even if it's so covered in jackets and coats that he can't see how shiny it makes me. He can see the smile on my face, and maybe that's enough.

Thanks to him, I actually start to feel pretty shiny myself. My Aunt Donna even does me a huge favor and switches sides. The bummer is that, it turns out, she was never really the most important bad guy.

I'm not super shocked to discover it was my dad spearheading this.

But when November eighth rolls around, I'm optimistic. Partly, it's that Ethan is just *so sure* his mom will take care of the problem. I guess in all the years he's known her, she's never lost. Or, that's what he says.

He tells me stories about how she got his English teacher to regrade his paper. How she terrified the school counselors when Izzy got made fun of for praying during school. How she argued with some curling iron company and got a free iron, a full refund, and an apology letter.

Plus, of course, she's a real *Harvard* lawyer, and my dad's just. . .well, a bully. A determined and experienced bully, but still just a bully. More than anything else, though, I have faith in Ethan. So when he asks me to go to ice cream *before* we've heard the verdict, I just agree.

"I mean, if this goes badly, at least I'll have a face full of ice cream to console me," I say.

"That's the spirit," Ethan says.

I'm driving, because his mom's using their car. "I can't believe you don't have your own car," I say. "I mean, you're eighteen."

"My mom's really old school about that stuff," he says. "I was hoping to be able to spend some of the money from the cattle we sold to buy something, but—"

"I know. That Derek guy shafted you, and then you and your mom did your best, but it's hard to do stuff like this the first time." I sigh. "I'm sorry that all went wrong." If I'd paid more attention to the details of my dad's business, I might have been able to help them. I didn't know they needed to make arrangements to water their cows on the day of the auction, either. I kind of assumed the sale lot would have water there, just like they did.

"It's fine," he says. "Unless you're not into me anymore, because I keep showing up on a clapped-out four wheeler. . ."

I roll my eyes. "It's fine."

"Oh, no." He presses his hand to his heart. "I knew it. You're taking me to get ice cream so you can let me down easy."

I know he's kidding, but when he says that, I think about how I'd feel if we were breaking up, and my heart almost stops. I shouldn't be in this vulnerable place right now. We were supposed to be planning a first date *today*, and only if his mom beats my dad.

But if it goes the other way, I'm going to be wrecked.

Not disappointed.

Not frustrated.

Wrecked.

I'm already *way* too vested in this guy. *Danger, Beth, danger!* Only, even thinking about that doesn't make me anything but happy to be with him.

And I should enjoy this—the first real, public date we've ever had. The first time I've let him take me out where people can see us. It's a little scary, going out like we're official. Taking Ethan to get ice cream at a place I loved as a kid. Driving almost an hour in winter for something cold.

It's kind of crazy, really. I hope they still *have* ice cream right now. When we reach the diner-looking place, Ethan's staring at me.

"What?"

"This says it's a *grill*."

I'm nervous, my hands still at ten and two on the steering wheel. "Yeah. It is."

"I said *ice cream*," he says. "That's a sort of noncommittal date."

What's he saying?

"This feels like a real-deal kind of date, and I may not be ready for that." He compresses his lips, and I realize he's kidding.

I roll my eyes and yank the keys out of the ignition.

"Beth."

I whip my head back his direction. "What now?"

He's leaned closer, and now his face is just an inch or two from mine. "Kiss me."

I swallow. "What?"

"Before we go in there, kiss me, here in this car, where no one we know is anywhere around, and tell me that you're as excited as I am for our first date."

"I am," I whisper. And then I shift a hair.

Ethan comes the rest of the way, nearly crawling over the center dash to reach me, his hand gently pulling me closer, his mouth covering mine. As strongly as it did the first time, my heart races.

This kind, funny, smart, *hot* guy really likes me. . .and we're going on a date. If this trial goes well, he'll be my boyfriend for real, and if he had a white horse and a suit of armor, we'd be like a fairy tale in a book. It all feels. . .surreal. Like it can't really be my life.

I practically float into the 1950s themed diner, not paying much attention to the red and white checked paper in the baskets, or the absurdly long menu. "I'll have a cheeseburger and a huckleberry shake," I say, when we reach the counter.

"Did you see they have a soda fountain?" Ethan asks. "Do you still want that?"

"What do you want?" I ask.

"A root beer float," he says, and then he licks his lips like he's four years old.

I've never wanted to kiss someone more in my life.

So I do.

Right there, in front of the cashier, in front of everyone in the diner.

Which is about four other people, but still.

Someone behind us claps.

When I finally drop back, Ethan says, "Wow, if I knew you were such a big fan of root beer floats, I'd have asked for one before now."

I giggle.

The lady behind the register clears her throat. "We don't got huckleberry. It's winter."

I sigh. "Figures. Alright, two root beer floats, then."

Ethan taps his cheek.

"What?"

"You said root beer float. Isn't that code for, 'I want to kiss you, you hot, hot man'?"

I roll my eyes and turn back toward the cashier. "Two cheeseburgers, and two—" I drop my voice to the barest whisper. "Two root beer floats."

Ethan laughs. "I still heard it."

The cashier rings us up, and I try to pay. "I said it was my treat."

"Our first real date can't be your treat. If it was

just ice cream, maybe, but we're getting dinner." He nods slowly. "You have to let me pay."

More importantly, the cashier takes his card.

I sigh in mock surrender. "Fine, but the next date—"

"Will also be paid for by me. What kind of boy do you think my mom raised?"

"The kind who can't even afford a car?" I scrunch my nose.

And Ethan frowns. "Rude. You're rude on our first date."

I lift my chin. "Honesty is never rude." I tuck my credit card back into my purse. "But if I pay half the time, you can get a car sooner, and then we can go on more dates."

He sighs slowly. "I'll allow it."

The rest of the meal is just as nice. We're both just finishing our root beer floats when my phone dings. It's Aunt Donna.

TESTIMONY DIDN'T GO SO WELL. HAD TO HANG AMANDA OUT TO DRY.

That's unfortunate, especially for Aunt Donna, because I know she likes both Amanda and Abigail, but. . .ultimately, I don't care. As long as Ethan can stay, I don't care about anything else. But no one texts after that.

When I text Aunt Donna asking for an update, she's silent.

The ride back to Manila's not quite as bubbly and exciting as the ride to Green River. In fact, now that we've eaten our ice cream and our date's over, I feel. . .unaccountably nervous. *What ifs* sneak into my mind, and I can't seem to get rid of them. I told Ethan that if my dad cost them their ranch, we couldn't date. But is that strictly true? I mean, I doubt Ethan will blame me.

He says he won't.

But it's not like, without a ranch, he'd have a reason to stay here. His family's from Houston, and there are better colleges there. No matter what he says, if he's not running a ranch, he's the kind of kid who will go to college.

At the end of the day, I'm just a high school senior in Manila, UT, and if Ethan's family loses this ranch, all their shiny goodness will move back to Houston, abandoning me to live here all alone in the pitch-black darkness left in the wake of their departure.

I breathe in through my mouth and out through my nose all the way back. We're passing through downtown Manila when Ethan's phone rings.

"Hey, Mom. I'm just—"

He's quiet. I wish I could hear what Abigail's saying.

"What?"

Still nothing. But his expression isn't good.

"Just tell me now," he says. "I'll be home soon, but I want to know what happened."

Silence, again, and a sinking feeling's starting in my belly. Eating an entire hamburger and float felt like a good idea at the time, but now I'm starting to think it wasn't my smartest move.

"So we lost it?" He barely pauses. "I don't understand. But you said—"

He swallows and looks out the window.

This time, his voice is very small. "Can we appeal it?" And now it's explosive. "How can you say that?"

His hand strikes the window, hard.

"Fine."

He pauses again.

"Why do you care? I'll be home soon." He hangs up.

I open my mouth to ask what happened, but I realize it doesn't really matter. They lost the ranch, clearly. And now I have to go home to the jerk who stole it from them—or, you know, who cost them the ranch, anyway—and listen to him gloat.

Why did I think this was going to go well? I know my dad. He'd stab a kitten in the eye for twenty bucks. Luckily, we're only a few blocks from the ranch Ethan just lost, so the pained silence doesn't stretch for very long.

"I'm sorry."

My words drop like water on a hot skillet, doing nothing at all. Hissing into the night helplessly and then gone.

"It's not your fault." Ethan turns toward me then. "You know, when Mom told me that the judge —" He shakes his head. "I thought I'd be really upset if we lost it, because I love that ranch." His broad shoulders slump a little. "I feel like I'm closer to my dad there, but when my mom said we lost it, the first thing I thought was, 'No way. I'm not leaving Beth.'"

My heart lurches, drunkenly, staggering as if from a blow.

"I'm not going," he says. "Mom can appeal it, or if she doesn't, then. . ." He throws his hands up in the air. "I don't know, but that's not it. I'm not done yet."

"Ethan."

He looks at me, his face not crestfallen or angry.

123

He's energized, ready to fight for what he wants. But I don't see the guy I've come to adore. The guy I think I love. The guy I've never been good enough for.

What I see when I look at his adorable, handsome, devoted face is Nippy, the coyote. I see his trust in me, his genuine goodness, and his hope for the future. And I know that, if given half a chance, my dad will do even more damage to Ethan than he's already done today. He'll shoot Ethan right in the head and never lose a minute's sleep over it.

Only, I can't survive something like that with just a few days of crying. I can't stand by and watch as something as beautiful, as good, and as amazing as Ethan is ruined. I'm older now. I'm stronger now. I'm braver now. And that's how I'm capable of doing what I should have done years ago.

This time, I run that coyote off before he can get shot.

ꙮ 11 ꙮ

ETHAN

After my dad died, I felt numb.

Like nothing really hurt me. But nothing really made me laugh or smile, either. It felt like I'd been wrapped in a huge roll of bubble wrap, and I was walking around totally untouchable.

Of course, not feeling anything is better than hurting.

But it's not great, either.

No pain, no joy. No sadness, no delight. No despair, no elation.

Beth unwrapped that bubble wrap, and then I got socked in the gut. I know it's stupid to say we broke up, since we were officially dating for like one day, but that's how it feels. I check my phone at least twenty times a day, and I send a message to her about half of those times, but she never replies.

I wonder whether texting her ten times a day would be grounds for her to get a restraining order. I could ask my mom, if we were talking. No matter how many times I begged her to appeal the judge's ruling, she just shook her head. "Let it go, Ethan," she said. "He's the finder of fact, and it's a factual issue. No appellate judge will overturn it. I did the best I could, given that we left for a month. The will was clear."

I know she's sad too.

I know she did her best.

I know I'm rubbing a sore spot raw.

I know she thinks it means we're not meant to be here.

I know that I'm not the only person badgering her, either. Steve's at least as upset as I am.

But the thing is, I can't seem to help it. I can't stop texting Beth. I can't stop dinging Mom. I can't stop doing any of it, because I hate how powerless I feel. I haven't felt this powerless since Dad got sick, and that time, nothing I did helped. I hate feeling like this, and I don't want to be here again. I can't stop chasing the high I felt when Beth liked me, when I had a future, and when I wanted to wake up in the morning and do exactly what I was doing.

I know what my stupid therapist would say.

He'd tell me to look to the future, not the past. He'd tell me that I need to work through my feelings, not get caught up in them. I'd really like to chuck my stupid grief journal at his face and tell him that my anger's justified.

The world is unfair.

Why would God even give us this ranch and introduce me to Beth, just to take it all away? Mom says He never gives us things we can't handle, but I think that's wrong. This was just mean.

It's like handing Gabe the ultimate Lego collection, and then melting it down to goo in a pot in front of his eyes. It's like showing Izzy a video of her winning the NRHA derby and then having her turn around and discover it's not really her. It's like Whitney being crowned queen, and then the country falls into civil war on the first day.

It's cruel.

Is God really this cruel?

First Dad, then this? It sure feels like He is. Mom would say this is when I *need* to be praying, but I think that's wrong. I'm not going to go talk to the guy who just socked me on the chin.

I'm too pissed for that. Anything I say will just make it worse.

"Ethan." Mom taps on my door.

"What?" I hate how surly I sound. I know Mom did her best. I know she's as upset as I am. But I also know that there's a part of her that's relieved, and that's why I can't seem to let go of my anger with her, either.

"Izzy helped me load up the back of the Tahoe, but we're making a lot of progress going through the girls' room. Can you possibly drive it over to Amanda Saddler's and unload it for me?"

She wants me to start moving all our stuff—the temporary move we're making so the girls and Gabe can finish this school term. The thought of that— moving again for just a few weeks—irritates me more. I hop up and open the door, ready to tell her exactly what I think about her plan to run back to Houston.

But when I open the door, she looks so *tired*. It's the mom I remember from the year after Dad died, and I can't yell at her. Mom's not the enemy. I know she's not. I hug her instead, and something about that makes me almost start to cry. I spring away and jog to the front door.

I can't cry in front of Mom. I know it'll make her cry, and she's spent way too much time crying in the past few years. If God socked me on the chin, he kicked her in the face, and she's still here. Going through the girls' room. Swimming against the current.

Fighting the fight, even when it really sucks.

Maybe for the first time, I understand a little bit why Romeo and Juliet took that poison. I still don't respect them. I still think the story sucks. But I *get* it in a way I didn't before. Sometimes, when it feels like everything is stacked against you, when it feels like none of it is your fault, it's tempting to just give up.

But I'm not like that, so I grit my teeth, and I inhale until I'm not about to cry, and I park Mom's car in Amanda Saddler's front drive. I have to kind of psych myself up to deal with her by myself. I know Mom and Aunt Amanda really like her, but she's a really weird old lady.

For instance, what kind of person wants a pet that turns into bacon? It's not even nice to rub. It's not as bad as a porcupine, but it's too close for comfort. And isn't that the point of pets? Comfort? So why have one that's neither cute nor soft?

Whatever.

She's letting us stay with her for a few weeks, and that feels better than up and moving right before the holidays. Although, the thought of spending our first Christmas up here in some stranger's house instead of in the home we've grown used to living in depresses me. I tried to convince Mom to try and buy the ranch in the auction, but she didn't even consider it.

"Ranches like this only make financial sense if they're paid off," she says. "And even then, it's a lot of work to make a smallish amount of money."

That, in a nutshell, has always been Mom's issue with this whole thing. She's all about maximizing gains. How much can a job bring in for the smallest amount of work? It's funny that, for someone who pays a lot of attention to that, she had so many kids. One kid might bring you joy, and you have to invest in it, but I can see why someone like her might have one.

But four?

It's way more work for a negligible increase in joy, especially when the four of your children fight and squabble.

Although, given how little I've followed in her and Dad's footsteps, maybe it's good she invested in children who might actually fulfill their potential. Jeff and Kevin told me they've been saving to buy a ranch of their own, and they're a little short yet, but they said if I could borrow some money myself, the three of us could buy the ranch together.

I really thought about it.

It's what I want to do, frankly, even if I'd be co-owning it with two other guys. They're decent people. I trust them. They know their stuff. They like the area. They work hard.

But if I did that, if I took out a loan on the ranch and stayed when my family went back to Houston. . .I can't help seeing it all over again in my mind—Mom's face when I whipped the door open. I may not be the college-boy clone Mom and Dad deserved, but I'm not a bad enough son to stay here while my mom does everything with the other three kids all alone.

"Hey, kid," Amanda Saddler says. "You gonna sit there all day?" She taps on the window with one knobby finger.

I jump.

For an old lady, she moves pretty quietly.

"Did you freeze to death in there?" Her head leans closer to the glass, and I open the door. Not enough to hit her in the head, but enough that she knows I'm coming out.

"Your mom said you had a load of stuff?"

I nod.

"It's going in the barn, I think." She points.

Duh. Mom and Izzy were packing stuff in suitcases for the few weeks we'll be living here, and the rest is just being packed up until we get a rental truck to haul it back. "Right. Sorry."

I'm about to close the door so I can pull the truck forward when her gnarly hand curls around the edge of the door. "Wait just a second. How about, while you're already right here, you come help me rearrange some stuff."

I should've expected something like this. She's being awfully generous, letting us stay here for free. We should have offered to help her haul some things out of the rooms we're occupying so Gabe won't break them. I slide out the door and zip up my coat against the brisk wind. "Sure, I'm happy to haul out whatever you need, too."

"Haul out?" She arches an eyebrow so high it almost hits her knit cap. "What are you saying, boy?"

I swallow. "No idea. Why don't you tell me what I should be saying?"

She cackles. "Yes, good boy." She starts for the house, her head bobbing, her weird little pig bouncing along after her. Watching them head for the door, I realize they make more sense than I thought. Amanda Saddler's not your average old lady, and it would be crazier for her to have, like, a fluffy little lapdog, than it is for her to have a pig wearing what I swear looks like a Lololime vest.

I'm not even going to ask.

"Now listen here."

I trot after her as fast as I can manage so I don't guess wrong again.

"You're bringing all this joy to my house, so I wanted to be ready for it."

Joy? What's she talking about? Has she met Whitney? Or Gabe?

Maybe she's having a stroke.

"I'm sorry?"

She's stopped in front of her brightly painted door. "For what?"

"I didn't understand. Did you say we're bringing *joy*?"

"Of course I did," she says. "You're bringing happy little children and—"

I can't help laughing. "You're in for a very rough few weeks, I'm afraid."

"You should stop being sorry and afraid, young man." She scowls at me. "You don't know what you have, so you should stop telling people things you don't understand."

Um, okay.

"I'm more excited for my houseguests than I

have been in a long time, and I need to rearrange some furniture to make sure you're all comfortable."

Two and a half hours later, I've moved three beds out of storage and set them up, and I've helped her put clean linens on the mattresses. We also cleaned off several end tables, chest-of-drawers, and desks, and moved them into the rooms that were deemed deficient.

"It looks like I need to order about ten pillows," she says.

"We have lots of pillows," I say. "We can bring our own."

"Are you sure?" She pins me with the glare I'm growing used to seeing.

"A hundred percent," I say.

"Hm." She sighs.

I see my opportunity to break away and take it. "Maybe I better head on over to the car and start unloading it."

She shakes her head. "Of course, of course. Sorry this took so long. You're a better sport than you look."

Does she mean I'm more athletic? Or is she commenting on my attitude? "Sorry," I say. "It's been a bad month."

She barks a laugh. "I guess it has. I know you're the one who had your heart set on that ranch."

I can't bring myself to say anything.

"Chin up, boy. Things have a way of working out."

"Maybe in movies," I mutter.

"Ethan Brooks." Amanda's straightened up to her full five foot three inches. Her hair's poking up at strange angles now that she's not wearing her hat.

Her bony elbows are both visible, with her baggy sweater shoved up above them, and her right eyebrow has a piece of lint dangling from it.

Even so, she manages to be pretty intimidating.

"What?"

"You, sir, need a better attitude."

"I need better luck."

If she starts lecturing me, I'm going to have to bite my tongue. I swear, old people think that if they talk to us long enough, our feelings will just age out and die. That's not how it works. But I also know that anything I say will probably be repeated to my mom, so. . .

"Your luck in life will always be shifting." As if the hot air inflating her fury somehow just *poof*, disappeared, she abruptly sits. "But your family's always there for you."

She's not wrong—and she is. "Unless they die."

Her head snaps up, her eyes flashing. "Yes, until they die."

I shrug. "I'll try to have a better attitude."

"Is it just about the ranch?" She looks curious. "And your dad? Or is it something more? Something else?"

I look at the door. I was so close to escaping. "Just the ranch," I say. "I'm fine."

"So it was something else." Her half smile's a little unnerving.

"Did you hear me? I said just the ranch."

"Oh, I heard you boy. You lied and said it was just the ranch." She pats the sofa next to her chair. "Sit."

"I've got an entire carload of—"

"Ethan Brooks, sit down."

I sit.

"What else is going on this month in particular?"

I haven't told anyone about Beth. At first, it was because it was kind of exciting to have a secret. But then, it was like it was too late. You can't really get sympathy for a loss no one knows you had. If I'd been more honest at the start, I might have a support system in dealing with my not-breakup.

I mean, I told Mom I like Beth.

But she thinks it's the same way I like Ford F-150s. Or the same as I like chocolate cake. Or how Gabe likes Legos.

She doesn't know I like her like she likes Dr. Archer.

That was my one hope, really. That she might want to stick around for him. I guess he's a little bummed about not being enough, too.

"It's that Ellingson girl, ain't it?"

I nearly jump out of my skin. "Are you telepathic?"

She cackles, and I swear, she sounds scarier than any witch on any Halloween movie I've ever seen. When she slaps her leg, I can't quite keep from shifting away from her by a few inches on the sofa.

"I knew it."

She's pretty insightful for a woman who lived next to the love of her life for fifty plus years without ever telling him, much less kissing him.

"So you're upset because you like that girl, and now her daddy lost you the ranch and you're moving. You mad at her? Or just yourself?"

"Neither."

"Your mom, then."

I shake my head. "I mean, I know she tried."

"But your mom doesn't try. She *wins*."

I look at my feet.

"And she let you down."

"I'm a jerk for even thinking it," I say. "I know that. I love her, and I know she did her best."

"Maybe," Amanda Saddler says. "You know, this isn't really her fault, though."

"No?" I meet her unsettling gaze. "Whose fault is it? Beth's dad?"

Amanda Saddler shrugs. "Snakes bite. It's what they do. Blaming them is a waste of time. But old Jed really screwed this one up royally. What that idiot was thinking, I will never know."

"If he'd just given it to us, like everyone thinks he should have, we'd have just sold it."

She stares at me for a moment. "You're smarter than you look."

"I look stupid?" I can't help being a little offended about that.

"Pretty boys are usually dumb." Her smirk brightens her whole face. I wonder what she looked like fifty years ago. I wonder if Jed loved her like I love Beth.

In that moment, I realize that I do.

I mean, I'm eighteen. I'm sure Mom would say that I don't really know what love is. But I think it's something that makes you happy. It's something that makes you want to work hard. It makes you want to run fast. It makes you want to break things if they get in your way. It makes you think about that person morning, noon, and night, and maybe it makes you text them so much that you could get confused with a stalker. And when you can't see them, you feel all broken and stubby inside.

135

If that's what it is, then I do know.

"I love her," I say. "And without Uncle Jedediah's weird will clause, I wouldn't have ever met her. I just wish that judge had tried to do what Uncle Jed wanted, and not just what it said in the will."

"Just because that idiot never took a vacation, he shouldn't have limited you guys to a week." She shakes her head. "He was such a stubborn fool."

And in that moment, watching Amanda Saddler thinking about the person she loves, and thinking about Beth myself, I wonder whether it's all a futile waste of time.

"Family's always a complicated mess," she says. "And you have a lot of family." She leans a bit closer. "But it's the best mess in the whole world. You may feel a little cursed, but really, you're luckier than most people I've ever met. Try to remember that."

"That's probably true," I say. "But it doesn't help me right now."

"Don't give up on her, then. Just because you're moving back to Houston—"

"I don't even want to move," I say. "I told her that, but she won't even text me back."

"Did you tell her you love her?" She isn't mocking me, and that's a relief.

"Of course not. I only just admitted it to myself."

She nods. "Smart boy. Don't breathe a word of that."

"No?" It feels momentous, like I should tell the world, like I should at least tell my mom. And of course Beth needs to know, too.

"No way."

"This is coming from the woman who let fifty years pass—"

She slaps my shoulder. "Stop. Just because someone made one mistake for a really long time doesn't invalidate all her other advice. Now, listen. I may not know you very well, but I've known the Ellingsons for a long time. And that sweet, shy girl?"

Now I'm hanging on her every word and she knows it.

"She's like a scared duckling. You're not gonna get her to come out with big declarations." She shakes her head. "No. You want her to come to you, so you're going to have to friend zone her."

"Friend zone her?" Clearly Amanda Saddler is an idiot. I stand up. "Good talk."

"I mean it, boy."

"I'm sure you do."

"It's not what I did with Jed," she says quietly, as if she knows what a bomb that will be.

"Wait. It's not?"

"I froze him out. That's totally different than this. The opposite, in fact."

I sit back down. "How so?"

"You're going to keep yourself in the game, you big lummox. You're going to be there, outshining all the other little boys she meets, and acting like it's totally fine, and that you don't even like her. That'll keep the little duckling from swimming away."

"Okay. Tell me more." I like the idea of being able to see her, even if I can't kiss her.

"Listen, I pushed and pushed and pushed with Jed and your grandpa, and I pushed so hard that it burned the bottom of the soup pot."

Huh?

"It's too many metaphors." She waves her hand.

"The point is, if I'd let them sort things out before I got involved, I might have had a chance."

From what I can tell, she had fifty years of chances that neither she or Jed took, but maybe she's right. Maybe I don't really understand that. "Back to the friend thing?"

"Let Beth settle things with her dad. Let her settle things with herself. Don't give up on being in her life, but don't push and try to date her. Can you do that?"

Not if I'm living in Houston, but I guess I still have a few weeks. "I think so."

"Good." She smiles and pats my back. Her grip's surprisingly strong. "Good boy."

I wish I didn't feel like a dog right now.

"Ethan?"

I stand again. "Yeah?"

"I can already tell you're a strong offensive player. You'll be able to get out of that friend zone when it's time."

My hands are shaking by the time I finish unloading all the stuff and drive home. Mom and the girls have managed to gut their rooms, and it makes me pretty sad. But even with the long day it's been, and even with trembling hands, I stare at my phone like an addict.

HOW ABOUT A DEAL?

I shoot the text off before I have time to think.

She doesn't reply, of course. I've conditioned her to ignore me, clearly.

I'LL PROMISE TO GIVE UP ON DATING YOU.

Still nothing.

Amanda Saddler is a moron.

I brush my teeth, and then I plug in my phone. I can always circle back around tomorrow. Then my phone bings. I knock my lamp on the floor, I'm so excited to rip it off the charger.

Mom taps on my door. "Is everything alright?"

"Fine, fine," I say. "Just tired and knocked the lamp over by accident."

She opens the door and her head peeks around the corner. "I'm sorry I had you do all that. I didn't know Amanda was going to ask you to do—"

I wave her off as nonchalantly as I can. I'm worried that I look like a junkie. "It's fine, Mom. Really." Steady eyes, Ethan. Steady. I force a smile.

"Are you constipated?" Mom opens the door further.

"Mom!"

"Okay, alright," she mutters. "Geez. Let me know if you need anything." She closes the door, finally.

AND?

That's it. One word. I was super duper excited for a response, and it's one single coordinating conjunction.

AND IN RETURN, YOU ACTUALLY RESPOND TO ME.

I DON'T UNDERSTAND.

WE'D BE. . .WHAT'S THE WORD? I KNOW THERE'S A WORD FOR THIS. OH, WAIT. I REMEMBERED IT. IT'S AN OLD WORD. A WEIRD WORD: FRIENDS.

NO KISSING.

I like that her mind went there first.

NO HOLDING HANDS.

I can work with that.

NO FLIRTING. NO PAYING FOR ME EVER. NO MEALS TOGETHER.

She's coming up with a lot of rules, and some people might find that discouraging, but I can't think about anything but the fact that after days and days of nothing, she's finally responding to my texts. Maybe Amanda Saddler's smarter than she looks.

But even if she starts talking to me again, will I be able to take this from the friend zone to the end zone when it matters?

I sure mean to try.

At least it means I'm still in the game.

12

ETHAN

When you grow up with siblings, you're accustomed to doing everything with a buddy. When I washed the car, Izzy came along. When I mowed the lawn, Izzy edged. When I learned to ride horses, Izzy was already better than me thanks to her posh lessons back home, and she made no effort to soften her advice to me or her criticisms of my failings.

But she's been my buddy for almost my entire life.

The hardest thing about all this Beth drama has been *not* talking to Izzy about it. Keeping our flirting and meet-ups a secret was kind of exciting, but it's taking a toll. I'm hunched over my phone when Izzy gets home from school.

"Who are you always texting?" She drops her enormous backpack on the floor by the door.

"You're going to make Mom's head explode if you leave that there."

Izzy rolls her eyes, but she reaches down and snags the tail that pokes out of the back right strap and starts dragging it like she'd drag a corpse behind her all the way to her room. "Fine."

"I'm trying to help you."

"Sure you are," she says.

That sounds cryptic, so I follow her, stuffing my phone in my pocket. "I am trying to help. What else would I be doing? I don't care if you leave your crap all over. Even when you can't find it the next day and you run around like a chicken with no head. Actually, I find that kind of funny, as long as you don't miss the bus."

"Whatever." Izzy practically slams the door in my face.

"Dude," I say. "What's going on with you?"

Before I have time to get a real fluster on, she whips the door open again. "What's wrong with me?" She leans closer, so her eye's only inches from mine. "You're all mopey half the time and then full of manic energy the next. You're clearly best friends with someone who's shady, or you're dating someone Mom wouldn't approve of, or you're selling drugs or something, because you won't tell me what's going on. That means it's bad." Izzy arches her eyebrow *just* like Mom. It's eerie, really. "And if you think you can hide it when we move to Amanda Saddler's, you've lost your mind, because there will be even more people in a smaller area."

"I'm not selling drugs, and I don't know any shady people." In Manila? Really?

She jabs her finger into my chest. "I knew it. Then who are you dating?"

I roll my eyes. "Please."

"You didn't say it wasn't that one, and now I'm

sure it is. Tell me who it is, or I'll go to Mom with my theories."

"You wouldn't dare."

She arches that same eyebrow again.

Sometimes I wonder whether Mom could strain an eyebrow. Probably, as a professional at the glare, she can't. But I bet a wannabe like Izzy could. Or maybe not. But she *might* have the guts to go tattle on me, even if it's only because she's butt hurt. "Fine," I say.

"Fine. . .what?" Izzy glances down the hall like she's worried the paparazzi might be on our tail.

She's right that soon we'll have even less personal space than we have now, so I guess I may as well tell her. I shove past her and close the door. "I'm *not* embarrassed, okay? But it is a bit tricky, because for some reason, this girl isn't totally sold on me yet." I can't help flexing my pecs and biceps a little. "No idea why."

It's idiotic, but it makes Izzy laugh. So, there's that. "Who?" She's like a cow with corn—fixated.

"Beth," I say.

"I *knew* it," she says. "Whitney thinks you're talking to Becca from back home."

I scrunch up my nose. "Ew."

"You did like her last year."

"You were obsessed with mom jeans and scrunchies last year. I don't mock you for that."

Izzy rolls her eyes. "So, tell me why all the secrecy."

"Do you really not know?"

"Because her dad's the devil?" Izzy frowns. "Honestly, I'm surprised you're okay with that. They basically forced us to move."

"Here's the thing," I say. "Her dad does suck, but people can't control what their parents do, and some parents can't even control what their kids do."

"I guess," Izzy says.

"And I'm not sure that I'm moving."

Izzy may have had a hunch about Beth, but that declaration takes her by surprise and then some. "You. . .what?"

I fill her in on how Kevin and Jeff have offered to spot me on a one-third interest in a ranch. "They have their eye on Birch Creek, and yeah it would've been better if I had just inherited it, but I was already looking at a partial share when you guys were going to inherit it, and I'd have two other people to help me this way."

She just stares at me. "Will you really stay here if we move home?"

I shrug.

"Mom is gonna *flip*."

"It's not for Beth," I say.

Izzy's eyes widen and she snort-laughs. "Sure it's not."

"I mean, not entirely."

"Okay."

"I wanted to come here from the start," I say. "And I've liked working the ranch and learning about cattle."

"But you were going to head home with us. . .if it weren't for her."

I can't really argue with her about that part.

"Listen, nothing's definite, but can you at least help me with a plan?"

"What is the plan?" Izzy falls back onto her bed, her head flopping against her pillow.

"So, the thing is, Beth wasn't talking to me. Like, at all. She decided she's bad for me, and that her dad is bad, so even though we were flirting and stuff—"

Izzy sits ups. "Whoa. You kissed her."

I feel my face flood with heat. "The point is, she cut me off, basically. And then Amanda Saddler suggested—"

"She knows about this too?" Izzy's eyes widen. "Mom's gonna be really hurt that everyone—"

"Shh," I hiss. "Geez, what's wrong with you? Do you *want* other people to overhear? Two people in the whole world is not everyone."

"Fine, but you need to tell Mom at some point."

"Listen, there's nothing to tell right now, you little yes-man. I know you hate the idea of keeping anything from Mom, but it won't be for very long. I just need you to help me get into the friend zone."

Izzy's face scrunches up. "Wait, you *want* to be in the friend zone?"

I twist her chair around and sit on it, backward, my chin on the chair back, and I smile. "Friend zone to end zone, baby."

"That may be the dumbest thing I've ever heard."

"Well, you can tell that to Amanda Saddler."

"That's what she called it?"

"The name might have come from me," I admit. "But listen, the point is, she likes me already. But she cut me off because I'm too much for her to handle in her delicate, guilt-ridden state. So I'll slide into the safe side of things, and then I'll transition."

"What can I do?"

"She's really into photography," I say. "She's great at it, too. And I know she's on the school paper. So maybe you join that, and then bam. You can invite her over here, talk to her, and generally pave the way to me getting back into her life."

Izzy looks skeptical.

"Come on, Iz," I say. "When have you ever not been my wingman?"

She huffs. "I guess that's true."

"So you'll do it?"

She inhales slowly, and then she exhales in a rush. "Fine, but I want it on the record that I am strongly encouraging you to tell Mom all about it ASAP."

I can't help my smile. Beth may be able to withstand me alone, but who can stay firm against the united power of the Brooks family? No one. I hold up my hand, and Izzy high-fives me back.

"How are you going to come up with money to help buy the ranch back?" Izzy asks.

"Dude, my college fund should be good for something, don't you think?"

Izzy's laugh is so loud that Mom actually pokes her head in. "Whoa, what's going on in here?"

Izzy pelts me with a pillow. "Nothing. Ethan's just being annoying."

"So, the usual," Mom says. "Carry on."

"Soon," Izzy whispers once the door is closed. "You have to tell her soon."

"Yeah, yeah," I say, realizing that Izzy is a very weak link. She loves me, but she loves Mom more. I'm on a timer, and when the time's up, Izzy's going to make sure the person who governs my college fund knows just what I'm planning.

But the next day, my gamble has already paid off. When the bus drops Izzy, Maren, Emery, Whitney, and Gabe off, Beth hops off with them. She's not wearing her pink and sparkle heart shirt, but she waves when she sees me.

"Hey Ethan."

It's not the warmest greeting, but it's not cold. We're off to the races—next stop, besties who braid each other's hair. I'd need to grow my hair out a lot longer for that to work, but you know, same idea.

Beth and Izzy seem to be having a great time, too. They talk about an article Izzy's supposed to write—I'm gonna get it for that one—and then Beth shows her how to work a pretty fancy camera.

"Don't break it, fumble fingers," I say, eager to be a part of things.

"You're calling me that?" Izzy asks. "You're the one who dropped the pickles last week."

"Only because Roscoe got in the way and I tripped," I say. "I'm not clumsy."

"What about the time you caught that football and then went through the neighbor's door?" Whitney asks. She's always happy to add an embarrassing story.

"Their *screen* door," I say, "and remember, I *caught* the ball."

"Yes, your professional football skills are not in doubt," Izzy says. "Just your general grace."

Beth's laughing along with the others, and I'm beginning to think I might have gotten the wrong end of this deal when Izzy points at Whitney and Gabe. "We need to go feed the animals. Maybe Beth can help Ethan make dinner and then he can give her a ride home?"

"I can walk," Beth says. "It's not really that far."

"I can take you," I say. "But where's your car?"

"It needed an oil change, and my dad's taking it in today."

The others kind of duck out—Emery and Maren go with them too. Emery loves to help with the horses, but Maren just hates making dinner. It usually annoys me when she ducks out, but today? Not so much.

"What are we making?" Beth asks.

"I'm a pretty simple guy," I say. "I can heat up spaghetti sauce my mom leaves in the freezer and boil noodles. I can make oven nachos. And I make a mean frozen pizza."

Beth laughs. "Wow. Your mom failed."

I laugh. "Right?" I shrug. "You just can't get everything, as it turns out. And she's such a great cook that I never had the motivation to learn a lot myself."

"That's really all you can make?" She cringes. "Yikes."

"Oh, I can also heat up my mom's chili, put a frozen lasagna she left in the oven, *or* bake a shepherd's pie."

"What can you do that she hasn't already done for you?"

"Did you not *hear* me say oven nachos or frozen pizza? Or are you kidding?"

Beth shakes her head. "How about chicken dumplings?"

"Who am I looking at right now? Is your name Betty or Beth?"

"Excuse me?" Beth frowns. "What?"

"Betty *Crocker?*" I wink.

She throws a towel at me.

"I feel like my sisters are teaching you bad habits."

"If you think I had to be taught to throw things at men, you underestimated me from the start."

"Snap," I say. "I guess I did."

And then I fetch and carry things to her from places in the kitchen. She's not impressed that my mom doesn't have any cans of chicken. "We mostly use frozen stuff," I say.

She sighs. "Fine, fine. It's just slower."

"They won't come back in until we call them," I say. "Believe me. They're like little bums. Once they're done feeding the animals, they'll basically ride around on scooters, swing, or play chase until we tell them dinner's made."

"Maren's riding on a scooter?"

I snort. "Well, maybe in the summer. In this weather, I'm sure she's hiding in a corner of the barn, playing on her phone. The others are probably playing some stupid horse game on top of the bales of hay. Maren would come inside, if she wasn't worried she'd get tasked to do dishes, make a salad, or like, fold laundry. She's a professional at skipping out on work."

"Said like someone who looks like a *professor* at it."

"Rude." I flex my chest and arm muscles. "I'm a hard worker."

The smile falls off Beth's face, and I realize I got too flirty. "I know you are, Ethan."

Friend zone, idiot. Focus. "It's fine. I get it. Slackers are always underestimating me, but that's your own confirmation bias showing."

She rolls her eyes, and we're back to dropping the dumplings into the boiling broth and chicken.

"And maybe we pull out some frozen sweet corn?"

"Sure," Beth says. "Or how about green beans and cornbread?"

"Dang girl," I say. "Are you trying to out-Southern my mom?"

She claps a hand over her mouth. "Oh, no. I forgot your mom's from the South."

Ethan snorts. "She's from California, but she lived in Houston for a while. Trust me, she's not snooty about Southern stuff. She had to learn to make it herself."

She bites her lip.

"Just make the cornbread. My mom has a great recipe."

But Beth looks like a nervous wreck while she's mixing it up. And when my mom gets home, driving the kids through the front door in front of her, Beth hides behind me.

"Wow, Ethan, you cooked?"

"Chicken dumplings," I say.

"Oh, no," Gabe says. "Can I have cereal?"

Mom laughs. "Well."

"Hey now," I say. "I had help." I shove Beth forward like a human sacrifice. "She made me do it."

"I hope she helped a lot," Whitney says. "Because otherwise, we're probably all eating cereal, and I think we're low on milk."

Mom's laughing. "Smells like cornbread?"

Beth nods, but she kind of looks like she might cry.

"Don't listen to the kids," Mom says. "It smells

great, and I'm sure with your help, none of us will be eating cereal."

Mom glares at Gabe, who drops his eyes immediately.

"Now, let's wash up and sit down to say grace," Mom says.

Aunt Amanda breezes through the door moments just after we say the prayer. It's no wonder Maren's an expert at avoiding work. I swear, her mom wrote the book on it. It's like the woman can *smell* when the work is done and that's when she sticks her nose in. "Oh, wow, what are we eating tonight?"

"I can't believe you cook for an army every night," Beth mutters. "How many frozen pizzas do you cook?"

"Usually four," I say. "But keep in mind that Maren and Amanda hardly eat anything. They mostly subsist on Red Bull and strong smells."

Maren hits me on the back of the head. "Shut up, you pig."

"I've been around a lot of pigs. He definitely smells too good for that," Beth says.

Izzy laughs.

And I realize that my plan is working. When I take Beth home, I focus on keeping things light. "Alright." I put the car in park. "Thanks for helping Izzy. I'm surprised to hear she's joining the paper." It's a little hard not to cringe, since I'm quite sure I'll be writing her stupid assignment to pay for this.

Still. Worth it.

"She's already pretty good at framing photos. She has a natural talent for it."

"Which you can identify because you're awesome?" I ask.

She rolls her eyes. "My mom's a photographer, you know. I just got dragged to a *lot* of courses."

"You don't like it?"

"Oh, no, I do. In fact, if I thought I might get in, UCLA would be my top college pick. Their photography program is epic. But when I mentioned it to Dad, he about died laughing. 'Pay two hundred grand so you can learn to take photos? Any idiot can do that.'"

"He's wrong," I say. "If that's what you want to do, you should apply. I bet you can get in."

Beth shakes her head. "Their admittance rate is like one in ten students. My grades are not the best, and my SAT is. . .not horrible."

I laugh. "I can relate to all of that, but as your dad so elegantly pointed out, there are other photography paths you can take. You don't need a top SAT to be a top photographer."

She smiles. "Thanks, Ethan."

"It's the truth."

"I mean for the ride, but yeah, also for reminding me of the truth." She's smiling when she waves bye.

I don't linger, because that's too boyfriend-esque. I can't quite help turning back for one last glance, and luckily, she's already walking toward her front door.

When I get home, Izzy practically corners me, ducking into the bathroom right before I drop my pants to pee. "Whoa, geez. You almost got an eyeful."

"What's wrong with you?" Izzy shakes her head.

"I'm sorry. Where would you rather I pee, if not in the toilet, behind a closed bathroom door?"

She laughs. "Yeah, I guess you're right. But listen, I doubt anyone else will barge in here." She drops to a whisper. "How'd it go?"

I can't help beaming. "So well. I think it worked, honestly. When is your article due?"

"I already wrote it," she says. "It was pretty fun."

"Wait, are you actually interested in the paper?"

She shrugs. "I mean, I wasn't, but it's pretty cool. There's only four people, and they do a paper once a month and then they put together the yearbook. I think it'll be fun. They were so excited to have me join."

"See? It's already working out for everyone. Now, if we can just get lucky and have no one else bid on the dumb ranch, then this might all work out."

"Will you really stay here with Jeff and Kevin?" Izzy sighs. "Because I'll really miss you."

"It's not like we can't talk." I point at the phone. "But, can I please pee?"

She laughs again, but when she opens the door to duck out, Mom's standing in the doorway.

And it looks like she heard us.

❦ 13 ❦

ETHAN

Oh, shoot. Day one, and I've already been caught. Living with my mom has always been a bit...overwhelming. She's intense.

Once, when I was like five? I decided to pee in the guest bedroom trash can. I have no idea why— why do five-year-old boys do anything? Anyway, I insisted it wasn't me who did it, but she pressed. I was so proud of myself, because no matter how hard she came after me, I didn't buckle.

Until she told me about the cameras she had installed in every single room of the house. She told me if she had to go back and review all the camera footage and found out that I was lying, she'd be way more upset than if I just confessed.

Yeah, I broke.

I didn't find out for years and years that the whole thing was a total lie. There were no cameras, but she said it with such conviction that we all believed her. Later, my sister was caught with the same gambit. I think that camera thing got us all, at one time or another.

You don't lie to my mom.

And I just tried.

In my defense, it was temporary. It's not like I was going to try and make her think I had moved to Houston when I was, in fact, staying here. It's just the timing I was trying to control.

"So, we probably need to talk," Mom says.

"Yeah."

Izzy runs, the coward.

"You can pee first. I'll wait." Mom closes the door, but her face says it's game on.

I wash my hands more slowly and thoroughly than I ever have in my entire life, and I lived through the Covid mess. Sheesh. But eventually, I have to dry them off and face the firing squad.

"So."

Mom tosses her head toward her room.

There's no saving me. Not if I'm getting sent to the inner sanctum for my trial. No jury. No appeals. I sigh as I follow her.

But when we get inside, Mom's storm-cloud face lifts. "What's going on?"

I sigh. "I don't want to move back to Houston, Mom."

She nods. "I know. So?"

"Jeff and Kevin are going to try and put an offer on the ranch, and they told me I can stay and work it with them."

She taps her lip with one finger. "Do they have financing?"

I frown. "I mean, I think so."

"Do they have a down payment?"

Oh, I know that one. "Yes."

"How much?"

I blink.

"And what's your share?"

"I was hoping to use my college fund," I say.

"There's a penalty to pay if you do that," she says. "You'd need to calculate what that is and then withhold that much for taxes."

I can't even process what she's saying.

"As much as I respect and admire Jeff and Kevin, I doubt they'll be able to make a competitive offer for the ranch," Mom says. "But if they do, and if they want to cut you in, well, you've earned that chance."

I must have misheard. "I have?"

"You haven't slacked off, and they obviously agree, or they wouldn't be offering to let you join them."

I guess that's true. I'm having trouble understanding why she's not freaking out, though. "So, you aren't mad?"

She puts a hand on my arm. "Ethan, what good would that do?" She looks tired. Really, really tired. "You're an adult now."

That's true.

"Why do you want to stay?"

I think back to what I said to Izzy. I can't remember exactly, but I don't think we talked about Beth. I could leave that part out, but I already feel guilty for leaving Mom out, especially when she didn't even explode. "Beth," I say.

"Beth. Donna's niece?" Mom's lip curls. It's slight, but it's there.

"You don't like her?"

"I don't know her," Mom says, "but I'm not a fan of her father."

156

"Neither is Beth," I'm quick to point out.

"That's hard," Mom says, "but I bet you know that already."

"She's not like her dad," I say. "That can happen."

Mom laughs. "I hope it can."

"Huh?"

"I'm nothing like my parents," Mom says. "But I learned from them, and you need to remember that. Beth will have learned from hers as well. She'll have baggage she'll need to check or chuck, and that part is both painful and dangerous."

I'm not sure I know quite what she means, but she's taking it all way better than I thought.

Amanda Saddler was right.

"Thanks, Mom."

"For what?" She arches her eyebrow. The OG eyebrow arch.

"For being you, I guess." Something about that makes me cry. I *hate* crying, but I especially hate to do it in front of her. I know she needs me to be strong, and it feels weak. Even so, I can't help thinking that, if I'm going to have only one parent, at least it's a really freaking good one.

Mom hugs me, and it almost makes up for the crying.

The next day, Mom walks me through the amount of money in my college fund and then explains all the details. There's more than I thought, just shy of a hundred grand, but the penalty is pretty crappy. After taxes and whatnot, I'd have around what I thought I had in the first place. When I meet with the guys, they're fine with it. They've saved a hundred and twenty between them, so they don't even demand I include all of it.

I know from what Mom said that we'll likely need it all to have a hope of being competitive, and we may still fall short. "Let's just make an offer including everything," I say.

"Then we can split the ownership that way, too," Jeff says.

I shake my head. "We split it three ways, because we're going to all be working the same."

Mom helps us go over the paperwork, and she even offers to co-sign. I don't cry again, but it's a near thing.

Only, when the auction comes, someone comes in and *smokes* us. They offer a full three hundred grand over us, and it's an offer made in *cash*. How anyone could have that kind of money is beyond me, but the offer's closed, so we don't even know who beat us. I'm in the grove, kicking snowdrifts and thinking how cold my toes are, when Beth shocks me by showing up.

We didn't have plans to meet, so I'm really taken aback. "What are you doing here?"

She's bundled up like that poor little kid on *A Christmas Story*. She actually looks like she might not be able to move her arms.

"You're wearing the scarf I loaned you." Beth's voice is quiet.

"Oh. Yeah." My hand goes to my neck involuntarily. I'm lucky it's blue. If she'd given me a pink one, I'd still have worn it, but Izzy and Maren and Whitney would *not* have let it go.

"Why are *you* here?" she asks. "We didn't have plans."

"I got some bad news," I say. "I guess this is

where I come to think now." Even when the stupid bench is buried in snow and the trees are all bare.

"Me too," she says. "Or, well, I guess mine's not really news."

I can't help my frown. "What happened?"

She kicks at a snow drift, too. "My grandpa died."

"Oh. I think I heard something about that from my mom. Donna's dad, right?"

She nods. "We just had the funeral, and I feel like I should have been sad, and like, I'm not."

"Oh."

"I know. Bad, right?"

I shrug. "I mean, I'm not sure there's right and wrong when you lose someone."

"But you were sad when your dad died."

"My dad was a prince among men," I say. "Everyone was sad when he died."

Beth's bark of laughter isn't gentle. "Yeah. That's definitely not my grandpa."

"How about this?" I ask.

"What?" Her eyes are hopeful when they meet mine.

"Let's make a deal. I won't be all depressed about my news, and you won't be bummed for *not* being depressed about yours."

Her lips move, but no words come out, like she's talking to herself. Then she nods. "Neither of us will be sad."

I smile. "Yes, that's the deal."

She doesn't ask what my news was, and I'm grateful. I can't really act all breezy and sweet about being friends if I confess I was trying to keep Birch

Creek. Plus, it'll remind her how we lost it in the first place.

"I'm not sure if people can just agree to be happy."

"But you just did."

She shakes her head, but she's smiling.

"See? You already feel better."

She swallows and opens her mouth like she's going to say something, but then she clicks it shut. "I guess I do."

"If you ever need to be reminded of our deal, just text me and I'll meet you here. Just coming here will help," I say. "But having me remind you will make you smile, and once you're smiling, you're halfway to happy, even if it's a little forced."

"That's not true," she says. But she's still smiling.

"It totally is," I say. "I read a study, so it *has* to be true. The study said that when you're sad or angry, even if you just force a smile or a laugh, it boosts your. . .smiling chemistry in your body and you get happier."

"That sounds made up." Beth pins me with a look. "It is, right?"

My lip is twitching. "You tell me?" I point at her. "Smile, and then tell me it didn't make you happier."

She swears under her breath. "Ethan Brooks."

"The word you're looking for is Elijah," I say.

"What?"

"Ethan *Elijah* Brooks," I say. "That's what my mom says when she's irritated."

Beth's grin widens. "You don't say."

"I mean, you're the one who's supposed to say it." I can't help smirking.

But when I get home that night, when I'm all

alone, or you know, as alone as I ever am anymore with Gabe snoring next to me, it hits me. I should be saying my nightly prayers, but I just can't do it.

"What's going on, God?" I mutter. "First you give me this ranch, and I'm like elated. Then you introduce me to a girl I really like. It's not an easy path, with her stupid dad, but we're working it out. And then." I sigh. "And whatever. I stopped being mad at you, because I made a plan. Like Mom says. Get off your knees and go to work. But now." I'm just, I could scream at him. Only, that would for sure wake up Gabe.

"But now, this? What the heck is wrong with you?" I clench my fist at my side. "Who the heck has that much money and why would they want my ranch?" Then I ask the real question that's been bothering me. "Do you hate me that much?"

I'm still angry.

I go to the clearing in front of Steve's almost every day for the whole week before Christmas. I never see Beth there, but Steve definitely notices. He waves the first time.

The second time he sees me, two days before Christmas, he pulls his coat on and comes jogging out.

I suppress my groan.

I like Steve. I mean, I actually really like him. It's just kind of hard to like him, because I can tell he wants to replace my dad, and that makes me want to punch him.

But he makes my mom happy.

I feel like that would make my dad want to punch him. And thank him. It's confusing. When he reaches the clearing, I try to shove back all my confusing thoughts and force a smile.

"What are you doing here every day?" Steve asks.

"I guess it's become my thinking spot," I say.

Steve nods. "It's not a bad spot. I used to do homework here when I was a kid."

"Really?"

He nods. "But listen, there's something I want to talk to you about. I've been a little bummed lately, and I think maybe for the same reason as you."

I can't help my smirk. "I doubt it."

"I don't want you to move to Houston."

I touch my chest. "I had no idea you liked me that much. I'm flattered, but I like *girls.*"

"A little humor to distract from the sore topics is always appreciated," Steve says. "But I'm being serious when I say that I mean to propose to your mother."

Wait, he means to *propose?* "Didn't you meet, like, five minutes ago?"

Steve smiles. "Maybe a few more than five minutes, but I know it's fast. Do you think it's too fast?"

I think about it—I owe him that much at least. After Dad died, I was so sad that I didn't really pay much attention to how sad Mom was. She seemed almost normal, really.

She woke up and showered. Some mornings she even went for a run. She made us breakfast. She packed lunches. She directed us to do dishes, to clean, and do our school stuff. She took us to activities and lessons. She worked all the time. She did paperwork. She called people and lined things up. She signed forms, and she led family prayer, and she hugged us when we cried. She did the girls' hair, and she tucked Gabe in, and she did it all with a forced, tired smile.

Mom never fell apart.

It's not what she does.

But thinking back, it felt a little like she was quietly dying inside, a little more each day. Like she had become the perfect, automaton mother who never let us down, but really she was slowly disappearing bit by bit. I realize that in all that time, there was no one there to make sure *she* was okay.

No one to pack her a lunch.

No one to tuck her in.

No one to hug her when her heart hurt.

Steve changed that, and lately, Mom has lit up again.

I loved seeing it, and I hated that it wasn't Dad doing it for her. But that's my issue. That's not Steve's, and I'm not a big enough monster that I don't want my mom to be alive and happy. Even if it's gross to think about, I guess I even want her to be tucked in or whatever.

"The enemy of my enemy is my friend, right?" I hold out my gloved hand.

"How am I your enemy?"

"The important thing is that we both want my family to stay here."

"I only use about half my acreage," Steve says. "You couldn't run the numbers you had at Jed's place, but you could have a small herd here, and it wouldn't cost you a dime."

"Except for buying the herd, you mean."

"Well, yes."

"What do I get out of supporting your leveraged buy-out?"

"My what?" Steve laughs as he gets what I'm asking. "Do you mean my proposal?"

I shrug. "Potato, potahto."

"You're a really weird kid," he says. "I think I might love you more for it."

"Gosh, I hope so," I say. "Anyone can get a normal kid. It's the odd ones who are really valuable."

"I'm beginning to learn that," Steve says. "And I had an idea."

"What's that?"

"I thought you might be more amenable to my, what did you call it? My leveraged buy-out of your mother—" Steve cringes.

"If you knew my aunt Helen, you'd get it."

"Helen. Your mom's sister."

"The one and only," I say. "But spit it out, Steve. What's your idea? You didn't happen to buy Birch Creek in cash, did you?"

Judging by the confusion on his face, he didn't. Rats. "No, but I did think it might be time for me to buy a new truck."

Not exactly the same level, but okay.

"And then I wouldn't need that one." He points at his perfectly good pickup truck.

"Wait."

"I thought my future stepson, who has no car of his own, might want it."

Play it cool, Ethan. Don't drool. "I mean, it's a decent truck for someone in this area."

"Nice," Steve says. "Then do we have a deal?"

As if I was really going to reject the horse doc on

my mom's behalf. She can do the rejecting herself if she wants. And on that note. . . "Now, let's talk about what happens if we strike this deal and my *mom* turns you down."

Steve laughs. "You can keep the truck."

"Are you for real?"

He nods slowly. "Yep. I'll have bought a new one by then already anyway."

"I don't regret backing you," I say. "I have to admit. Classy move."

"Nice question, though. You may want to ranch instead of studying, but you are still your mother's son."

"Darn straight," I say.

"Now, tell me the thing you're upset about."

I figure I have nothing to lose. I fill him in on the plan—friend zone to end zone.

He smiles like he's proud. "I'm going to be swinging big soon, so as one man to another, don't wait too long."

We talk for another few minutes, and he helps me decide. If my mom says yes to Steve, if we're sticking around, I'll try and use all that holiday magic to make my move, too.

The next few days crawl by, as opposed to the usual pre-Christmas race. But finally, the big day does come, and I'm probably as nervous as Steve. After all, he's not the only one who has something riding on this.

I try to pull Steve aside and ask him when he's going to do it. But before I can, Amanda Saddler leaps out of her chair and starts for the tree. I swear, she moves with as much energy as Gabe. There's no way she looks eighty-something.

She plucks a box out and thrusts it out to Mom.

Mom stammers, and she never does that. "Y-you —of all people, didn't need to get us a single thing."

"I beg to differ," Amanda Saddler says. "In fact, from the day Amanda brought me those letters of Jed's, I've been thinking. I loved Jed, but he and I screwed everything up royally. I figure that's probably why he was like he was, all confused and stupid."

Mom looks a little off-guard, unsure what to expect. I'm sure she's wondering if she got Amanda a nice enough gift.

"Here." Amanda Saddler basically drops the present on her lap.

"Well, you didn't need to do anything at all," Mom says, "but thank you."

"It's for all of you." Amanda Saddler waves at Gabe, Izzy, Whitney, and then she winks at me. "The whole Abigail Brooks clan."

Mom sucks at accepting gifts. It's fine, because usually she doesn't get much. I mean, our money comes from her, and Dad's dead, so he's not about to surprise her, but even when he was alive, she mostly picked out her own stuff.

When Mom finally opens it, she stares blankly at the box with the word 'Macy's' written across it. I wonder whether that means something to Mom.

It's for all of us, but I have no idea what Macy's is. I think maybe it's a store for old people? Did Amanda Saddler get us. . .dentures? Oh, no. What if it is some weird, old person thing?

But it's a stack of paper in the box.

"What is this?" Mom looks almost frantic, her eyes searching Amanda Saddler's face. "This isn't—"

She covers her mouth and shakes her head. "We can't accept it."

I'm done sitting and waiting for Mom to explain what our group gift is. I grab the box.

"What is it?" Aunt Amanda asks.

I'm not a lawyer, but it only takes me a moment to realize what I'm looking at. It's a deed—for the Birch Creek Ranch.

The pieces all click in my head at the same time, and I realize what an idiot I am. *Amanda Saddler* is the person who has cash to pay on a ranch. Three hundred grand over our offer.

Of course she is.

And who else *should* fix Uncle Jed's idiocy?

I can't help it. My joy just bubbles over, and I race around the room, leaping up and waving my arms. "Whoop!"

"What's going on?" Aunt Amanda asks again.

"Amanda Saddler bought Birch Creek Ranch in the auction," Mom explains. "And she gifted it to us —to our whole family."

"As Jed should have done." Amanda Saddler nods.

I kiss the old lady right on the mouth after that. She may look shocked, but she doesn't look upset.

Steve's proposal gets a little mixed up, but it goes alright, too. And by the time it's done, I'm holding a new set of keys, and I'm not moving to Houston.

After Steve gives me the nod, I text Beth that I'd love to meet her at our grove. When she says okay, I throw her gift in the truck, and I practically peel out in the pile of old, dirty snow.

But when I climb out of the truck, Beth does *not* look happy.

In fact, she's bawling.

"Whoa," I say. "What's wrong?"

She's hiccupping in her attempt to stop. Instead of talking, I just drag her head against my coat-insulated chest and pat her head until she finally stops.

"Are you alright?" It's a stupid question. It looks like her day was as bad as mine was good.

"Mom's home, but I guess she shouldn't be," she whispers, "and Dad—he's even worse than usual."

I'm not sure what that means. "Do you feel safe there?"

She laughs. "Ironically, the only one who hit people was my grandpa, and he's dead."

And now she's bawling again.

It takes a while, but she finally calms down again. "Do you want to talk? Or just be with someone?"

She shakes her head. I think she probably doesn't know. That's fair. I had plenty of nights like that after my dad.

"I'll just say this." I squeeze her gently. "A lot of people think grief is like this thing, like I don't know, a ladder. You just climb it, up and out."

She's listening. I can tell by how still she is.

"But it's not like that. It's like, we used to go to the beach in Galveston. Once, after a storm, we went to the beach and the waves were really weird. Some were small. Sometimes there would be a few small ones, and then *bam*, one huge one would knock you down. Plus, there was something called a riptide. My dad made us get out of the water. He said the red flags meant it wasn't safe."

I'm not my mom. This analogy isn't really that great, but Mom's not here. I'm all Beth's got.

"Grief is like that ocean after a big storm. Sometimes it's little waves. Sometimes it's huge ones that knock you over. And sometimes a sneaky little rip tide you can't even see will pull you under and drown you. You just don't know, and you have to try and stay standing no matter what hits."

"How?"

I search her face, which she's turned up toward me, and she seems to genuinely want advice. Maybe my B-team analogy wasn't so bad after all. "I mean, you try to keep your balance. You try to anticipate. But friends help."

She meets my gaze for a moment, and then she nods.

"So do gifts." I smile. "Want yours now?"

She tenses. "I didn't get—"

"Stop," I say. "If you knew my mom, you'd know that our love language—pounded into us by her—is giving gifts. Ironically, my mom doesn't seem to care about getting them much, but boy does she give good ones."

"It's just that—"

"You must not have many friends," Ethan says. "This is what friends do."

She freezes. "I don't, no."

You're an idiot, Ethan. Change the subject, quick. "Okay, well. Wait here for one second."

As soon as I grab the gift, I wonder if I made a huge misstep. I bought this thinking that I'd tell her how I felt and *then* I'd give it to her. What will she think about it now?

"Why are you so happy?" she asks. "Are you just a huge fan of Christmas?"

I feel a little bit like a jerk, sharing my news when her day was clearly bad. "Well. The thing is, apparently Amanda Saddler bought the ranch for us, so it was a pretty good Christmas, as stuff like that goes. Oh yeah, and we aren't moving back to Houston. Steve proposed to Mom, and she said yes."

Beth straightens immediately, her eyes widening alarmingly. "What?"

She's frozen like that for at least five seconds, and I'm worried she's disappointed. Was she happy to be rid of me?

Then her entire face lights up. "I wish I'd known that earlier. I might not have melted down at all. What awesome news! Congrats to your mom, too."

"Thanks."

She reaches her hands out. "I'm ready for my gift now."

I cringe a little bit. "The thing is."

"Just give it."

I swallow. "But you might think—"

"Ethan Elijah Brooks."

She finally used my whole name, and it feels like she's claiming me, somehow. Like she's acknowledging that I'm hers.

She cocks her head, clearly tired of waiting. "Hand it over."

I do, but my heart beats frantically while she opens it.

"What is this, exactly?" she asks.

I cringe a little. "So, I had a *ton* of shirts from high school. My mom made me a quilt with one of them—"

"No way," she says. "That's something—"

"Dude," I say. "Let me finish."

Her mouth snaps shut.

"But these were leftover from that. They're my B-string t-shirts."

"Did you *make this*?"

I laugh. "No way."

"Then how. . .?"

"My cousin bought this stupid-fancy quilting machine, but she couldn't afford it. My mom 'invested—'" I make air quotes. "—in her machine, under the deal that Samantha would make her any quilts she ever wanted."

"Oh." Beth shrugs. "Okay, so these are leftovers."

"I figured if you ever need a friend and I'm busy, you can curl up under this and remember that you do have one."

Beth's smile is like a hundred-watt bulb, and it makes me happy inside, even if I didn't make the move to the end zone yet. Even if it's not time for *us*, I'm okay being here for her.

However she needs me.

BETH

My friend Hannah's an only child, just like I am. Her parents throw her a huge birthday party every single year. Last year, when I said, "Mrs. Stillman, you always throw Hannah the best parties," her mom responded with, "Of course I do. My little Hannah Banana will be gone soon, and all I have are a few more years with her."

My parents went a different direction.

I've never had an actual birthday party. I mean, my mom and dad always give me something. Usually it's something nice or at least enough cash to buy something nice. My mom often buys me way more than she should, frankly. But my dad's not big on friends, and my mom's never really doing well enough to try and organize a huge party.

Not for me, at least.

But this year, Izzy told me that if I didn't have plans, I should come over to her house on my birthday. I pretended it would be hard to get away, but I knew Mom and Dad might not even remember what day it was. When I wake up on my birthday, my words prove prophetic. My mom's still sleeping, and my dad barely nods at me when I walk past.

I look in the mirror on my way out the door.

It may be wishful thinking, but I feel like I *look* older. More mature. More confident.

I took too long curling my hair, and I'm actually late to school. It's not like it really matters. The most they do for tardies is send a letter to my parents, and I'm the only one who ever gets the mail and carries it inside. Plus, if they did happen to grab it, what would they say?

No one at school realizes it's my birthday either, at least, not until lunch when Izzy drops an apple on the edge of the table in front of me.

"What the heck is that for?" Maren asks. "I really hope it's not, like, a birthday present." She pulls a pink package out of her bag and sets it on top of my lunchbox.

"Hey, what's that?" Izzy asks.

Maren shrugs. "I guess you'll have to WAFO."

"WAFO?" I ask.

"Wait and find out," Maren says with a smirk.

"I got you this." Whitney plonks a bottle of lotion down next to me.

"That's used," Maren says. "Gross."

"Shut up," Whitney says. "Or I'll tell your mom about—"

"About what?" Maren asks. "Because if you're talking about the thing I think you're talking about, you wouldn't dare."

"It's perfect," I say. "I love honeysuckle." I squeeze some lotion on my hands and rub it in. "Thank you."

"It's barely used," Whitney says. "I mean, I had to make sure it didn't smell gross."

In my entire life, I've never had anyone argue about what people are giving me, and no one has ever brought me anything to school. Well, my friend Hannah brought me a banana once, if that's not too ridiculous for words, given her nickname. It was pretty mashed, though. I figured it was probably hers from lunch, and she just didn't want it.

"Wait, how are you even here?" I ask.

Whitney turns bright pink.

"Yeah, how are you here?" Izzy asks. "Is this why you asked what time our lunch is?"

Whitney stands up again. "I better go."

"You're just going to run across the street?" Izzy asks. "That doesn't sound very safe. Do you want me to walk you?"

Whitney shakes her head. "I just said I had to go to the bathroom." She shrugs. "What are they going to do? It's not like I'm skipping school. I'm still *at* school."

"Dude, if you get caught you are *so* busted," Maren says.

"Getting caught is literally the definition of the word busted," Izzy says. "But my mom will kill her, if that's what you mean."

"Have you ever thought about being Candace from *Phineas and Ferb* for Halloween?" Whitney asks Maren. "I doubt you'd even need a costume." She sticks her tongue out, flounces around on one heel, and ducks out of the cafeteria.

That kid may get a lot of heat from her siblings, but she has some real moxie.

"Open it," Maren says.

"Wait," Izzy says. "First I need to explain the apple."

"I really don't think you do," Maren says. "We all know what apples are."

"There's going to be a cake at home," Izzy says. "So I didn't want to give you a cupcake or it would be overkill, and your real present was too big to bring to school."

Maren scowls. "Liar. You just didn't get her anything."

Izzy folds her arms. "I guess we'll see."

"Whatever." Maren pulls out her phone. It's her go to when she's upset. I doubt she even knows why she's scrolling social.

I open her present anyway. "Oh, I love these." And that's true. She may be a little snotty, but Maren has an eye for fashion, and she has connections. The clips and barrettes in the cute pink package are both classy and cute. All I have at home is a pile of scrunchies and some huge, overblown bows my mom made when I was seven years old. "Thank you so much."

"Do you really like them?" Maren actually looks up from her phone, and the expression on her face looks genuine.

"I really do. Thanks."

I float my way through the rest of the day, and then I give all the Brooks kids a ride home. It's the first time I've ever had six kids in my car, and I'm lucky that Izzy's willing to sit on the hump between the driver and passenger seats. "Are you sure it's okay that Gabe doesn't have a booster seat?"

Maren rolls her eyes. "Please. Like those do anything anyway."

175

He's sitting on a geometry and an algebra book stacked on top of one another, so the seat belt hits him at the right place, at least. I hope his mom doesn't see and freak out. But it felt wrong to drive to their house while they all rode the bus, and after I asked Izzy about it. . .they all kind of just followed me over.

Big families are awesome.

And sometimes hard to navigate.

I have basically no experience, so that's not helping me.

When I reach the house, everyone pours out of my car, and I'm reminded of the cartoons I saw as a kid where three dozen people would exit a clown car. I wonder if that's how Abigail feels *all the time*. I would like it, I think, having so many children around. I'm sure it's exhausting too, but in my book, exhausting sounds better than lonely. As I exit the car, I notice that Abigail's SUV isn't parked in the drive. I wonder whether she had some kind of meeting.

"The birthday girl brought you guys home?" Ethan's standing in the doorway, talking to his siblings.

But he's looking at me. Smiling.

I have to remind myself every single time I see him that we're not dating anymore. He's just a friend.

A friend I dream about.

A friend who makes my palms sweaty.

A friend who makes my heart race and my knees weak.

Just a friend.

But when he smiles, it's hard to remember

anything at all. "Happy birthday." He waves. "Now you're finally able to vote."

"Yeah, but who do I vote for?"

Ethan throws his hands up in the air. "Ah, ah, don't ask that. Have you met Amanda Brooks?" He cringes. "Politically, we're a house divided."

I can't help laughing as I walk up the porch steps.

"Now, Izzy says you told her not to go overboard, so I got my deposit back on the jugglers, the petting zoo, *and* the bouncy house. But." He lifts one arm to block me.

I'm forced to look up and meet his eye. "What are you talking about?"

"She texted me to tell me you're coming, and well, winters are slow on ranches, so I had some time on my hands."

"What does that mean?"

"I whittled you a chair out of an old oak tree."

"You—what?"

He laughs. "I'm kidding, but I did make you a cake." He drops his hand and gestures all in one big movement, and I duck past before he can do or say anything else ridiculous.

On the counter, there's a chocolate cake.

Sort of.

It's supposed to be a three-layer cake, I think, but instead of being smooth and round, it's peaked and high on one side, and saggy in the middle, with a kind of lumpy spot on the other end. The frosting's sliding off the low side, and it's pooled in the center. The closer I get, the worse it looks.

"Wow," I say. "I mean, really, wow. Is it the first time you've ever made a cake?"

"Why would you think that?" His forced smile shows me that he knows it looks terrible, at least.

"It's. . .unconventional."

"I was trying to copy the cake Hagrid made Harry."

"Right," I say, "well, then you nailed it. Except, there's no frosting writing on it."

"That part was harder than it looked," he says. "Besides, we all know who the cake is for, right?"

"And she's welcome to it." Maren's leaning against the counter by the sink, a look of pure contempt on her face.

"I'm sure it tastes great," I say. "And that's the only thing that counts."

"What if it doesn't?" Izzy asks. "Because in my experience—"

"Hush, you," Ethan says. "It'll be great." He pulls ice cream out of the freezer and plonks it on the table.

"Are we eating it now?" I ask, a little surprised.

"I mean, it's kind of starting to collapse." Ethan points.

"Right. Better to eat it while it's still standing upright," I say. "Let's do it."

"We have to sing first," Gabe says. "And we need candles."

It takes three kids opening at least fifteen drawers before candles are located, and they don't match. "It's fine," I say. "Really."

"Where's Amanda?" Izzy asks. "She doesn't eat much cake, but she loves parties."

"She had to meet a contractor," Maren says. "That's why she said we could come over."

I forgot they're living at Amanda Saddler's now.

"Contractor? Do you mean the tile guy?" Emery asks.

"Sure, whatever," Maren says.

How strange to have a mom who's always changing her career. First an influencer, then a cookie shop owner, and now she's meeting tile guys. I wonder whether Maren and Emery like it or hate it, but I don't ask. Generally speaking, I try not to ask questions about things when I have no idea what the answer might be.

"Alright, here we go." Izzy starts poking candles into the cake, but the structural integrity of the cake wasn't ever that great, and apparently it wasn't really up to taking additional damage. When she pushes the fourth candle in, it splits, the lower, saggier one third shearing off and falling onto the floor with a splat.

"Um." Gabe tilts his head sideways and scrunches up his nose. "That looks gross. I don't want any."

"Hey, now," Ethan says. "That's not very nice. It's a great chocolate cake."

Roscoe sees his shot and snags a huge chunk.

"Wait, that's chocolate," Emery says. "Dogs can't have chocolate."

No one told Roscoe that fact, because that cup-sized chunk is already gone, and he's darting toward it, going for more. Ethan leaps into the fray to stop him, and I'm a little worried he's about to lose a finger.

The front door opens, and Abigail and someone who looks a little like her, but somehow scarier, step through the door, both of them holding bags. "Good afternoon." Abigail's eyes swivel back and forth, taking in all the kids and the dog and the ruined cake. Just then, another soggy chunk of it gives up and falls.

Onto Ethan's head.

He shoves it off and says a not-very-nice word. Then his eyes widen. He stands up slowly, his hands both turned palm out. "Things are fine, but the cake I made did not turn out very well, and Roscoe was eating it, which is bad, because dogs can't have chocolate." He looks more like a toddler than I have ever seen him look.

I should not be smiling.

No one else is.

Until Abigail starts laughing.

The woman next to her is looking at her like she's insane.

When they see their mother laughing, Izzy, Whitney, and Gabe start laughing too. Ethan gets a beleaguered look on his face, like he's the long-suffering butt of a lot of jokes. "I'll just go take a shower."

"Well, you could do that." Abigail wipes her eyes. "But then you'd miss the birthday song and the cutting of the actual birthday cake."

"What are you talking about?" Ethan practically juts his bottom lip out. "I already messed that up. See?" He points at his head. "I'm wearing it."

Abigail ducks out of the room, into the area that used to be a corner, and reappears, carrying a huge, fluffy, white cake. "I made this last night and left it out there so we'd have room in the inside fridge."

"Ooh," Izzy says. "I love the Angel's Delight cake."

"What's that?" I ask.

Abigail sets it on the counter.

"Yeah, what is it?" the woman asks.

"Beth, this is my sister, Helen," Abigail says. "She's in town, visiting. Isn't that a great surprise?" I've never seen Ethan's mother being sarcastic, so I'm not totally sure, but she almost looks like she means that it's *not* great.

"Nice to meet you," Helen says. "A friend of Izzy's from school?"

"And Ethan's too," Gabe says.

My cheeks heat up, and I hope no one notices. "Yeah," I say. "We're both on the school paper."

Izzy rolls her eyes. "I just joined and I'm clueless. Beth's the best photographer ever. She's been helping me out some."

"Well, it's a good thing you weren't really counting on Ethan for the cake." Helen pokes what's left of it. "This is. . ." She snorts. "I mean, it's probably better than what I could make, but." She looks at Ethan. "I have the decency to know what I can and can't do. I'd have bought one."

"Listen," Ethan says. "I've seen Mom bake a million times. I figured, how hard could it be?"

"Hard," Helen says. "Impossible, if you don't know all the things people who bake assume you know. Like how to measure the flour, how to tell when it's baked—all ovens bake differently, apparently—and what happens when you're at elevation." She tsks. "Rookie mistake, kid."

"What kind of cake is that?" Emery asks. "Angel's what?"

"It's an angel food cake," Abigail says, "but you slice and layer it. I've been craving strawberries, so I did those when I saw some decent ones at the market. But you can also do chocolate."

"You chose strawberries instead of chocolate?" Maren curls her lip. "Why?"

"Because her mother taught her not to be rude," Helen says. "Oh, I'm sorry, I thought you asked why you should keep your mouth shut when you have nothing helpful to say."

Ethan laughs out loud. "I love you, Aunt Helen. Please never leave."

Helen wraps an arm around his shoulders. "Love you, too."

Abigail carefully places eighteen pristine red candles in the cake, and then she lights them with the grace of a head waiter at a five-star restaurant. She lifts one hand, and as if her kids have some kind of communication device the rest of us don't, they all start singing.

"Happy birthday to you, happy birthday to you, happy birthday, dear Beth, happy birthday to you." On the second happy birthday, Emery, Maren, and Helen have caught up. Which is kind of too bad, because Maren can *not* carry a tune.

But it still feels nice.

So many people. Two cakes, even if one isn't exactly picture perfect. When I blow the candles out, I'm fighting back tears. And before Abigail can slice it, I stop her. "Can you get a photo of both cakes?"

"I must have misheard you," Whitney says. "There's no way you want to remember *that one*." She pokes at it.

"Careful," Izzy says. "Last time we touched it, there was a landslide."

"A cake slide," Maren says.

"Precisely." Izzy smirks.

Roscoe looks at it expectantly, but it holds.

"I did mean that one," I say. "It may not be a work of art, but I want to eat both, and I want to have a photo with both. I've never had two cakes before."

"I have," Gabe says. "Lots of times." He holds up his small hand. "Once, when I wanted a Pokémon cake *and* a Ben Ten one. And once when I loved chocolate and strawberry and couldn't pick."

"And last year, you had three parties," Whitney says. "One at the restaurant, one with family, and that one with your friends."

"Only cause Dad died and everyone was all sad, so Mom kept saying I could have one more. And I only got cake at the first one."

Talk about a conversation doorstop.

"Anyway," Ethan says, "we all hope your birthday is great." He hands me a plate with a slice of each kind of cake. Even though the chocolate piece is kinda mushy, I eat both of them with a smile.

Izzy ducks into her room after that and pops back out with a gift that she probably could have brought to school, but I'm glad she didn't. It's almost two feet tall, and probably eighteen inches wide. It's also totally flat, so I'm guessing it's a framed poster or something.

"Here." She thrusts it toward me.

Everyone's staring at me as I open it.

"I know you probably have a ton of better presents at home," Izzy says. "But I found this online and I thought it was really funny."

Funny?

I prepare myself for something awkward.

When I open it, it's not a framed anything. It's a metal sign. It has a camera on the front of it, and the words, "I shoot people" in huge bold letters above it. And below the camera, it says in smaller lettering, "And cut off their heads."

I can't help smiling.

"Oh," Gabe says. "Because you take photos. It is funny."

Whitney and Emery laugh at Gabe's reaction more than the pun, but it is the perfect sign for me. "Thanks." I hug her.

As soon as I release her, Whitney hugs me, too. It should feel awkward, but instead, I feel like I might cry. I've always wanted a sister, and if I could pick any sister at all, Whitney and Izzy would both be near the top of my list.

"Can I?" Emery looks like a lost puppy, all wide-eyed and vulnerable when Whitney lets me go.

I open my arms, and she shoots toward me, her bony little arms wrapping around me tightly. I half-expect Maren to hug me, but when Emery finally lets me go, Maren rolls her eyes and walks down the hall.

We eat pizza for dinner *after* cake, which I think is a little brilliant. We play a terrible game of Twister, which Ethan insists on calling the colors for because Maren isn't trustworthy. Whitney smokes us all, of course. That kid bends like a rubber band. We feed the horses and chickens, and then we all watch an episode of this old television show called *The Flash*, which Gabe is obsessed with.

"I mean, he can run so fast you can't even *see* him." His eyes are wide and excited. He reminds me a lot of Aiden, but if Aiden's dad wasn't a waste of space and he felt a little more comfortable in his own skin.

As soon as the show starts, the Brooks kids drag out several baskets of laundry.

"Here." Whitney hands me a basket.

"Uh, she doesn't have to fold on her birthday," Izzy says. "Geez."

"Why not?" Whitney frowns. "I still did."

"She's not even family," Izzy says.

I grab the basket. "I don't mind." Because in that moment, I've never wanted something to be true so badly. The problem with happy families is that, if you're in one, you don't realize how rare it is. It does make it that much harder, later, when I have to climb into my car and drive home. Alone.

"Hey, wait." Ethan jogs toward the car. "I got you something."

"You made me a cake," I say.

He shrugs. "What can I say? I'm a saint among men."

I roll my eyes. "What is it?"

He hands me a small, hard rectangle wrapped in thick paper.

"You can open it later." He half-grins and steps back, waving goodbye.

I wonder what it is all the way home. By the time I finally park, my fingers are practically itching to open it. But my mom yanks open the front door the second I show up.

"There you are." She does not look pleased, and she's yelling loudly enough that I can hear her from inside my car.

"Oh." I climb out. "I'm here." I glance at the

clock on my phone. It's seven forty-one. "Were you waiting on me for some reason?" No one had even said a word this morning about it being my birthday —Mom wasn't even *awake*.

I check my phone.

Not a single text.

"Did we have. . .plans?"

Dad's standing behind her, arms crossed, glowering.

"Apparently we need to have plans in advance to see our own daughter," Dad says. He sighs and turns around, disappearing back into the house.

Mom's practically glaring as I walk into the house, abandoning Ethan and Izzy and Whitney and Maren's gifts in the back of my car. I hope the lotion won't freeze. . .

That's when I notice the table. My favorite burger from Brownings. Mom's favorite salad. Dad's steak. All of them are sitting on the table, and they broke out Mom's fancy china. There are tall ivory candles in silver candlesticks in the middle of the table.

"Did you guys—?" I turn around, but no one's in the room. I'm standing all alone. I raise my voice. "Did you guys plan a dinner for me?"

Dad comes back out, and I notice he's wearing pajamas. "We did."

"It's not even eight," I say. "We can still eat."

"I'm sure you already ate." Mom's still wearing jeans and a fancy silk blouse, and somehow that makes me feel worse.

"I could eat again," I say.

"Where were you?" Mom asks.

I don't want to tell them. Dad acts like the fact

that Amanda Saddler bought the Birch Creek Ranch and gave it to its rightful owners is some kind of injustice in the world that personally offends him. Never mind that he's the one who instigated all their problems, he's holding a grudge against *them*. If he found out I was at their place. . .it would be bad.

"I had no idea you guys wanted to have dinner. I'm really sorry."

"That's the point," Dad says. "We wanted to surprise you."

"You did that," I say. "I'm very surprised."

"Clearly." Mom's voice is still flat. "Well, if you don't mind that the food is cold, let's sit, then."

She didn't press me for where I was, thank goodness. We sit down, and I bow my head, expecting them to pray like Abigail's family does.

"What are you doing?" Dad asks.

"Had a crick in my neck," I lie. "Oh, good. I love their fries." I can barely choke them down cold, though. Ugh.

"This steak is disgusting," Dad says.

"There's this thing," I say, "called a microwave." I stand up and hold out my hand. "Here, let me show you its magic."

Dad and Mom stare at me like I've sprouted a third eye. The Brooks would have loved that joke.

"I'm kidding. I mean, about the magic part. But I really will reheat your food."

"It's fine." Dad grits his teeth and plows his way through his cold, tough steak.

My family loves being martyrs. It's practically a hobby for them. Well, it's not for me—I microwave my burger. If I'm going to add another half inch of cellulite to my backside by eating two unhealthy meals in one night, I'm at least going to enjoy doing it.

Although, *enjoy* might be a stretch. I'm shocked my parents made an effort, but I'm kind of wishing they hadn't. They're so mad that I didn't come home, although they didn't ask me to, that no one really says anything. And I know it's not great to compare, but I can't help noticing the contrast between the Brooks' laughter-filled evening, replete with good-natured ribbing, and my family's passive aggressive irritation.

I mean, I came home late on my birthday, but it's not like I had any reason to believe I shouldn't. I'm just eating my last bite when Dad holds up his glass of wine. "To eighteen. Just one more year of teenage sulking and rudeness, and we're finally in the clear."

"Wait, I can't sulk and be rude after I turn twenty?" I ask.

Mom shakes her head. "Nope, so that means you have less than two years to go."

"Then what's Dad's excuse?" The second I say the words, I wish I could take them back.

But I can't.

It's too late.

Dad slams his wine glass down, the red liquid sloshing over the side. "Here." He stands up and yanks out his wallet. "Here's what you really want from me." He throws a wad of bills down on the table and storms off.

My family has never been like the Brooks. I don't expect it. But that feels like a slap in the face.

"He's had a rough week," Mom says. "Don't be too mad at him."

"He has?" Maybe I'm as guilty as they are, if I don't pay enough attention to know he's struggling.

"Your aunt is being. . .difficult," Mom says.

"Wait, Aunt Donna is?" That's a surprise. She's really, really awesome. Probably my best family member, now that Grandma's dead. "What's she doing?"

"Well, you know she made a deal when she went off to school. She told your grandpa that if he paid for her school, she didn't want an inheritance. She lived like a queen up there, and thanks to your grandpa sending her copious amounts of money, she caught a husband at Stanford from a rich family."

I can't help quirking a brow. "You mean the guy she just divorced?"

Mom sighs. "Well, now she's trying to say that she should get some of your father's parents' estate."

"She's trying to take the ranch?" That surprises me.

"Not the ranch, no," Mom says, "but the life insurance proceeds."

"Wait, you think Dad should get the ranch, the money from it, and all the life insurance? Shouldn't she get *anything*?"

"I told you." Mom sounds annoyed. "She made a deal."

"Still, she made that deal when she was, what? Eighteen?" It hits me then. She made some kind of deal with her dad when she was *my age* and my parents want to hold her to it?

I stand up. "I think Dad's probably being the jerk." I wipe my mouth and throw my napkin on the counter, ignoring the wad of money Dad threw at me.

189

If he treats his own daughter like that on her birthday, how can I trust that he's being fair to Aunt Donna?

"You owe him an apology."

"I do not," I say. "You guys didn't tell me to be here at any particular time." A red-hot flash of indignance shoots through me, out of nowhere. "It was my birthday, but Dad just grunted this morning when I left. I didn't think he even knew."

"You're his only daughter," Mom says.

"I used to wish for a brother or sister, but now that I'm older, I'm glad you didn't have any more. I'd have to feel even sorrier for them than I do for myself."

Mom looks like I smacked her, and I feel a little bad. I probably went a little too far.

"How dare you," my dad says from the doorway into his room. "How *dare you* speak to your mother like that?"

Something slams into the wall behind my head and shatters.

It reminds me of the last time, and I shudder.

"Patrick," Mom says, "that's too much."

"She never said where she was." Dad's scowling. "I think she should tell us why we had to wait."

I shouldn't say it. I should keep my mouth shut. But I'm tired of being the only one who does what she should do while my parents behave like spoiled children. Even Maren's not as bad as they are. "I was at Abigail Brooks' house, where the parents like the children and they never throw things at their head." I set my jaw.

"You're as bad as your Aunt Donna," Dad says. "And if you don't watch out, you'll end up being on the wrong side of things just like she is." He drops his voice. "And if you think I'll spare you, you're as dumb as your aunt." He grabs his coat and stomps out the door.

Mom just sighs.

"What did that mean?" I ask.

"He got her fired today," Mom says. "She deserved it. She was being terribly disloyal."

It takes me a beat to process what she's saying. "Dad got his *sister* fired, because she wants some of their parents' inheritance?"

Mom just stares at the table in front of her.

"He cost the Brooks women their children's inheritance, too. Has it ever occurred to you, Mom, that *Dad* might be the bad guy?"

I wait in my room for an hour and a half before sneaking outside to get my gifts out of my car. I carry them as quietly as I can inside the house and set them all on my desk. Then, finally, I open Ethan's gift. I'm hoping there will be some sign, some message that he still likes me. That maybe, some day in the future, I might be able to date him again for real.

It's a simple photo frame with a small photo inside.

The one I took of his family.

Looking at that image, which Ethan had asked me to send him weeks and weeks ago, breaks my heart. It's everything I'll never have. The boy, the family, the shiny future. A tiny knock at my door startles me, and I drop the photo frame. It lands face down on my floor. Before I can even pick it up, the door's opening. It's my dad.

Of course it is.

"What do you want?" I ask.

"Your mom's asleep, and I hope you're happy with yourself. She must have had some pills stashed somewhere, because when I came back inside, she was out cold."

"I'm sorry," I say. But I'm not as sorry as I probably should be. I'm tired of being sorry for what Mom does. I'm tired of apologizing when other people react to something I did. I'm tired of everything always being my fault.

"You know, you might not think I was such a villain in all this, if you knew why I was doing it."

"Doing what?"

"If I was married to someone like the Brooks women, I could be generous and share my inheritance with your aunt. But I'm married to your mother, and she needs more than most people."

"You mean because she's always binge shopping? And going to pricey rehab places?"

Dad frowns. "Your rudeness is really disgusting."

"But that is what you meant."

Dad sighs. "You keep right on acting all self-righteous and important." He smirks. "Because you're just like Donna."

After he leaves, I lean over slowly and pick up the photo. The glass over the front of it is broken, and it just highlights how different my world is than the world staring back at me from the photo. Their happy, bright joy can't even survive in this house when it's behind glass.

My life shatters theirs, and that thought makes me bawl even harder.

✣ 15 ✣

ETHAN

I f I had grown up out here, I probably would have played football in high school. I'm tall, I'm coordinated, and I'm athletic. I played high school basketball back home, but it's Texas. So to play high school football, you need to live, breathe, and sleep football.

I did not.

Even so, I'm familiar with how it works. My friend who made the team had to go over plays every day to remember them all, and then several times a week, they'd run each one in turn.

When Izzy jogs inside to grab drinks, I snag her arm. "Hey, can you go over the plan with me one more time?"

Judging by her eye roll, she thinks it's overkill.

"Okay, so here's how it will go."

"Ethan." She doesn't even say my full name, but I swear, with the emphasis she puts on it, Izzy thinks she's as scary as Mom.

"Just one more time," I say. "I want to make sure I didn't forget anything."

"You didn't forget a single thing, I promise."

"So I ask her to meet me at the grove."

"You mean that bench near those three trees at Steve's?" Izzy was unimpressed when she saw our meeting spot.

"We call it the grove."

"I can't call it that just because you two are stupid." She folds her arms. "You call her over there. You tell her that you really value your friendship, but that you never stopped caring about her." She pulls the flower bouquet out of the vase and clutches it to her chest. "You give her flowers and then you tell her 'no harm no foul' or some other dumb cliche about the ranch, because, well, we still own it. And then you kiss her." She makes a gagging sound. "And then bam. You're planning your summer wedding."

"I'm not proposing," I say. "Geez."

Izzy drops the flowers back into the water. "Right? So why are you obsessing so much?"

I sigh. "I don't know."

Izzy punches my shoulder. "She either likes you still or she doesn't, and after tonight, you'll finally know. No more faking or stressing or obsessing."

I think that's the part I'm most excited about. Instead of buzzing around Beth, always giving her my 'hey buddy' smile, I can finally look at her the way I want to. Touch her the way I want to. Call her my girlfriend. Heck, I'll be able to call and text her without worrying what she'll think. Because she'll know the truth about how I feel.

A slow smile spreads across my face. "Okay. You're right. Thanks." I throw two thumbs up and smile.

"You're kinda dorky," Izzy says. "Let's hope Beth

hasn't noticed." She jogs out the door and back to Maren. I'm not sure why they're getting along so well right now, but I guess it's probably good.

I do think about what she said, though. Is it just Maren rubbing off on her, or is she right? Am I dorky? I used to be reasonably cool, other than the no drinking, no swearing, no drugs thing, but I had friends. People liked me. Now that I'm here, shoveling actual poop and fixing fences. . .am I kind of a loser?

I text Beth before I have time to fret about it too much. My mom's out of town, and while she's supportive, I'm still nervous to start things up with Beth again under her very watchful eye. I don't wait very long before my phone buzzes and Beth says, SURE, SEE YOU AT SIX.

When I race out to the barn to finish up my chores, Kevin's out there, getting the new supplies unspooled so we can use them to fix the fence tomorrow. "Here, I can help," I say.

"Oh, great."

Kevin's awesome to work with. He's patient, he's great with farm and ranch stuff, and he never gets angry about anything, really. But he and Jeff are brothers and they kind of do everything together, so we haven't really hung out a bunch.

Then again, it's not like I've ever asked him to do anything.

Maybe I should have.

"Hey," I say. "What do you think about Beth Ellingson?"

Kevin pauses. "What do you mean?"

"I might like her," I say. "But I'm a little nervous to tell her that."

A slow smile rolls over Kevin's face, totally transforming it. "Really? That's great. I'm sure she likes you, too."

"You are?" I can feel my heart swell a little. "Why do you think so?"

Kevin shrugs. "I seen her smile at you a few times."

Hope deflates. "Do you date a lot, Kevin?"

He laughs. "Not really, no."

"Well, I'm about to either start dating her or get shot down pretty spectacularly."

"Nice work," he says. "Shoot your shot, man."

"Did you play basketball?"

Kevin shrugs. "Some."

"We should go play sometime."

"Jeff's not bad either, and we got a few friends from school who shoot hoops every Saturday. You could come."

"I'd like that," I say. They may not be the coolest guys in America, but spending time with more guys my age—or, you know, closer than Gabe and Aiden, anyway—can't hurt.

"Alright," I say. "Well, I'll finish this up, and then I'm going to go shower and get ready."

Only, I'm nearly done when Aunt Amanda traipses through, talking about the ranch, which is awkward, and then dragging Gabe back to the house. I hope she won't be all strange and demand I stick around all night tonight. Usually when she's 'watching' us, she's barely even here. Which is just fine with all of us.

I'm just stacking the last pieces when she shoots back out, a crazed look in her eye.

"Hey, Ethan? You in here?"

I try to avoid any conversations with her when she looks like that, but apparently luck is not on my side. That's alright. I can handle some crazy interactions with Amanda as long as my bad luck is confined to her. "Everything alright?"

"You're eighteen," she says. "You're an adult."

For some reason, that sounds borderline creepy. "I am, yeah."

"And you're capable of keeping the kids alive and making sure they do their homework and eat, right?"

Um, what exactly is she asking me that for?

"Earlier, you said that winter's slower on the ranch, and you had time, didn't you? Because I had an emergency come up, and. . ." She points at the door to the barn as if that makes sense. "I need to go somewhere."

"Go somewhere?" I hate that I'm repeating what she's saying, but I don't understand what's happening. "Is everything alright?" What could have happened that would make her act all crazy and suddenly leave? Aunt Amanda has never been the most attentive, but she's never just bailed when she was supposed to be the responsible adult, either.

"I just put a pan of nachos in the oven. They'll be ready in twenty minutes or so. Tomatoes and lettuce and ranch are already out on the counter. Gabe's in the bathtub and is ready to get out whenever. Can you hold things down until tomorrow night?"

"Yeah, sure, of course." I wonder what kind of emergency she's dealing with. I hope no one's sick or dying. I've never heard her talk about her family, but I think someone said she has brothers. I hope they're all okay. "Are you alright? Is your family okay?"

"I sure hope so," she says.

Oh, man. Now I'm even more worried. "Go," I say.

She disappears like Roscoe sprinting after a squirrel, her car shooting down the driveway even faster than Aunt Helen's does. And that's when I remember that I'm supposed to be at the grove in. . .I check my watch.

Twenty-six minutes.

Which is totally fine. I can shower in three and a half minutes, throw on clothes, pull the nachos out, and then I can hop on the four-wheeler and haul balls to the grove. If I'm a minute or two late, it's fine. It's not like the girls can't hold things down until I get back.

They're teenagers. Even Gabe's not the walking wrecking ball he used to be.

I shower, I pull the nachos out—the cheese isn't totally melted, but close enough, and I call everyone in. I make a point of getting Izzy's attention. "Hey guys, so something came up, and I'm going to have to step out for a bit. Izzy and Maren will be in charge until I'm back and—"

"My tummy hurts," Gabe says.

"Well, you're in luck," I say. "Because dinner is ready."

Gabe grimaces. "Not that kind of hurt."

"Um, are you sure you're not hungry?"

He shakes his head slowly.

"Well, like what, then?"

"I think. . ." Gabe doubles over. "I think I need to go poop."

I groan. "Okay, buddy. Let's go." I walk with him

to the bathroom and stand next to him, patting his back while he goes. Groaning.

Being a fill-in mom is super gross.

When I look up to check the clock on my phone —I have four minutes to get over there—I notice something strange.

There's a cow looking at me through the window.

Yeah. That's not *ever* supposed to happen.

I swear under my breath.

"Whoa, what does that word mean?" Gabe asks, his moaning temporarily stopping.

"Just focus on what you're doing, okay?"

"But you just said—"

"I know what I said, but look." I point, and when Gabe sees the big brown head with white splotches eyeing us through the glass, his eyes widen.

He repeats my word.

Mom is *not* going to be pleased if she realizes I taught him that. Ugh. "Let's not say that any more, okay?"

He says it again. Of course he does.

I glance at my phone again. Two minutes until Beth will be waiting on me in the grove. This time, I wish I could say even more creative words, but my little sponge brother would for sure love to hear those. I suppress any more grumbling I want to do and force myself to text Beth.

SOMETHING CAME UP. WE'LL HAVE TO MEET ANOTHER DAY.

Then I spend the next two hours rounding up cows. But that's nothing to the very next day, when the poo Gabe is currently making starts to bubble up as very smelly sludge out of the toilet. That's when I find out what septic sprinklers are, and what happens when your septic can't empty and needs to be pumped.

I'm replacing a septic sprinkler head—thanks YouTube—when my phone starts ringing. I wouldn't answer, but I know that ringer. *I'm Walking on Sunshine.* I wipe off my hands and swipe.

"Hello?"

"Is everything okay?" Beth sounds worried. "It's not like you to cancel last minute. Then you never called me or explained, either."

I groan. "Aunt Amanda randomly ditched me last night, and my mom's out of town, and so is my Aunt Helen, and Whitney forgot to lock the gate and about fifty cows got out. One of them trampled the septic sprinkler, and with the snow melting. . . Basically it's a literal poop storm over here."

"Storm?"

"Poop soup? What sounds worse?"

She laughs. "All of it sounds pretty bad."

"Well, anyway, sorry for canceling, but trust me. You are lucky not to be here."

"About that." A horn honks from our driveway, and I look up.

Her cute little car's parked, headlights on, in front of our house. I'm dirty. I stink. I'm exhausted, and my house is a mess.

"You sounded like maybe you could use a hand." Beth walks toward me, her eyes wide. "I was on my way over anyway."

"Can you hand me that screwdriver?" I ask. "I need to adjust this."

She spends the next half hour handing me tools

and rewinding videos to show me what to do. I'm pretty proud of myself for getting the sprinklers fixed before Mandy's people arrive to pump the septic.

Unfortunately, Mom gets home just in time to help me scrub the bathrooms and floors. Even then, Beth insists on staying to help. When it's finally done and the house is clean—just in time, because we're all super filthy—I apologize.

"I'm sure that's not anywhere on your list of how you'd like to spend your weekend."

"Actually," Beth says, "it was probably more fun than I would have had at home."

"Ouch," I say. "Are things really that bad?"

She nods slowly. "I ticked my parents off, but they deserved it. It's been bad lately. My mom. . .isn't happy. My dad. . .is greedy and that makes him miserable. It's just." She shrugs. "It's bad."

As awful as the past weekend was, maybe it's for the best that I got delayed. When I look at Beth I feel at peace. I feel calm. I feel warm and happy. I guess that means that being her friend for a little longer isn't so awful.

And maybe what we both need the most right now *is* a friend.

❧ 16 ❧

BETH

There's something freeing about realizing the truth about people. For years, I've known my dad wasn't the hero most girls believed their dads to be. But he also took me to daddy daughter dances. He bought me dolls. Clothes. Jewelry. He put a roof over my head, and he never beat me or attacked me like I know some dads can.

He told me he loved me.

It made it hard for me to know what to think about him. And then when Aunt Donna came home, I watched her dad treat her like an indentured servant. I saw him yell horrible things at her. I saw him take swings at her, the very person who was caring for him.

I know there are worse people than my dad.

So I made excuses for him.

But hearing that he got his own sister fired because she had the audacity to ask for part of their inheritance?

And then discovering from Izzy that he had been

lying all along—Grandpa and Grandma had changed their minds. They didn't want to cut her out. They wanted Dad to share what they left with her. He knew that.

And he lied to her anyway.

And he lied to me about it.

My dad may not be a serial killer, but that doesn't mean he's a hero.

There are many shades of gray in between absolute good and absolute bad, but I do know that I want to fall on the side of white, or as close as I can get to it.

I'm eighteen now, but I'm still living at home, waiting to graduate. So my revelation didn't really change a whole lot, but it did impact how I spent my time. Instead of spending a lot of time at home, begging for scraps from Dad and hoping Mom would have a few good weeks, I spent more time away. I spent time with Izzy. Time with Aunt Donna and Aiden. Time with friends on the paper at school.

And I applied to UCLA.

It's a long shot, but I had to at least try. I also applied to a half dozen other, less prestigious schools. But to be honest, even that was a little half-hearted. The more time I spend taking photos, the less I want to do anything else. I know UCLA and other colleges have great programs for photography, but I'm not sure they're really the best way to learn. Even if that's where Mom went to study art, and even if she had a promising career before her accident, I'm not sold on college at all.

So when the letter comes from UCLA telling me I'm on their waitlist, it doesn't wreck me.

UCLA doesn't have the market cornered on photographic skill.

The world isn't black and white, but there is truth out there, and I see it much more clearly through the lens of my camera. People lie all the time, but their faces, their expressions, and their actions rarely lie.

I think if I've learned one single thing from my life to this point, it's that we get to choose how to spend our time, and I want to spend mine with people that bring me closer to white and further from black. Sadly, that person isn't my dad. I wish it was.

Badly.

But until he starts making better decisions, I refuse to sit around bawling about how he keeps letting me down. That's not bringing me joy, and it's not helping anyone.

Maren's part of the team that helps get us fitted for our caps and gowns, which surprises me for some reason. "What are you doing?" I ask.

She shrugs. "I'm thinking about doing fashion as a career, and the closest thing to that I can do around here is costume design for theater. They asked our club to help with taking measurements." She tilts her head. "There's really no way to make a cap and gown look like anything but a balloon with a Lego on top, is there?"

I turn toward the mirror and decide she's right. "It's not really something people wear for fashion, that's for sure."

"It's hard to make your hair look decent with this dumb thing on your head." Maren's hair always looks perfect. *Always.* Emery's always looks great too, but

Maren's is perfect because she's very aware and she has good genetics. I get the impression Emery's appearance is pure genetics and maybe some luck.

"I'm not too worried," I say. "It's not like I'll be making a love match at graduation."

"Won't Ethan be there?" Maren's sideways smile is sly.

I'm afraid, thanks to her question, that my face is close to matching our bright red gowns. "Why would you ask about that?" I shake my head. "We're just friends."

"Oh, I know that," Maren says. "What I can't figure out is *why*, when he clearly likes you." She frowns. "Don't tell me you don't like him. I mean, he's super annoying as a cousin, but he's not bad looking, and all that cow work stuff has given him muscles for days."

I choke.

She pats my back. "Look, if I'm off base, whatever. Fine. But if I were you, I'd want to look better in this getup than you do right now. That's all I'm saying."

"What exactly would you do to look better?" I ask. "If you were me?"

She ignores the other twelve or thirteen students still waiting, letting poor Betty measure them all herself, and tells me exactly how to do my hair and what to do with my cap.

"Hey," I finally ask when she's done. "Why didn't Betty complain you weren't helping?"

Maren rolls her eyes and tosses her hair at the same time. I feel like I might sprain my eyeballs if I tried to emulate her. It must be an advanced move. "She's way too afraid of me to complain, trust me."

Poor Betty. I know just how she feels, and I'm two years older than Maren. "Well, thanks for the advice."

"Here's one more suggestion." Maren drops her voice. "Playing hard to get is a great plan. Bravo on that. But don't draw it out too long. That can be as bad as just falling in their lap." She shrugs and flounces off.

Does Ethan think I'm playing hard to get?

He can't really think that. I liked him more than he liked me. It's just that it feels like our families have been on opposite sides from the very day we met. First my dad cost them the ranch. They only have it because Amanda Saddler has more money than sense.

And then, after I thought we might be able to move past that, my dad went head-to-head with Donna over this inheritance, with Ethan's mom as her biggest champion. I hate how much damage my dad keeps causing, but I can't really do anything about it.

When Izzy texts me asking if I'd come help her go over her very last article for the paper, I might reply a little too quickly. Lately, it feels like the only time I really get to see Ethan is if I have the excuse of going over for something Izzy needs. I know it's a busy time for the ranch—I've grown up very familiar with the rhythms of cattle. The cows are milling around, ready to go up to the summer pasture, and the new calves are all being born. But it doesn't change the fact that I'm stupidly yearning for moments when I can see him and his beautiful smile.

I see his dimples in my dreams.

Sometimes I wonder whether Izzy invites me to hang out just so she doesn't have to ride the bus. I know Gabe and Whitney never mind, and since Amanda Saddler's place is next door, I always offer to take Maren and Emery, too. I've gotten used to the bus full of kids being in my car.

On the days I'm not taking them home, it makes me a little sad.

This time, when we reach Izzy's house, Ethan's nowhere to be seen. I hate how much my heart sinks.

"Are you looking for Ethan?" Maren whispers.

I glare.

"I heard there's a calf being born right now." She shrugs. "He's probably out there, muscles flexed, ready to, I don't know, catch it or something."

It is a warm day. Maybe he's not even wearing a shirt. . .

"Beth?" Izzy asks.

I jump like I've been caught hiding pills or something.

"Coming."

Maren's laugh follows me into the house.

For the next forty minutes, I'm worse than useless for Izzy. She's probably wishing she hadn't even invited me over.

"—just go out there."

"Huh?"

Izzy's smiling. "He asked me to be your friend, you know."

Suddenly I'm all ears. "Wait, who did?"

"My brother. He said I'd like you, and he was right."

So it was charity, then.

"But really, he just wanted you to have a reason to come over."

My mouth goes dry.

"You should just go out there and find him. Clearly you're not paying any attention to the parking spot assignment stuff. It doesn't help that it's literally the most boring article ever." Izzy laughs. "Just go."

I stand up before I realize how incriminating that is. "The thing is—"

Izzy shrugs. "For the record, I think that liking you is the first time Ethan's ever really had good judgment, so just go find him."

My heart races. Am I really going to just wander out in the pasture, like I'm *looking* for him? Like I just want to see him? I mean, friends do that, right? I *could.*

But it would be weird.

Just then, the front door bangs open and Ethan walks through, peeling his shirt off as he does. It's coated in mud and something reddish—probably blood. Birthing's messy. "Geez, we can't catch a break," he says. "First it's storming, and now the mosquitos—" He freezes. Then he swallows, his Adam's apple shifting slightly.

I've always known he was fit, but it's hard to see much under sweaters, sweatshirts, and coats. But with his shirt off, his hands extended over his head, I can see *everything.*

Abs. So many abs.

Arms. Rippling arm muscles.

And his chest. Ermagosh.

Ethan's face is frozen, his eyes darting between me and Izzy. "Give me a little warning. Geez." He throws his filthy shirt toward the hall in front of the laundry room and sprints to the bathroom.

Izzy, meanwhile, busts out laughing so hard that I worry she may asphyxiate. It would serve her right. I'm blushing so hard my face feels like it's going to melt and drip onto the floor.

"That was epic," Izzy says. "If you didn't know he liked you before." She slaps her thighs and descends into maniacal laughter again.

I walk out the front door faster than I ever have before, my heart beating out of my chest. Why did I just stand there, staring? Why did my mouth fall open? Why didn't I look away or act like it was no big deal? Could I have possibly looked more idiotic? I thought I was going to storm out there and let him know I liked him, that I was done pretending that we were just friends.

But instead, I feel like a complete idiot.

I'm in my car, my fingers turning the keys, when Izzy reaches me, her hands slapping against my window. "Hey." Her face looks distraught. "What are you doing?"

"Isn't that obvious?" That's when I realize that I'm crying.

"No." She shakes her head slowly. "I have no idea what's going on."

I wipe my eyes and inhale deeply.

"Beth. Open the door."

I clench and unclench my hands a few times, and then I nod.

Izzy opens it. "Why are you leaving? I thought you liked him."

"I looked like a weirdo back there," I say. "I can't

just sit in there now like I didn't just completely stare at him."

Izzy's mouth curls into a smile. "Wait, *you're* embarrassed?"

How did she not know that? I nod slowly.

"Beth, I was laughing at *him*. Did you see his face?" She giggles. "Did you see him yell at me?" She snorts. "It was the funniest thing I've seen this month, at least." The humor falls off her face. "But if you leave, then he'll never talk to me again. Don't go."

"I don't think he wants to see me right now," I say. "Trust me."

"You're wrong," Ethan says. His hair's dripping on his shirt as he jogs toward me. "I always want to see you."

I can't breathe.

"I didn't want to look like an idiot. And I thought—" He shakes his head. "Your graduation's Friday, right?"

I nod.

"I'll be there. And my mom's wedding is the next week. Would you like to be my date?"

His *date*. The word feels heavy, like real whipped cream. Like solid gold jewelry. Not the fake stuff. Not the pretending we've been doing. I drag a breath in, and I open my mouth, and then I force the word out. "Okay."

"Okay, as in yes?" He beams. "Okay, great. Yes. That's great." I wish I had my camera in my hand right now, so I could capture this expression to look at forever.

And then my hands are moving as if I just don't care how corny it is. I swipe my phone and snap a photo.

His face falls. "What are you doing?"

"I'm saving it," I say.

"Saving what?"

"This moment," I say. "So I can remember how I felt in this moment." The tears on my cheeks started from distress, but now they're full of joy.

Ethan leans forward and snatches the phone out of my hand, and then he spins it around and snaps a photo of me. "You can't remember how *you* felt with a photo of me."

I shake my head. "You're wrong. I feel all the things when I see you looking like that."

"Well, then I deserve to have one, too." His grin when he shrugs and texts the photo to himself is one of the most endearing things I've ever seen.

"What should I wear?" I haven't been to a wedding since I wore my hair in pigtails.

Ethan shrugs again. "Overalls? A pair of jeans and a t-shirt. I don't care as long as you come."

"Ethan," Izzy says. "Stop being an idiot." She leans against the front of the car where she moved so she'd be out of the way. "Wear a dress and heels. That's what everyone else will be wearing."

"Thanks," I say.

"No, thank you," Izzy says. "If I have to go over any more plans with him for how to ask you out." She sighs dramatically. "I might strangle him."

Ethan's glaring at her with so much intensity that it makes me laugh.

"I better go," I say.

Because if I stay here any longer, I'm going to pounce on Ethan like a barn cat on a baby mouse. I keep seeing the same image of him over and over—

his shirt up over his head. I can practically feel my hands moving down, down, down, to where they can stroke those beautiful abs.

"Wait," Izzy says.

"Your article's fine," I say.

"No one's going to read it anyway," Ethan says. "It's the last week of school." They're bickering when I pull out, and it steadies me, like the world hasn't tilted on its axis. Like what just happened really is real.

Ethan asked me out.

To his own mother's wedding.

Not as his friend.

I'm almost floating when I walk through the door at home. Mom's back home again, thankfully, and she might even have some ideas for what I could wear.

Only, Mom's not going to help me. I know it the second I walk inside. My mom gets sad sometimes, and she lies around a lot when she's drunk or high. When she's not, but she's trying to stay clean, she shops. One thing Mom never does is yell.

And right now, she's yelling. "—told you that the very first time you ever did that, I'd leave. And now?" She tightens her hand into a fist and trembles. "We're through, Patrick. I already called my parents to tell them we'll be there tomorrow."

We? They're through? What's going on?

"Mom?"

Dad's head whips sideways. "It's not what you think."

"Is Mom leaving you?" I ask.

"It's exactly what you think." Mom doesn't look at me. "Your dad swore to me when we got engaged that he wasn't like his dad. He promised he'd never hit me."

"Dad *hit* you?" I ask.

"He hit his sister," Mom says. "Close enough."

Dad hit Aunt Donna? I feel sick.

"You don't understand," Dad says. "We need that money."

Mom throws her hands up in the air. "Maybe *you* need it, but I don't need you anymore." She finally turns toward me. "Go and pack, honey. We're moving."

"No," I say. "We can't move."

"What?" Mom freezes. "Why not?"

"I graduate in two days," I say. "And Ethan's mom is getting married."

"What does that have to do with anything?" Mom asks. "Plus, even if you don't walk, you'll still graduate."

"Amelia, you're not thinking this through," Dad says. "I know you're upset, and I'm so sorry." My big, strong, horrible father drops down to his knees, tears rolling down his face. "Please, please don't do this. Don't leave me."

"Patrick, I'm not doing this to you. You did it to yourself." Mom turns around and disappears into their room.

I follow her, too numb to think straight. "Mom, can't you talk to him?"

She spins around. "He's been planning to steal from your aunt. She was supposed to get half his parents' estate, and he's been lying to us all. He knew it, and he kept it from her. Then when she found out, he threatened her and when she came to confront him, he hit her." Mom's trembling. "What part of that should I talk to him about?"

I'm not even sure what to say.

"Mom." What I want to ask is why this is happening to me. Why, when things are finally going well for me, do they always fall apart? How come, every time I'm almost happy, the sky falls down on my head? "Dad was wrong." I stop then, because what else can I say?

I turn around, trying to decide what to do. Do I pack? Do I stay here with Dad, at least until graduation? I have no idea.

The second I walk out the bedroom door, Dad grabs me and hugs me. It's one of the most vulnerable things he's ever done. I wish he'd done it without facing his own personal hades. It would mean a lot more.

"Dad."

"Wait, Beth. At least let me explain."

"Explain why you hit Aunt Donna?" I can't help hating him. It's been growing for a long time, but really, it all comes down to this. He's the devil. He's just like his father.

"It's not that simple," he says.

"I think it is."

Dad releases me. "Give me half an hour. Listen for thirty minutes, and if you still want to leave, I'll help you pack."

I'm not even sure I want to leave right now, but I don't tell him that. "Why do you want me to stay?"

I hate how badly I want him to tell me he loves me. I hate that even now, even when I know what a jerk he is, I'm desperate to hear that he wants me to stay *for me*.

"If you're still here, your mother will come back for sure."

Something deep in the corner of my heart, something that thought that just maybe he might love me for being his daughter and no other reason dies. "Okay, Dad." I nod. "Half an hour."

He bobs his head frantically. "Yes, half an hour."

I follow him into his office. "Look." He spreads papers around. "I've never shown you this, but just, look."

"What is it?"

"Your mother." He swallows. "You know that I love her. When I met her, I felt like I was total trash."

Because of Grandpa. "Okay."

"She told me I wasn't. She said I was strong. She said I was brave. She told me that I was the best thing she'd ever seen. The handsomest. The smartest. The most amazing."

"Dad."

"She was raised by two people who always wanted *more* from her. They dressed her up and trotted her out to parties, to business events, always touting her achievements. They used their own daughter." He shakes his head. "She wanted to be free. I freed her from them, and now she wants to go back."

I don't bother arguing. "Alright, Dad."

"But when she broke her back in the car accident, the one after her first gallery opening, she was in the hospital for weeks."

"I know."

"That's when she got addicted," he says. "It wasn't her fault."

"You told me that, too."

"What I didn't tell you, what I never told your mother either, is how much all her rehab cost." He points at the documents, and I finally look.

The figures are staggering.

"Her own parents said she was broken. They said she was a lost cause, and that spending all that was a waste."

"But Dad."

"That's why I married her. She could be on my insurance, and I could pay for it."

It never worked, in spite of all his faith, in spite of his herculean efforts and ongoing rehab. I don't point that out.

"She got better," he says. "We had years, sometimes, before she relapsed." He looks like a junkie himself as he explains this.

"Dad, you still—"

"But it wasn't just the rehab." He sighs.

"What?"

"In between bouts with using, when she'd get upset, sometimes after a relapse, sometimes before she'd use again, she'd go shopping."

"I don't understand."

"She bought things we didn't need. Things we couldn't afford. It made her feel, I guess. That's what she said."

"But—"

"I couldn't afford to pay the bills." He looks broken. "I didn't know what to do."

"So you. . .you decided to steal from Aunt Donna?"

He shakes his head. "No, Dad told me he was leaving me everything. But then, later, he changed his mind." Dad's face crumples. "But he didn't tell Donna. And at that point, I had his power of attorney."

Oh, no.

"Donna had that rich husband and she had that fancy education."

"Dad."

"Even now, she's got a job. She and Aiden are fine, but I'm about to lose your mother. And she wouldn't budge at all."

"Budge?" I shake my head. "You lied to her."

"Which is why I need your help."

"My help?" I feel sick even asking that question.

"Don't you want to stay here?" He has no idea how badly I want that. But we don't get what we want just for wanting it. "If you could talk to your aunt, if you could explain. . ."

Mom stomps down the hall, then. She's carrying a bag. "Elizabeth Amelia Ellingson, let's go."

"Mom." I walk out of the office, and I take a good look at my mother. This whole time, I've been seeing her as this pathetic victim who just can't stop herself and my dad as the mastermind, but was that wrong?

When I look back at my dad, I wonder. "Let's report Dad," I say. "He can confess to the police that he hit Aunt Donna, and then—"

Mom shakes her head, the blood draining from her face. "We can't do that." She drops her suitcase, and walks across the hall to me. She places one hand on my cheek. "Promise me that you won't do that."

"But you said that's why you're leaving. Let the law sort that out, and maybe he can take classes or go to therapy."

Mom shakes her head. "Once someone crosses that line, they can't go back."

For decades now, Dad has given up everything to try and help her, and the first time he crosses her line, she's done?

"Beth, come. Right now. We can buy you new clothes once we get there." She grabs my arm.

She has always liked to shop.

Looking back, I see some of it in a new light. Was she always running, running, running? Was Dad always being the jerk. . .for her? It was misguided, clearly, and it didn't fix anything. But did he think he was being a white knight?

I shake her off. "I'm staying."

❧ 17 ❧

BETH

When I was fifteen, we went to Seattle to celebrate Mom's birthday. Grandma and Grandpa took us out on a boat to celebrate with some friends who had just upgraded their boat. I haven't thought about that trip in years, but lately, it keeps coming to mind. Grandpa spent a lot of time talking about Mom's photography skills, her gallery of photographs that won critical acclaim, and the amount of money she made from her sales. Usually Grandpa didn't talk about money, so I noticed that he kept using numbers.

He told his friend about seven times that I was just like her.

I'd never thought of it as Grandpa showing off, but after my talk with Dad I realize that he was.

That was also the trip where I learned about rudders. A rudder's a tiny little thing, compared to the size of the boat, but without it, the ship can't turn. It directs where the boat moves very simply and very completely.

Life's like that, sometimes.

Our lives are these huge strings of moments, but then one small decision can dramatically alter the direction our life takes. Mom could have stayed with her parents, but she chose to marry my dad over their objections. I could have gone with my mother, but I stayed with my dad.

And I can tell my dad to jump off a cliff when he asks me for help.

Some choices we make.

Others are taken from us.

I wanted to go to my graduation and walk the stage in my robe while Ethan and his family clapped. I wanted to be Ethan's date to his mother's wedding. Heck, I wanted to be his date way back when, before Dad stole their ranch.

But even when other people—like the currents of the ocean, or the winds on the sea—shove us in one direction or another, we still have choices to make. Our choices set us down a path, just like that tiny little rudder changes the boat's direction, even on a storm-tossed sea.

And I made a choice on the day I was supposed to be Ethan's date.

Several, really. I canceled our plans. I skipped my own graduation. I told Ethan I was terribly ill. I told him I didn't want to see anyone. He dropped off soup on my front porch. But really, I just didn't want to ruin his week, his mother's wedding, or his life in general.

One thing Ellingsons do quite well is ruin other people's futures.

First, my dad's dad. My grandmother was the sweetest lady in the world, but she never stopped him from dictating everything. Then my mom's dad who never seemed nearly as bad to me, but might have set my mom on her path to the cycle of misery her life has become.

And then my mother herself. Even if her parents shoved her down the path she took, she never broke free. Finally, my dad. He tried to be different from his father. He tried to be a good husband in all the ways his dad never was. His patience and care for his own wife was like a love letter to his own mother, I realize. He treated his wife the way he wished his father had treated Granny.

But even that wasn't enough.

They all tripped and fell right into the same traps. They were dragged down in the same ways. Because I recognize them, I know they're the same ways I'd wreck Ethan, if I let him love me.

My dad made a fake will. He wants me to testify in court that my grandpa gave it to me. He wants me to perjure myself in front of God and witnesses, swearing that Grandpa *did* mean to leave everything to Dad after all. He wants me to save him from the mess he's made at the expense of his own sister—again. He still thinks he can fix a lie with another, bigger lie. When at first you don't succeed, up the stakes and go again.

But I've been studying rudders. You can't change the course of the boat unless you change the way your rudder turns—your own behavior. So on the day of the wedding, I tell him my decision. "No," I say. "I won't do it."

"But if you—"

"Dad." I shake my head. "I've heard you out, and I even considered it, as sick as it made me, but it's wrong." I shrug. "I know you'd sacrifice me a million times over to save Mom, and I've known that for a long time, I think. I've come to terms with it even, but it doesn't mean I'll help you do it."

"You'll go down when we do," Dad says. "When your aunt takes over, we'll be homeless. That means you'll have nowhere to live. Did you consider that?"

"Homeless?" I ask. "Did you become terribly crippled while I slept last night? You can get another job, something other than ranching. I can do the same. Most people aren't born with a ranch, you know. Most people start with nothing and make something for themselves instead of spending and taking from others their entire lives."

Dad's face brightens and flushes. "You're one to talk. You've never done a thing—had a single penny —that I didn't give you."

"I'd rather be poor and honest than lie so I can steal from Aunt Donna." I shake my head. "But I will go and talk to her about the truth, just like you talked to me."

"You think your aunt will just *give* me the life insurance policy to repay the ranch debt?" Dad's laugh is harsh. "You're a bigger idiot than I thought."

"You're acting like she's like you, but she's not." My voice is flat. "Just because you'd never do that doesn't mean she won't."

Dad's jaw muscles work like crazy. "You're the biggest disappointment of all." He turns and walks into his room.

I should be gutted.

He meant that as an insult to wound me.

But it backfired. Because disappointing my dad may be the best thing I've ever truly done.

The next two hours are not high points. I sneak

into the wedding I was supposed to attend as a guest, and then when I find a lull where I see Donna standing near the edge of the ballroom, I grab her and drag her outside.

I'm pretty sure my dad's right. I mean, if I were her, I'd never hand over the inheritance Dad tried to steal. . .to Dad. But to my utter shock, my pathetic plea for clemency works. She agrees to give Dad the ranch *and* the majority of the insurance money. And a few weeks later, she follows through on her promise.

But it turns out, the only real chump in this whole thing. . .is me. Getting the money back does win Mom over. Or maybe it's the promise Aunt Donna wrangled out of him to attend anger management. I'm not sure which. Either way, Mom takes him back.

I didn't think she would.

But then, Dad stabs his sister in the back again, and he betrays me in the process as well by listing the ranch—that he just got improperly and paid off out of the largesse of his sister's heart—for sale. I feel so guilty about being a part of it that I can't even bring myself to call Aunt Donna. I appealed to her goodness, and then Dad spat on her yet again.

"I don't know why you're sore about it," Mom says. "Your parents are happy, our debts are paid with a nice pile of money to invest besides, and we're headed to Seattle. *Finally*."

"Where you can start your freshman year at a pretty darn good school." Dad's cheesy grin makes me think of the cartoon dads in almost every Disney movie ever.

"I don't want to go to the University of Washington," I say. "I only applied because you kept badgering me."

"It's a good thing we did," Mom says. "I didn't really think you'd get in."

"Your grandparents are proud," Dad says, as if he wasn't badmouthing them a few weeks ago.

"How about this?" Mom asks. "Come out for the weekend with us. See how nice it will be when we move there."

I still can't believe Dad just agreed to Mom's terms.

Actually, scratch that. My dad would probably agree to fur transplants and start making the transition to being a furry, if that's what Mom wanted. What I can't believe is that he did it without even putting up a fight. Without even a grace period.

That's when I realize that's precisely *why* he agreed so fast.

He's embarrassed every time he sees his sister, and he agreed to move to Seattle *to run away*.

The whole thing disgusts me. "I don't want to go for the weekend, and I certainly don't want to move there."

"Well, too bad," Mom says. "Because we won't pay for your college if you don't move." She folds her arms like she's played their trump card.

"Are you deaf?" I stomp. "I just said I don't want to go to college there."

"We won't pay for it anywhere," Dad says. "Even if you got into UCLA."

"But if you come, I bet your grandparents will get involved enough that they'll pay for it," Mom says.

There it is. Their actual plan. If we move to

Seattle and engage the sympathies of my mega-rich grandparents, they'll probably pay for my school so they can brag about my successes. The exact trade Dad was boasting about sparing my mom earlier.

"Oh, I dearly hope so."

As if she can't even hear the tone of my voice, Mom beams. "Get your bags packed," Mom says. "That's the end of it."

I head for my room, tired of arguing with them. I missed the perfect date I'd waited for so long. Everyone saw me as Judas, thanks to Mom and Dad, complicit in their mess, and now they're going to take away the roof over my head if I don't follow them like Mary's little lamb? Fine.

Instead of packing, I start searching for jobs in Manila.

It's not super inspiring, to be honest. There's not much out there in a town this small. But I did hear from someone that Bob at Gorge Tours was thinking of expanding. Maybe I could get his number from his niece Hannah.

A tap at my door has my hands clenching. "I'm not going."

Dad opens the door and pokes his head in. "White flag." His nervous grin irritates me more.

"What do you want?"

"Listen, kid."

Oh, good grief. Does he think I'm too stupid to know when he's trying to manipulate me? "Dad, just go without me."

He slides through the door and closes it behind him. "So here's the thing, kiddo."

If he calls me that again, I'm going to scream. As it is, I'm already gritting my teeth.

"Your grandparents are willing to help us get settled in Seattle, because we think it'll be better for your mom. I met with a handful of the best addiction and recovery experts in the country when I went last time. They think the small town life she's been living has been a trigger."

For once in his life, Dad actually looks entirely serious. I imagine he's drowning in guilt, if he thought he was helping her, and now experts are telling him he may have been the problem.

"I don't know what else to try." Dad's voice is small.

As badly as I wanted to rage and yell and pull my teenager card, his stupid little confession took a lot of the wind out of my sails. "I don't want to go, though," I say. "I'm tired of always being the one person whom no one cares about. Why doesn't anyone ever ask what I want?"

"Because when a family member's in distress, you put your resources there," Dad says. "I've never had hobbies, or friends, or anything at all, because I was always trying to get your mom stable."

Twenty years of subjugating all his wants for her? Yeah, I'm pretty sure that's not healthy, either. The biggest problem with Dad is that he's always searching for the golden ticket. He always thinks the game changer is right around the corner. It's true in ranching, in life, in business, and in relationships. "Has it ever occurred to you that she might not be fixable?" I don't want to break his brain, but he needs someone to say it. "Until *Mom* decides to change, nothing we do will make a difference."

"It's not her fault she hasn't been able to change. Alcoholism is a disease. Besides, she does want to

226

heal," he says. "That's the word they'd like us to use. Not *fix*."

Sometimes I think these experts need a big smack. "Whatever."

"If you come this weekend, I'll sign your college fund into your name. You can use it for any kind of education you want, anywhere you want to go."

As much as I hate it, that promise catches my eye. That sounds a lot like freedom, and it's the first time anyone has ever offered it to me. "All I have to do is come this weekend?" I arch my eyebrow. "I want you to transfer it to me first."

"I knew you'd say that." He pulls a folded paper out of his pocket. "This is the transfer form. The second we pull into the driveway at your grandparents, I'll sign it."

I hate how much I want it, but I've been looking at photography classes, and they aren't cheap. Even if Bob's hiring, I doubt I'll be able to pay for my housing and living expenses, and have anything left over to save for classes like that.

"Listen kiddo, your mom needs all our support. And who knows? You might actually like it there. You haven't seen much of your grandparents, and maybe you'll like them."

"The people you were just telling me are the devil?"

He winces. "I never said they were the devil. For your mom, we both need to try."

I insist on driving my own car over, unwilling to rely on their assurances that they'll bring me back at the end of the weekend. Since my dad drives like he's already an octogenarian, I pull in right next to him in front of Grandma and Grandpa's palatial home in the center of Redmond. I haven't been here in a long time, and looking at it now as an adult, I'm positive it cost an absolute fortune.

The lot is enormous, for one. Acres and acres. It's heavily treed, like most of Redmond, and the drive is lined with old, picturesque trees. The house itself has a three-car-wide circular drive out front, with a ridiculous fountain in the center of it. It looks like something that would fit in as a centerpiece in a town square, but it's here instead, in front of a single home.

The red brick house has not two, not four, not even six, but eight enormous white columns that run from the ground to the roof, shoring up a massive, super wide porch in front of a bright, red brick facade. The bushes are shaped into sea animals, as if they need to draw more attention to the fact that they have a huge boat. Dolphins leap on either end of the house. Crabs stand, claws extended, on either side of the double front doors. And in possibly the strangest trimming of all, an eel-like bush runs from the dolphins to the crab.

I wonder how much they have to pay their gardener.

And Dad made me beg my aunt to give up her inheritance to 'save' my mom? It makes me even angrier. I hate how often in this world the little guy's asked to sacrifice for something while the fat cats sit and lick their paws.

I tap on Dad's window, and then I make a signing motion. I want that transfer document. He opens the door and signs it, and then stuffs it back in his pocket. "I did what I said, but I'll hand it over on Monday morning."

Why didn't I expect something like this? It's classic Dad. Before I can yell at him, Grandma and Grandpa walk out the front door. The last few times I came to visit, I'm positive they had a butler or someone like that who let us in.

"You came." My grandma's face barely moves when she smiles. Probably another reason she loves sea creatures—isn't that where Botox comes from?

"Always a delight to see my little urchin." Grandpa holds out his arms like I'll rush over and hug him.

I force a smile and wave instead.

But I can *feel* Dad's glare on my back, so I slowly walk toward him and let him hug me. It's hard to know how much of Dad's story is true, and how much is an exaggeration. Maybe Grandma and Grandpa aren't guilty of much more than being rich and judged by their daughter. He seems genuinely happy to see us.

"Alright," Grandpa says. "Are we all ready to go?"

"Go?"

"We didn't tell her yet." Mom smiles. "We thought it would be more fun for her to find out from you."

Find out?

Grandpa claps. "We just bought a new boat, and we're all going out to christen it this weekend."

"Oh, no," I say, shaking my head involuntarily. "I can't."

Mom glares.

Dad scowls and pats his pocket.

Grandma looks confused. "Why not? What's wrong?"

Dad looks practically apoplectic by now, and he makes a tearing motion with his hands.

I scrunch my nose and snap, "It's just that I forgot to bring my boat shoes."

She beams. "Oh, don't worry about that. I have so many pairs I haven't even worn them all yet. You can have one of them. I'll let you pick."

"Oh, yay." I was trying for forced enthusiasm, but it just came out forced. That earns me another scowl, since Mom can clearly tell I'm being sarcastic.

We don't discover that we're not the only people who will be on the boat until we reach the dock. It's been two years since I've seen him, but I feel about the same now as I did then.

Jackson's taller and broader than he was before, and his dark hair still falls across his eyes, but his sullen look is the same as he lugs his suitcase up to a man in a uniform and practically drops it into his hands before turning away like the attendant is a bug.

"You didn't tell me *she'd* be here." His disgust is baked into the words.

"I was also not informed," I say.

"Oh, young people," Grandma says. "I know you two didn't hit it off last time, but haven't you heard?"

"Heard what?"

"Enemies-to-lovers is all the rage right now." She winks at me.

Like I'm about to *fall in love* with her friends' entitled, irritating, frat-boy grandson? I don't hand my suitcase to the man on the deck. It's a stupid kind of rebellion, but I can't help it. I'm too annoyed, and I can't think of any other way to show it so I clutch my bag to my chest like a conspiracy theorist.

"Why didn't you hand that over?" Jackson asks. "Is there something good in there?" He looks. . .hopeful.

"Something good?" I frown. "I don't have a bag full of cash, if that's what you mean, and I left my good jewels at home."

"Pills," he says. "Weed."

I blink. "Are you serious right now?"

His furrowed brow tells me that he is.

"Ugh, you're even worse than before."

I spend the rest of the night ignoring him. At least there are enough people that I can put them all between us at the dinner table. It's pretty awkward, sitting at a table with four old people, my parents, and one kid my age. Especially since he bugs me to death.

The next morning, I find out that we're docking in San Francisco. "Should be cool," Jackson says. "I hear your grandparents have a city tour planned."

"You think a city tour in San Francisco sounds cool?" Yeah, right.

He shrugs. "I mean, it's not like a rave with edibles or anything, but maybe I've been trying too hard to look cool."

I stumble in shock. That, and a wave hit the boat at an angle.

Jackson catches my elbow. "I'm actually not that big of a partier. I did that a little too much my first semester and almost failed out."

"Well, I don't like partying at all," I say.

"Maybe we both have a little bit to learn." Jackson's face, when he smiles for real, isn't quite so irritating.

My phone starts going crazy as we dock, and I fumble around trying to figure out where I put it.

Jackson reaches over and tugs it out of the side pocket of my backpack. "Been out of range. Sounds like people have been missing you."

When I pull my phone out, I have dozens of messages. All of them are from Hannah. Did her uncle give her more info on the possible job? I swipe with a little too much hope burgeoning in my chest.

I'm beyond ready to have my own income and get my own place.

UNCLE BOB SAYS YOU CAN MEET NEXT WEEK. HERE'S HIS NUMBER. She shares the contact.

HEY, YOU'RE FRIENDS WITH THE BROOKS GIRL, RIGHT?

She doesn't bother waiting for a reply, clearly.

BECAUSE I JUST MET HER OLDER BROTHER. DID YOU KNOW HE'S HOT? LIKE, SMOKIN HOT?

My hands start to shake.

IS HE COOL? WHAT STUFF DOES HE LIKE? BECAUSE OMG, GIRL, I CAN'T THINK ABOUT ANYONE ELSE. HOW HAVE I NEVER SEEN HIM BEFORE?

Hannah's five foot six. She has waist length black hair and green eyes. She could move to LA and model. No lie. Stupid Hannah Banana. Every guy in school follows her around.

OMG, HO, IS HE SINGLE? HAVE YOU BEEN HOLDING OUT ON ME???

I want to throw my phone in the water, but I can't stop scrolling.

WHY DOES HE KEEP ASKING ME ABOUT YOU? I DON'T WANT TO TALK TO HIM ABOUT YOU. I DON'T WANT TO *TALK* TO HIM AT ALL.

I might be sick.

The last text she sends is a photo of the two of them, his arm slung around her shoulders, and Hannah beaming bigger than I've ever seen. She's also looking up at him with a disgustingly mischievous smile that I'm sure guys like.

"Who's the hottie?" Jackson asks.

I drop my phone.

And it falls in the bay.

Jackson's mouth forms a big o shape. "Sorry."

I have no idea what to say.

"Oh, no, dear, did you lose your phone?" My grandmother tuts. "Maybe we can stop in the middle of the tour today and find you a new one."

I feel like sobbing. I want to run back to my room, but there's no way they'll allow it.

"You can use mine if you need to call someone," Jackson says.

"Like I know anyone's number," I spit.

"Oh, right." Jackson shoves his back in his pocket. "I really do feel bad."

"Don't bother," I say. "Really."

"Look." He grabs my wrist. "I know I was a jerk last time, okay? I'm sorry about that. But we're stuck together until tomorrow night. We may as well be friends."

"What are you getting out of this?" I ask. "I'm

only here because my parents will sign my college fund over to me if I stick out the weekend."

He laughs.

"What's funny?"

"I get a car," he says. "Geez, they must really want us to hit it off."

"Well, too bad for them."

"Your grandparents are really rich," Jackson says.

"I'm guessing yours aren't exactly eligible for food stamps."

Now that the air has been cleared, the rest of the day isn't awful. Jackson's still not ever going to be my dream match, but he's not a troll. In fact, he makes the rest of the Saturday more bearable.

When I do get a phone, I don't turn it on. I decide not to check it until I get back home. It's not like reading more about Hannah and Ethan's first date is going to cheer me up. I focus on getting through today, getting that signed form, and being out from under Mom and Dad's thumb.

"I thought you'd be burning down the cell phone tower, now you have that," Jackson says.

"Huh?"

"You're not calling whoever it was who sent you that photo?" Jackson bumps my shoulder. "Why not? You clearly like that guy. Right?"

We're headed back to the dining room for dinner, only this time I sit next to Jackson. It's better than constantly being distracted by his grandfather's dentures making that bizarre thwacking sound.

"Is the girl your friend?"

"How did you know that?"

He shrugs. "Guys and girls aren't that complicated."

"No?"

"Guys want to get into the girl's pants, and the girls want them to stick around after."

I roll my eyes. "You're an idiot."

He shrugs. "It's more true than you want to admit, apparently."

"The idiot part? I'm happy to admit that."

He laughs.

"The thing is, there's this guy I've known for a long time. We've gone back and forth a lot." I'm about to say more, but I'm distracted.

"No, no," my dad's saying. "I can't drink this."

"Wait, are you broken like Amelia?" Grandma asks. "Is that why you've been so supportive?"

That's the first time I realize that Grandma and Grandpa don't understand alcoholism at all. I'm sick of hearing about it, so I used the word fix earlier, but I know that's not quite right. I knew even then that I was being unfair.

But they're her parents. Shouldn't they be championing her defense?

"She's not broken," I say. "It's a physical illness, like having eczema."

"Like what?" Grandpa asks.

"I'm saying that Mom's not broken." I glance between him and Grandma. "Saying that is kind of hurtful."

"You can't drink either, can you?" Grandma asks. "Are you just like her?"

"Beth's fine," Dad says. "She's like me."

"Dad."

"Wait, is your mom an alcoholic?" Jackson asks.

235

I roll my eyes.

"You guys are more interesting than I thought."

"I want to see her drink a glass," Grandpa says. "So I can believe it. That she's fine."

"Excuse me?" Dad asks.

Mom stands up. "It's fine. Beth can do it."

"No," Dad says. "She doesn't need to—"

Jackson hands me a glass of wine. "Here. Just try this to shut them up." He's smiling, like this is all really funny.

I should say no. For the first time ever, my dad's actually defending me. My dad, the guy who never has my back. But my mom said to do it, and I realize she's tired of them treating her like crap.

And now they're implying that her alcoholism ruined me, too. That means the only way out for her is for me to show them that I can drink some and not turn into a drunk. I just can't believe they're badgering their alcoholic daughter's daughter to try drinking. Maybe Dad wasn't totally wrong when he said he was trying to save her from them.

"Beth?" Grandma looks so encouraging. I could almost imagine she's telling me to put my chin up and walk the stage in my cap and gown.

My dad, on the other hand, looks ready to take a swing at my grandpa. I think about what it must be costing him to sell his family ranch, to move to Seattle, and to work for his father-in-law, basically admitting that his intervention made his beloved wife *worse*.

"Beth, you don't have to—"

My grandpa claps an arm on Dad's shoulder. "Ease up, Patrick. Geez. Your daughter's not like her mother. Watch."

In that moment, I want to show them that I'm not. I want to defend my mother the only way I can think to do it. So I press the glass to my lips and drink it all.

I'm not sure exactly how many drinks are shoved at me, but I drink at least two more glasses of wine before I stop and stand up and shove away from the table. Things are a little hazy, just like the last time I drank.

The night Ethan found me.

The night he almost hit me with his car.

It's a stupid memory, but it makes me smile, anyway.

"Why are you so happy?" the good-looking jerk asks.

"Ethan," I say. "He's that guy."

"The blond one?"

I nod.

"The one who's dating that other girl?" The jerk cocks his eyebrow.

"Shut up," I say. "Maybe they're not."

"Then stop being a chicken and turn on your phone," he says. "Find out."

I shake my head. "That's dumb."

"You could send her a photo, too," he says. "You're with someone else."

That's true. I'm not *so* pathetic that her dating Ethan would wreck me. I have options. I power my phone up, and Jackson presses his face against mine. To him, my dad's not a villain. To him, my family's not an embarrassment. In fact, our grandparents want us to date or something.

I snap a photo.

He snatches my phone and looks at it. "That's

not going to make anyone jealous." He points. "You need to get the deck and the stars. Then they'll realize we're on a boat." He stands up and heads out, and no one stops us. I'm not sure anyone even notices that we're leaving.

I stumble after him, trying to grab my phone back. "It's fine."

"Come on." He pulls me against the rail and snaps another one. Then he pokes my cheek. Again. And again.

I finally turn. "What?"

That's when he kisses me.

"Hey." I slap at his chest until he releases me.

"What?" He's smiling. "That was nice. You're not half bad."

I finally succeed in getting my phone back. "Stop." But it's too late. He's already texted someone a photo. It's not like I have Hannah's number, but when I squint with my bleary eyes, I realize she's texted again. More stuff. He sent the photo in response to a string of texts she's sent. At least it doesn't look like it's a photo of us kissing, but still. I'm about to unsend it when he yanks my phone back.

The photo was sent with the text: YOU'RE NOT THE ONLY ONE GETTING ACTION.

Ugh. "Hey."

"What?"

"Don't delete those photos." He's smiling. "You'll be glad you sent that one later."

"Why?"

He frowns, and then looks at my phone. A smile spreads across his face.

"Because check out what you just got in

response." He hands my phone back and taps on the front of it.

Now I can't *not* look. Hannah sent me another photo. And in this one, she's wearing a *bikini*, and Ethan's in the background, smiling. I drop my phone again.

This time, Jackson catches it. "Whoa, there. You're dangerous, you know?"

"Dangerous?"

"To phones, I mean." He tucks it in his pocket, and then he runs.

I have to chase him to get it back. But somehow, we wind up in his room. And when he kisses me again, I can't think of anything but Ethan and Hannah.

Beautiful, uncomplicated Hannah.

Sunny, handsome, smart, kind Ethan.

He deserves someone like Hannah, and I should stop acting like I might ever be good enough for him. The best I'm ever going to deserve is someone like Jackson. Someone who steals my phone. Someone who verbally bullies me.

Someone who's exactly as crappy as my family deserves.

✿ 18 ✿

ETHAN

With the world population above seven billion, on any given day, there are somewhere around twenty million people who share the same birthday. It varies by the day of course, but it's somewhere around that range.

It really isn't that special.

But as mine approaches, I can't help thinking that when I was eighteen, I hadn't even met Beth. I did badger her into celebrating it with me later, but that was really just an excuse.

Now I'm nearly nineteen, and I'm still hung up on the same girl, but I'm no closer to being with her. It's not Amanda Saddler level dedication to a lost cause, but it feels like I'm definitely heading down a bizarre path—far closer to the last owner of this ranch than I'd like to be.

"It's time," I say.

"I've never heard that before." Izzy laughs.

"I mean it this time," I say. "I don't care what she says. We know she likes me, right?"

Izzy shrugs. "Do we? I mean, I think Hannah's

her best friend in the world, pretty much, and that girl would not ease up. If Beth really liked you, I'd have thought she'd have told her."

"She was relentless."

"That's what a girl who likes you looks like."

"Annoying?" I ask. "Badgery?"

"I don't think that's a word," Izzy says.

"Neither is 'yeet,' but that didn't stop Hannah from using it every time she chucked something my way."

"She was trying to get your attention. She's not that annoying at school."

"I hope not," I say. "Or I'd assume she'd get punched pretty often."

"I thought you were going to punch her." Izzy suppresses her laughter, though why, I'm not sure. She usually brays like a donkey when she's amused. "When she came out in that bikini and took a photo with you—"

"I should have punched her then for sure," I say. "But Dad was pretty adamant that I never could." If I hadn't heard his voice in my ear, I'd have done it. First she dumped that stupid, sticky red punch on my shirt. Then she said she'd go wash it out. When she came back out in a bikini and took a photo, like we were on some beach vacation instead of the community trash clean-up event, I wanted to crush her phone.

Because I know she's friends with Beth.

The last thing I need is for Beth to get the wrong idea. But then Hannah showed me that photo Beth sent her. She's apparently fine to date—just not to date me.

"Or maybe I do just need to let it go," I say.

"Why do you like her so much?" Izzy rubs Leo's forelock. Mom doesn't usually let us ride him, but when I told her we wanted to go for a trail ride, she actually offered him to Izzy.

And Steve's letting me ride Farrah. It's kind of awesome to have these great horses. I feel a lot better out here. "It's like this ride," I say. "Being around Beth is like being out here, I mean."

"It's peaceful?" Izzy's lip curls. "Because I'm not sure that 'peaceful' is really the beginning to an epic love story."

"I don't want epic," I say. "I want chemistry, sure, but there's plenty of that, too. When I see her, I want to kiss her. I want to hold her hand. I want to run my hand—" My sister looks like she might be sick. "That's probably enough of that. But what I mean about the trail ride is that it calms me to come out here. Actually, just being around horses and cattle is like that. Back in Houston, my brain was always full of so much noise. Being around Aunt Helen, or Aunt Amanda, or even Mom sometimes, it's like that. There are constant questions and pushing and, I don't know. Interrogations? But when I'm with her, it's like being in the sunshine. It makes me happy."

"You know, Mom might say that's not enough," Izzy says.

"I know." I groan. "But for Mom—"

"I said *Mom* might," Izzy says, "but I think that's the best reason I've heard. You didn't say you like her face, or that she keeps your interest because you can't catch her. You didn't say anything specific, just that she makes you happy. Isn't that the best reason to want to be around someone? And if someone like

242

Beth, whose family has been such a disaster, can still make you happy, there must really be something about her."

"She's my Juliet," I say. "The world wants to rip us apart, but I won't let it." I clench my fingers tightly on the reins, and Farrah's head jerks. "Sorry, girl." I pat her neck.

"Don't take it out on Farrah. She didn't do anything."

"I know," I say. "I told her sorry. But about the Beth thing, I think I took Amanda's advice to give her time a little too much to heart. I need to just lay my cards on the table. It's time. She's avoided me all summer, and I let her, because I was too afraid to press. But she's had time. I thought that, when I heard she was staying with Donna, maybe it was for me. But she never came by. She never texted, and she barely even responded to me."

"You do need to find out what's going on," Izzy says.

"But how, when she won't even reply to me?"

"Trick her," Izzy says. "It worked last time. I'll help you again."

"You will?"

"I'll tell her we're having a party, and that since you're working, I don't want to be lonely."

It might be a sign that Izzy has to tell Beth I won't be somewhere to get her to come, but I refuse to just let it go because of that. I don't think I'll be able to let it go until she tells me herself that she doesn't like me. "Do it," I say.

"Where?"

I think about that for a while. We wind around the little stream crossing, and we're on our way back when I have an idea. "Don't tell her it's a party. She might remember my birthday's around now."

"Okay, then what?"

"Tell her to meet you for dinner at Brownings."

"Since when do I go to dinner with people? I'm not thirty years old, and I can't even drive. Or did you forget that?"

"Just text and ask. Since it's not me, she might say yes."

Izzy stops Leo.

"What?"

"This is your problem. You don't think these things through, and then they fall apart."

I spin Farrah around. "I've overthought everything, and every time I've gotten close, something has gone wrong. For once, let's just try it the easy way. If I have to, I'll go over to her house with a big speaker and stand under her window."

Izzy grunts. "I'm not sure Donna would appreciate that. I think Aiden goes to bed pretty early."

"What, then?"

"If you want simple, why don't I just ask her to meet me for coffee?"

"Have you ever seen a romantic comedy with a breakfast declaration of love?"

"Do you love her?" Izzy looks incredulous.

"Don't I?" I'd never thought of it in those terms, but I think I must. "I can't stop thinking about her, and it's not a crush. I've known her for a year. I've kissed her. I've spent as much time with her as I could. She's tried to push me away a million times."

Izzy squeals, and both our horses startle. "You *love* someone, Ethan Elijah Brooks."

"I knew I'd beat you to it."

"I love her, too," Izzy says. "But maybe not the same way as you."

"You do like her, though, right?"

"Mom does too, you know."

"Does she?" I doubt Mom would say it to me.

"She has her reservations, but she will with anyone we like. She says good things about her, and she loves Donna."

"That's true."

"Steve likes Donna, too. So it's not like her whole family's a mess."

"Not exactly like they're the Capulets," I say.

"Wait, isn't Romeo the Capulet and Juliet's the Montague?" Izzy scratches her ear.

I shrug. "It's been like five years since I studied that."

"Either way, it's not as bad as their situation, so that's good."

And even better, when Izzy texts Beth, suggesting they meet for coffee, Beth agrees right away. I spend the next few days running through ideas for what to do when we meet. Flowers? Too corny. Plus, last time I got flowers, it didn't end well. A big pile of balloons might embarrass her. Brownings is kind of the central hub of Manila, so everyone would be sure to notice them.

In the end, I just put on a nice pair of jeans, a polo shirt I got from Amanda, and a clean pair of cowboy boots. My more elaborate plans have all crashed and burned, so I decide to keep things simple. I'm sitting at a table that's facing the door when Beth walks in, wearing a cute summery dress with a little peach sweater. Her sandals clack as she walks, her eyes scanning the tables.

Until they meet mine.

Her eyes widen, and her mouth drops open. "Where's Iz—" She sighs. "Really?"

I stand up. "It's just coffee." *Please, please sit.*

"Ethan."

"Please?"

Beth looks at the ceiling, and. . .is she tearing up?

I walk toward her. "Are you alright?" I reach for her arm.

She yanks it away and steps backward.

I'm not going to lie. It hurts a little, being treated like I'm some kind of pariah or something. I can't tell *why*. I didn't do anything bad. The last I knew, we were finally going on a date.

As if I've accosted her or something, she asks, "What do you want?"

"Just have a muffin or something," I say. "If you don't want to see me after we talk for a bit, well, I won't do anything like this again."

She looks like a startled deer, unsure whether she should run or freeze.

Freeze, I think. *Don't run again. Not yet.*

As if she could hear me, she shakes her head. But then she sits down. "One cup."

I suppress my smile. Barely. "Okay."

Luckily, the second she sits, the waitress rushes over. It's one of the benefits of being in a tiny town and a small diner. "What do you two want?"

I order two drinks and two muffins.

"What kinda muffins?" the waitress asks. She must be new, since I don't know her. She looks like she's about Beth's age, and I wonder whether she's a recent graduate too.

"Apple cinnamon and poppyseed?" I look at Beth for input.

"I don't like apple in muffins," Beth says.

"Great, then I'll take that one."

She rolls her eyes.

When the waitress walks out of earshot, I decide not to make small talk. I need answers, and with her being all weird, I may not get them if I wait.

"What's going on? We were friends at the very least, and we had a *date planned*." I cringe. I wasn't going to say that. It sounds accusatory. "But then you got sick, and then." I throw my hands up in the air. "Then it was like I had some kind of communicable disease or something. Did I grow horns?" I pat my forehead.

I thought it might get me a chuckle at least, but Beth's too busy staring at her hands to laugh.

"Beth."

She glances up and then looks right back down.

"What did I do? At least tell me that much."

She's still staring at her fingers like they contain the secrets of the universe.

"Did I say something? Did I—did someone tell you something? Because I should at least be allowed to defend myself."

When she looks up this time, her eyes are narrowed. "Like what?"

"I know you like Hannah, and Izzy says you're close, but listen. I don't know what she might have said. I didn't even talk to her really. She was like velcro, sticking herself to me." I shudder. "I told her to knock it off, but she didn't listen."

Beth smiles.

"Okay, so was that it? Because I know she took

some kind of weird photo of herself in a swimsuit, but I was only shirtless because she spilled stuff on me. We didn't—"

"Ethan."

"What?"

She shakes her head.

"Just say it."

"We weren't a good fit from the start."

"No," I say. "You're wrong about that. We were a great fit. Always. It was the other stuff that wasn't a good match. Timing. That's all."

She snorts. "You think it was just timing?" She shakes her head. "That's a stretch. Even at the beginning—"

"At the beginning, you were like light to me. Like air. You were all I could think about, and now—"

"Now, what?" Her nostrils flare. Her hands press so hard on the top of the table that her fingers turn white. "How do you feel about me now?"

The waitress cuts her check in half by showing up right then, as if she has *no* sense for reading people whatsoever. "Alright, that was a mint tea for the lady, and a hot chocolate for the handsome man."

"He is handsome, isn't he?" Beth says. "Too handsome for me, right?"

The woman blinks.

"See? Even Iris knows."

"What are you talking about?" I hiss. "Thanks." I wave at Iris, who thankfully walks off. "Beth, stop."

"Stop what?" She sighs. "I'm not a match for you, Ethan, and you're the only one who doesn't see it. Your family is bright and shiny, which I said from the start. And before you start again, me wearing a

248

sparkly shirt would be like dressing a toad up to be a robin. It's stupid. Toads can't fly. They aren't lovely. They croak and have warts, and no costume change will ever be enough."

"This is a lot of nonsense," I say. "We're both *human*, Beth. You've just been told by a lot of idiots that you suck, and you're buying into their crap. But those idiots moved to Seattle and left you here, and now you're with your aunt. Does she think you're a toad? Because if she does—"

"I slept with someone, Ethan." Her words are barely loud enough to hear, but they're like daggers.

"You—" I choke. "You what?"

"That guy Hannah showed you a photo of?"

I shake my head.

"I went to Seattle, and my parents introduced me to this rich guy they want me to date. That was him."

It's like she slapped me, only worse. "You love someone else?"

"Love?" Beth's laugh is loud. "I don't even like him, really."

"Then why—"

"Because I'm a *toad*, Ethan, and that's what toads do. We wallow in the muck." Beth stands up, plonks a five dollar bill on the table, and walks out. She turns and looks back at me, her eyes pained. "Please stop trying to make me fly. I may only be a toad, but it still hurts when I hit the ground."

BETH

My mom doesn't bake.

My dad doesn't cook *or* bake. He can grill steak, boil hot dogs, or make a frozen pizza. That's the extent of his skillset surrounding food.

Compared to them, I'm practically a chef. They tended to eat a lot of frozen dinners, takeout, or leftovers from going out to dinner before I got old enough to make food.

The place I learned basic cooking skills was, of all places, home economics in seventh and eighth grade. But the first time I ever made a cake was catastrophic. See, they had things labeled, but because it was all set up through the school, they kept the ingredients in huge plastic tubs. There were a lot of kids there, and sometimes the labels fell off.

That day, the label came off the sugar.

And the salt.

There are some mistakes that are no big deal, like the time I used milk chocolate instead of semi-sweet in cookies. Dad liked the cookies better, I think. Or the time I forgot to cook the lasagna noodles before baking them. They were a little crunchy, but it was edible. But when you use salt in place of sugar, a cake tastes and looks. . .well, not like a cake. Life's like that. You can laugh off some mistakes.

Others, not so much.

When I woke up next to Jackson, I was mortified. Sickened. Full of disgust and rage. Grandma and Grandpa were delighted when they saw me scamper across the deck and dart back inside my room.

That night was like substituting salt for sugar.

It wasn't a mistake that I can come back from.

The whole cake was ruined.

I never thought I was good enough for Ethan, but now? I can't even face him. I thought I could just hide. I thought he'd let me be, but that's not his way. Looking at him, listening to him tell me how great I was, it made me feel even worse. I realized in that moment that the only way I'd ever be free of the anchor dragging me down was to tell him the ugly truth.

That I'm not who he thinks I am. I don't deserve the pedestal.

But now, instead of getting in my car, I'm stumbling down the main street of Manila until I kick some pot that's sitting on the sidewalk. It tips over and breaks.

"Hey!" Dolores Jenkins is the scariest woman in Manila. Her hair's grey, but not a soft grey that you see on grandmas the world over. No, hers is gunmetal grey, battle-ax grey, and it has been exactly that same color since she was young, or so people say. She's totally insane—she talks to her plants like they're people in broad daylight and yells at almost anyone else she meets.

Some people say she killed her husband and put his body parts into pots all over her garden until the plants hid the evidence that she killed him. Some people say that she's so mean because her husband left her for someone who spent less time around plants and more time around people. Some people say she has her husband tied up in a room and doesn't ever let him out.

I've always wondered why everyone thought she had a husband.

She's holding something long, and she's practically running toward me. I stumble backward and fall on my butt in the street. Luckily, Manila's not exactly a bustling metropolis, and there aren't any cars driving in either direction.

"You alright, girl?" She's bending over me now, the long hoe she's carrying drooping slightly. Her face doesn't look angry anymore. She looks concerned. "Here." She offers me a hand, and even though it strikes fear into my heart, I take it.

She flings me back up to my feet easily. She's surprisingly strong for someone who must be in her sixties or seventies. Actually, maybe she's older than that. She looks almost as old as Amanda Saddler.

"I'm so sorry about your pot," I say. "I wasn't watching where I was going."

"No, I guess you weren't." She eyes me up and down, her face softening even more. "Why don't you come inside and have something to drink."

I open my mouth to tell her that I can't. I don't want to be locked up and kept in a room or chopped up and hidden in pots. But then I see Ethan walking down the road, kicking rocks.

Coming right at us.

"Okay, great." I barely squeeze past her bright red door and close it behind me before he would have seen us. I turn and lean against the back of her door, sighing.

That's when I take a good look around her house.

Now that adrenaline is receding, fear rushes back to replace it. Are there people tied up in here, like Ursula's garden of lost souls? Does she have a wall covered in newspaper clippings, with crazed notes scrawled and yarn connecting them all?

But no. It's more mundane than that.

From the floor to the ceiling, there are piles of things made with yarn. So many different things. Blankets. Scarves. Sweaters. Potholders. Hats. Mittens. What looks like. . .a book cover? Do people make those out of yarn? Against the windowsill, there are stuffed animals made of yarn standing in tight rows. Ducks, dogs, cats, owls, and even fruit. Pineapple. An apple. A giant variegated green ball that sort of looks like a watermelon.

"Oh," I say.

"I don't invite people in much," Dolores says.

"Okay, well thanks for making an exception for me." Because otherwise, I might have had to talk to Ethan, whom I just hit with a baseball bat of traumatic information.

"What happened?" The woman walks into the kitchen, carefully skirting around stacks of scarves and hats. "Do you like tea?"

I nod.

"Great." She shoves a teakettle under the sink and turns the water on. "Lemon?"

I shrug.

"You don't have to tell me anything if you don't want to, but at least you know I won't tell anyone."

I'm pretty sure she doesn't have anyone she *could* tell. "I thought you only liked plants."

"Plants fill my soul," she says. "Crocheting soothes it."

"Right."

"I'm not crazy," she says. "And I know that normal people don't often have to say that, but it's still true. I've been to see several doctors, and they said that crocheting and gardening are both healthy outlets for me."

She has a therapist? One hundred percent would not have guessed that. It doesn't look like he or she is earning their money. "Okay."

"I want to give some of the crocheted things away, but it's hard for me."

I nod like that makes perfect sense. Who knows? Maybe it does. I've never crocheted anything. Maybe if I did, I'd hold onto it with a kung-fu grip.

"It's apparently common for people who have lost a child."

And now I feel like a giant jerk. "You lost a child?"

She blinks. "You didn't know?"

I'm not sure *anyone* knows. She's lived here since the beginning of time, and she has no friends. How would any of us know anything about her? I wonder how often I've assumed people knew something about me and that they were judging me for it, when really people had no idea and weren't thinking about me at all.

"I'm sorry for your loss," I say.

"It's okay," she says. "I feel silly saying anything about it, now. I'm seventy-one next month. I lost Stanley almost forty-five years ago, and he was only three."

Now I'm crying again, which is really embarrassing. "I'm so sorry."

"Please don't be sorry, dear. I didn't care about that pot."

I shake my head. "I mean for all the crying. But, also about the pot."

"I have too many pots already, and too many plants. I do know that." She pulls out a chair and gestures for me to sit.

I do.

"Again, you can talk to me if you want, and if you don't, that's fine too."

If I tell this little old woman who lost her child at three years old what's going on in my life, she'll probably crochet me a scarlet letter and sew it to my sparkly heart shirt. The thought makes me laugh.

"I'm hipper than you might think, if that's why you're worried." She nods. "I've seen *Sex and the City*."

Now I'm really laughing. I sound unhinged, to be honest. I think that's a show people watched like, twenty years ago or more. It's so funny that she's using that to say she's hip. It'll probably be on *Nick at Night* soon.

"I'm just upset because I had to hurt someone I care about." There. Maybe that vague piece of non-information will scare her off.

She pats my hand right as the teapot starts to scream. She hops up pretty quick for an older lady, and a moment later, she's pouring steaming water onto a tea bag in a little mug. "Here, dear. There's not much in this world that tea won't help."

I'm not sure that's true, but it seems rude to argue with her in her own home. She sits with me for almost half an hour while we both sip our tea, and she never asks me for more information. She doesn't ask me for anything at all.

But when I finally stand up, she says, "If you don't have anything else you need to do, I could use a hand with some things in my garden."

I'm not sure whether it's true, or whether she's just lonely, but I feel like I can't tell her no. A few moments later, I'm helping her lift and haul peat moss, and then I'm helping her shovel compost into a wheelbarrow and transfer it into pots. It's not really a very clean task, but it feels good to be outside, in the sunshine, getting dirty.

It feels a lot better than I expect it to feel.

"Sometimes just moving helps." She smiles.

That's when I realize that *she* didn't need help. She thought that *I* did.

And she was right.

This time, when I start to cry, words just pour out with the tears. An hour later, I've told her all of it, even the worst part—that I slept with Jackson.

"I'm not even sure why I did it," I say. "I didn't want to—I don't even like—I didn't mean—"

We're sitting on an iron bench behind her house, and she pats my back and clucks. "There, there. It's going to be fine. At least you're not pregnant."

"Did you hear me?" I shake my head. "It was my first time."

She frowns. "What does that mean?"

"Of course I'm not pregnant."

"Because. . ." Her frown deepens. "I don't understand what you're saying."

"You can't get pregnant your first time." Duh.

She freezes. "Have you—" This time she's the one choking. "You've had your period since then, though, right?"

I *cannot* believe I'm having this conversation with her. "It's erratic. It always has been."

She closes her eyes.

"Listen, it's fine. I'm sure I'm not pregnant." I shake my head.

"How could you be sure?" She sighs. "You should take a pregnancy test."

I roll my eyes. "There's no way. . ." And then I think about what she's saying. "Wait, you're saying that you *can* get pregnant the very first time you ever. . ."

She nods. "What are they teaching you at that school, girl?"

"I mean, I didn't pay a lot of attention, to be honest. The boys kept laughing. The girls were making jokes, too." I groan. "I'm sure that. . ." I look at my flat stomach. "I haven't been throwing up, and I haven't gained weight."

"It hasn't been long yet, and some women don't get sick like that."

"I'm not sick *at all* though."

She shrugs.

"I haven't gained weight."

"You said this happened in June?" She sighs. "I think they have tests at the—"

"Can I take it here?" I have no right to ask that of her. I barely know her.

"Of course." She tilts her head like a concerned bird.

Two and a half hours later, I've finally bought a pregnancy test. I couldn't bring myself to do it in town, so I drove all the way to Rock Springs where I knew no one would recognize me.

Dolores Jenkins places her hand over mine. "It's going to be fine, dear. No matter what that test says. And think how much easier you'll breathe when it's negative."

I nod.

"But while you were gone, I was thinking about what you told me."

"What?"

"About how that boy calls you Juliet and how your families have been at odds."

"Okay."

"That's all nonsense."

"What?"

"Your families don't matter. Only the two of you matter."

"That's over, though," I say. "I told him this morning. Weren't you listening?"

"And then what did he say?"

"What do you mean, what did he say?" I snort. "That's a mic drop moment. I told him, and then I left."

"You weren't officially together when it happened," Dolores says. "Maybe he didn't care."

I'm trembling now. "You don't know him. I'm sure he cared."

"I'm beginning to think *you* don't really know him. From the things you've told me, it seems like he surprises you a lot."

"What?"

"He liked you from the start. I bet he was friends just to keep you talking to him. And then he tricked you into coming for coffee. You seem to be the one making a lot of erroneous assumptions."

Is she right?

"Maybe instead of dropping mics, you should do a little more listening."

Instead of snapping back with something right away, I think about what she said as I go into the bathroom. I think about it as I pee in a cup, and then as I wait for my results.

I mean, Ethan has been pretty consistent. I'm the one who's all up and down. I'm the one who keeps ducking out and begging off. But obviously I'm doing him a favor. Right? Or could it be that he never minded my horrible dad, or my terrible mom, or my lack of a plan for the future?

Maybe he never cared that I was a toad and he was a robin.

Was it all nonsense?

The timer goes off on my phone, and I look at the stick. Two lines. What does two lines mean? I barely breathe as I look at the long paper with the instructions on it. Two lines, two lines, two pink lines. . .means. . .

That I'm pregnant.

I shove the test and all the instructions in the trash. I dump the pee in the toilet and rinse out the paper cup before throwing it away, too. My hands are tingling. My stomach is tied in knots. And then, numb, I walk out of the bathroom. How can my flat, normal looking belly have a baby inside of it?

I stumble again as I walk down Dolores Jenkins' hall.

She grabs my arm. "Are you alright?"

I turn toward her slowly, and she sighs.

She knew. Somehow, she knew already.

How did she know when I had literally no idea?

"I know you're disappointed." She pulls me against her for a hug. She smells like mulch and sweat and mothballs. It's not really a combination of smells I've typically thought of as comforting, but I probably will from now on. Because no matter how long I stand there, crying, she never lets me go.

But finally, I pull away. "I'll be alright," I say.

"Will you?" She frowns. "What will your parents say? How will they react?"

I shake my head. "They're gone."

"Gone?" She closes her eyes. "Oh, dear. You can come live with me if you want."

I shake my head again, as if that's all I can do. "I'm living with my aunt."

"Okay, well, if anything changes, let me know."

I turn and start shuffling for the door.

"Here, dear. Take these." She carefully hands me a stack of crocheted baby blankets, and my heart breaks.

I'm eighteen.

I can't be pregnant.

This wasn't supposed to happen.

How can this be my life?

"I haven't given away a baby blanket since I lost

Stanley." Dolores' voice is soft. "I want you to listen to me, Beth. No matter what you decide to do about this, no matter whether you keep this baby or whether you give it up, it will be okay." She presses a hand to my cheek. "I promise."

I wish I could believe her.

❧ 20 ❧

BETH

When I was a kid, I thought that when I grew up, I'd be able to do whatever I wanted. I thought that ranchers were ranchers because they chose it. I thought my teachers were teachers because that's what they wanted to do.

After all, why else would they do it?

I convinced Hannah's uncle Bob to hire me to run fishing tours to the reservoir by telling him that I could earn him extra revenue by taking photos and selling picture packages. I told him I wasn't entirely certain that my photos would be good enough to 'lure' people, and I cringed when I made the bad fishing pun.

But the people who come out here are super corny and they love puns. And lucky for me, they *love* my photos. Most of them don't want to risk using their phones while toting all their fishing gear. By the time I'm halfway through my spiel, they usually fork over the fifty dollars for the complete photo package.

Bob lets me keep half of the fee for the packages, and he pays me for taking them out on the tours. It's not exactly the kind of photography I wanted to do. But it's putting money in the bank, faster than I thought it would, thanks to Aunt Donna's generosity in letting me stay with her for free, and it's photography. Sort of. Plus, I learn to drive a boat.

But, still.

What I do not expect the morning after I confess my crime to Ethan is for my private party hire to be. . .Ethan Brooks.

Given our history, maybe I should have expected it.

"No." I press my lips together to keep from saying anything else.

"You can't refuse me," he says. "I've already paid."

"I can refuse you." I scowl. "Because I have a stomachache."

"Look, I just want to go fishing, I swear."

"You just want to go fishing?"

"I used to do it with my dad," he says softly.

"You did?"

He stares at me.

Now I feel lousy. "Really?"

"I didn't even know you worked here."

Oh. So, I'm the jerk. Ugh. "Okay, fine." Also, fate hates me.

This is going to be a long day. I don't even offer him the photo package. If Bob complains, he can suck it.

Ethan's a complete gentleman all the way out. Once we reach the part of the reservoir where people usually fish, I relax a bit. He hasn't said a word. Nothing at all. It's rare that I come out here with only one person. Usually it's as many people as they can cram into the boat. The talking, and the jokes, and the entertaining can be exhausting. I mean, this is a little awkward, given who it is. Also, the timing's super suspicious. But he hasn't said a single word, so maybe—

"Now that we're out here," he says.

I freeze.

"Don't I need a fishing pole or something?"

I laugh, and stand up to go open the boxes. "Right."

It takes a moment to run through the equipment and rules. If he's fished with his dad, he probably knows more than I do, but I'm required to do it.

"I know how to work it." Ethan stands and takes it from me. "Beth."

My eyes snap up to his.

His voice is soft. Gentle, even. "I didn't come here to fish."

I *knew* it. "Ethan, I can't."

"You can't what?"

"I can't talk about this anymore. I think I was clear yesterday."

"Yesterday you told me you're a frog and I'm a bird." He laughs. "Pardon me if I don't think that's the last word on the subject. I feel like my jokes about the Romeo and Juliet analogy have confused you." He drops the fishing pole and takes my hand.

The warmth of his hand on mine, the gentle rocking of the boat, his kind words, they all confuse me. For just a moment, I imagine a future for us.

The future I thought about fondly off and on for almost a year.

"Beth, I like you. I've liked you for a long time, now."

"I know," I say, "but—"

He presses a finger to my lips, and then he replaces it with his mouth. His arms wrap around me, pulling me closer. "Beth." His mouth shifts from mine just enough to speak, so it's like my name falls across my own face. "I don't just like you. I *love* you."

My heart shifts inside my body, changing, reshaping. It's like all the dreams I've had for years couldn't possibly anticipate this moment, where the prince from the stories comes down on his white horse and tells me I'm the one for him. It's as ridiculous as any Cinderella story I've ever heard.

"I can't handle any more nonsense about birds and frogs, okay?" He kisses me again, and I forget where we are. I forget who we are. I forget why I didn't want to date him.

But then it hits me.

He knows about Jackson. It seems like he doesn't care about that, like Dolores said he might not.

But he doesn't know *everything*. I push him back. "We still need to talk."

I can feel it coming.

It's like the scene where the dragon shows up to roast the prince. Only, instead of the dragon being slain, the prince is going to throw down his shield and run away in disgust.

"Okay." He smiles. "I always want to talk to you. Talking may be the thing I like to do with you the most." He looks down at my mouth. "Or maybe the second most." His boyish smile melts me.

"Ethan."

"You can say my name all day, in any way you want." He bites his lip. "Now try it like you're mad. *Ethan!*" He grins.

"Sit." I shove away from him, my fingers noticing the defined ridges of his muscles. I shiver.

Focus, Beth.

"I like you too," I say. "But did you hear me yesterday?"

He nods eagerly, like a little boy about to tell his mom about his Lego tower. "I did, and I thought about it. You don't owe me anything, not even an explanation. I mean, we weren't dating."

"You thought about it and you decided 'it's fine'? Just like that?"

He shrugs. "It's not the eighteen hundreds, Beth. Was I surprised? Sure. But is it a problem?" He shakes his head. "I mean, no. And you don't need to wear a scarlet letter, either." His smirk is classic Ethan.

And I was just thinking about the same stupid school-assigned book. Ugh. Sometimes I hate how alike we think. It makes it really hard for me to shove him away. "Ethan, the thing is—"

He stands up then, reaching for my hand.

I'm not strong enough to stop him this time. I like the feel of his strong hand holding mine. I like any part of him touching me. I like seeing how happy he is. I like pretending, and maybe it's easier because we're out here in the middle of nowhere.

I know I can't have him forever, and for some reason, it makes it harder for me to end things. Knowing these are our last few minutes makes me want to cherish them or something stupid like that.

"I think you did it on purpose," he says, "subconsciously, I mean."

"What?"

"I think you kept telling me over and over that you weren't a good fit for me, but I didn't listen. So when the circumstance arose, you just let things happen that you didn't even want—to keep me away."

He thinks this is his fault?

"You said you didn't even like him, right?" He looks so hopeful. So pathetically, school-boy hopeful. It breaks my heart all over again.

"You may have built me up in your mind as someone I'm not," I say.

He squeezes my hand. "No way, and look. Maybe I'm wrong about that. Maybe you just got caught up. Or." He shudders. "Maybe you were really attracted to him." He shudders again. "But I really don't care. It's just that it really seems like you were looking for a way to push me away. You kind of threw that at me, like someone who's trying to protect themselves from the big, bad wolf by distracting him with a big slab of bacon or something."

Is he a super genius?

I think about his mother. Some of that probably rubbed off on him, I guess. "I mean, maybe I did throw it at you," I say. "But not to protect myself. To protect you."

He pulls me against himself and hugs me. "Or to protect you, if you didn't really think we'd work out in the long run. Easier to get rid of me now, before it hurts so much."

He's right.

How could he be so right? How could he have known that about me when I've never told him?

I shove back. "Well, then how about this one?"

"What?" He pats his chest and then points at me. "Tell me. I'm ready."

"All the things I told you are true. And yesterday I found out another piece of information I really didn't know yet when we spoke." I sigh. Can I really say this aloud? It becomes real once I admit it to someone. I mean, Dolores Jenkins knows. But she's a weird old woman who never talks to anyone and for some reason, I keep referring to her by both her first and last name, like she's Charlie Brown or something.

"What?" Ethan's heart is right there on his face. "I mean it. Tell me. Whatever other big, bad secrets, whatever's holding you back, whatever you're worried about, tell me. It can't be as bad or as big as you think."

Oh, boy. I wish that were true.

And what strikes me the most clearly is that my reasons for staying away from him were so stupid before now. What was wrong with me? This boy has been constant. True. Undeviating.

Why didn't I accept it before now?

How often are we our own worst enemy? How often do we stand squarely in the way of our own happiness?

My mom with her dependency.

My dad with his anger and entitlement.

Myself with my insistence that I'm not good enough.

Then with our actions, we make our perceptions, our fears, and our inadequacies come true. We doom ourselves. But it's not fair to Ethan for me not to tell him everything now. And then instead of standing in my own way, I'll finally trust in him and see what he says.

Knowing it may already be too late.

"I'm pregnant." My eyes well with tears, and I brush them away as quickly as I can. I don't want to make him pity me. I don't want to manipulate him. "I don't even like the father, and I don't know what I want to do yet."

His brow furrows. He opens his mouth, and then he closes it. And then his shoulders slump. He blinks. He nods. He looks around, his mouth opening and closing again.

Poor Ethan.

A year ago, we met. He's been doggedly pursuing me more or less that whole time. I've turned him down, shut him down, accepted him, then shut him down again.

And now, this.

"It's okay if this is too much for you," I say. "I understand." I can't help dropping one hand over my stomach. "I know it seems really sudden and really strange."

"Not to me," he says. "What do you know about my parents?"

His parents? I shake my head.

"My mom and dad were dating, and then my mom got pregnant." His fingers drum on the seat of the boat. "They decided to get married, and that's why I'm here."

I had no idea.

"Mom says marrying my dad and keeping me was the best decision she ever made."

Oh.

"I know we're not very old," Ethan says. "But I'll raise that baby with you." He smiles. "I have a ranch. We have family close. It'll be fine."

I don't know what I thought he'd say, but that wasn't it. And even though it sounds right, for some reason it *feels* all wrong.

❧ 21 ❧

ETHAN

My mom's kind of scary.

I didn't realize it at first. When I was really small, she was just my mom. But as I got older, my friends who came by to play were scared to ask her for a drink. By middle school, she terrified them all, pretty much. And in high school, forget it. My friends thought she was the scariest person they'd ever seen.

She hasn't ever really scared me, though.

Probably because she's always been on my side. Having her on my side always made me feel safe. It always made me feel like nothing in the world could really hurt me. Up until the ranch lawsuit with the alien people, I'd never seen her lose a fight.

Even after that, I'd still bet on her every single time.

When I first decided I liked Beth, I wasn't sure what to expect. I was nervous that Mom might not like her, or that because of Beth's family, Mom might misjudge her. I was wrong, of course, and from the time Mom found out how I felt, she was on board. She cheered. She gave advice. She was sad with me when things didn't work out. It reminded me that she's more open-minded about things than a lot of people give her credit for, especially when it comes to her kids.

So after I find out Beth's news, which definitely took me by surprise, Mom's the first person I talk to. I know she'll be supportive because she basically lived this already.

I lay the groundwork first, explaining that we were supposed to have our first date, but that she got sick and then ghosted me. And then I hit her with the big news. "Beth's pregnant."

Mom's face is as pale as I've seen it, at least since the day we got the news that Dad had cancer.

"It's not mine," I say, explaining the rest as quickly as I can.

"So you weren't dating, and she. . .met some other guy. And then. . ."

"Yeah, but she doesn't even like him. It was a mistake, and obviously she didn't think she'd end up pregnant."

"Obviously." Mom's brow is furrowed. Her color's coming back—she's always recovered fast from surprises—but she doesn't look the way I thought she would.

She always gets this look on her face when she's preparing to deal with something, like a general going into battle, ready to inspire and direct troops. Only, that's not what she looks like right now.

She looks. . .sick.

"Are you alright?"

She startles. "Me? Yes. Are *you* alright?"

"I mean, I'm fine," I say. "I didn't really think I'd

have a kid before I turned twenty, but sometimes life throws you curve balls, right?"

Mom blinks.

"I mean, you didn't really mean to have me, either."

"Your dad and I were in love," she says.

"I love Beth, too, Mom. This isn't, like, some kind of crush."

Her lips compress.

"You think I don't know what it feels like to be in love?"

Mom shakes her head. "I'm not saying that, but you're looking at this as though it's the same as what your dad and I did with you, and the two situations aren't at all the same."

"What?"

"First of all, I was in law school," she says.

"I know. You were at Harvard for grad school, whereas I'm your kid who has no future because I don't want to go to college at all."

Mom frowns. "That's not what I'm saying. I was much older, and your dad and I had been dating and were in love already. And the baby was his and mine."

Oh.

"I never considered anything but keeping you at any point. The only question in my mind was your dad's level of involvement."

"Mom, I really don't think Beth's going to get an ab—"

"I'm not even talking about that," Mom says. "Though, I'm not sure how you can be positive of anything at this point. Either way, I was saying that

Beth may not want to keep it herself, Ethan. She may want to put the baby up for adoption."

"What?"

"She's eighteen," Mom says. "She's very, very young, and this was not expected."

Now I'm the one frowning. "But it's a baby," I say. "It's *Beth's* baby."

"Has she told the father?" Mom asks.

"I'm not sure."

"If she did, what he said and how he reacted might be relevant. His level of involvement is going to be very, very important to her for the rest of this baby's life."

I hadn't thought about that. It was an accident, so I just assumed he didn't want anything to do with it. "I guess I should find out."

"Ethan." Mom's eyes are sad.

"This isn't some tragedy, Mom," I say. "I refuse to act like she committed some grave crime. It's not eighteen thirty-one."

"It's not," Mom says. "But relationships are complicated, and this adds a whole new layer of difficulty. You're only nineteen, and this is a *lot* to handle."

"I know, but—"

"As I understand it, you've never even really dated her."

"But I've liked her for a year," I say.

"Yes, but liking someone and dating them are very different. When you're dating, you're finding out whether your rhythms match. Whether your goals are in alignment. Whether you want the same things. Whether, day-to-day, you get on one another's nerves. You find out—"

"Mom, stop. You're making it sound like she's barely an acquaintance, and that's not true."

Mom stops talking, but her eyes are full of opinions.

"Listen, I came to you first, because I thought you, of all people, would understand."

"I think I *do* understand this situation, much better than you do, sweetheart. I've had four children, and I love them all dearly. I'm a woman, and I know what that feeling is, staring down the barrel of this kind of monumental life decision. More than most anyone understands, believe me when I say that *I do*. And I am empathetic. I'm trying to be supportive, but that means that I can't be a yes-man."

Somehow, every word she says makes me want to punch the wall.

"You're a kind, generous, smart, hard-working boy, and you came from a happy home. She comes from a home that may not be as happy, and that has its own share of challenges, but when you add a baby to the mix—"

"Mom!" I stand up. "Stop talking about her like she's some kind of charity case."

She stands up, too. "Then stop acting like you're some kind of knight in shining armor. I know that feels good. I know you want to be invincible, and protecting something helps you feel that way. But you have no idea how depressing, how demoralizing, and how agonizing it can be to be a parent. And that's when the child is yours."

"Don't you believe in adoption?" I've heard her advocate for it. She and Dad even talked about fostering kids with the thought of adopting more. "How would this be different?"

"Ethan, before you heard Beth was pregnant, would you have even *considered* adopting a child with her right now?"

I hate arguing with my mom. It's like trying to hold back the tide, armed with an umbrella and a spray bottle. "Look. I'm not going to stand here and go back and forth with you. I thought that talking to you was going to help me, but clearly I was wrong."

"If by *help*, you meant that you wanted me to charge in and tell you what you wanted to hear, then no, I won't do that. But here's your first lesson in parenting. More important than making sure your kids like you, your job is to advocate for what's best for them, even when they *hate* you for it."

"Well, you thought college was best for me too, remember? You think you have all the answers, but sometimes you're wrong."

"I didn't say you should go marry Beth and raise a baby with her, or whatever it is that you wanted me to say, because it's a lot more complicated than you think. The situation under which your father and I chose to marry and have you was a different situation altogether than what you're dealing with, and you should be able to understand that."

"It's twenty years later, too, in a world that's more understanding and more honest," I say. "There are lots of other differences, too. I never said it was exactly the same."

But it's still deflating to watch her poke a bunch of holes into my plan for our future instead of being our strongest ally.

"Ethan, I'm always on your side."

"But I don't want there to be sides in this." I grit my teeth. "I'm on Beth's side, which means I need you on *our* side. Do you think you can do that?"

She sighs heavily.

"You know what? Whatever." I kick the edge of the sofa on my way out, which probably earned me a scowl from Mom and definitely hurt my toe.

As I storm out and climb into the truck I only have because Steve decided to give it to me, I think about what she said. I don't want to think about it, but I can't seem to help it.

Beth's child isn't mine.

We haven't really dated.

She's implying we may not even be compatible, and that now, everything for us will be far harder because we have a baby coming. A baby I shouldn't have at all.

There's no way we'd be considering adopting if Beth wasn't pregnant. Mom's right about that. But no one sits around planning for the joys of a snowstorm. You don't, like, prepare for the roof collapse right around the corner either.

I realize that even in my head, I'm comparing the baby to some kind of uncontrollable natural disaster, as if it's bad and as if Beth had nothing to do with its creation.

She did sleep with someone.

Another guy.

And while I'm not about to start calling her Hester Prynne and acting like she's some kind of evil woman, what does that say about her feelings for me? Maybe they aren't as strong as mine are for her.

Or maybe she did it because she felt inadequate —certainly her words support that assumption.

But that kind of worries me, because I've consistently told her that I like her, that she's great, and that I don't think I'm better than her, but if she never believes me, then where will that leave us in the future? I don't need to forgive her for this, but I don't want to spend my life cleaning up after someone who keeps doing dumb things because she thinks I'm going to leave her eventually.

Did Mom get to me? Did she confuse me?

Or was she right?

Without even thinking about where I was going, I realize I've driven to Steve's. It's probably the place I drive to the most, other than maybe the True Value in Manila.

But coming here was stupid.

He's not my dad. He didn't go through this situation, and he's probably busy, working on a horse. His truck's here, but when he's here, he's working. My dad was always a bit of a workaholic, and now my stepdad's the same. I suppose the kind of person who would fall for my mom is someone who values hard work. It makes sense.

I put the truck in reverse, but before I can back out, I see someone waving from the corner of my eye. Someone near the barn. Someone who's now walking toward me.

My stepdad's pretty cool.

He's tall. He's in great shape for an old guy. And he's funny. He's also really smart. I guess he's what my mom would want me to emulate. Someone who went to college and then grad school and then a residency and then also works in the outdoors with his hands. But I'm not like him with horses, a skill he started learning when he was a very young boy from his grandfather, and I'm not big on studying, either.

Actually, I'm not sure why Beth thinks I'm so great. I'm none of the things people in *my* family think are amazing.

We're more like two toads than a toad and a robin.

"Ethan?" Steve's close enough for me to hear him.

"Sorry." I crank the window knob around and around until the window rolls down. "I'm not sure why I'm here."

Steve's half smile is wry. "Why don't you get out and we can try and figure that out."

I will give him this. He never rushes people.

"I'm sure you're working with your horses. It's fine."

Steve drops his dirty hand on the window frame. "I'm not too busy to talk to you. I'm never too busy for that."

"So, when you're on shift, I should just come on by?"

He laughs. "I mean, I might not be able to talk very long when I'm working a shift."

The ER gets wild, and he manages it all really well. Really calmly, too. Maybe he would be okay to hear about this. When I get out, Steve heads for the house.

"Maybe we should talk in the barn," I say. "I'm sure you've got things to do—I can help with them. And then you won't get things inside your house all dirty."

Steve nods, and I can tell he appreciates it.

There's always work that needs to be done in a barn. Always.

"I was moving feed over. Want to help?"

With as many horses as he has, he's constantly moving the feed out of the bags and into sealing containers to keep bugs and pests away from it. "Sure."

"Then I've got some hay to rearrange because we've got another cut coming." Steve arches an eyebrow. "Is this a grain transfer kind of conversation? Or a grain transfer, hay moving, and barn clean-up length talk?"

I snort. "Not sure."

He nods. "Well, let's find out. What's on your mind?"

We're done moving the grain into bins before I finish explaining what's going on.

"Your mom didn't even tell me you were dating Beth."

I sigh. "I mean, I wasn't, really. We almost dated, but then we didn't."

Steve's brow furrows. "Um. Okay."

By the time we've moved the old hay, I think he's caught up. "And you told her you wanted to keep the baby and raise it with her?" His eyebrows are practically climbing his forehead.

"I mean." When he says it like that, it sounds a little odd. We haven't really dated, but I told her we should have a baby? I want to swear under my breath. Did I mess things up? "Mom didn't think that was very smart."

Steve's laugh is hearty, like him. "I suppose she wouldn't."

"Wait, do you think it's smart?"

280

Steve drops a hand on my shoulder. "I think it's admirable, Ethan. Very admirable, that you're willing to do that, and that you care for her enough to be willing to sacrifice your freedom to care for a little person you've never met."

I realize, in that moment, that I am ready to do just that. "I love my family," I say. "I guess I knew I did, but I didn't realize how much until my dad died. So when Beth said she was pregnant, I thought, well, the more the merrier." An image comes to me, then. Beth, holding a tiny Beth. "The only thing better than Beth would be more Beths."

"I can see that," Steve says. "I mean, when you love someone, it's natural to want more ties to them, more connections, and more things you can share."

"I guess."

"And you have a great family, so of course you'd like a bigger one."

"Right?"

"And you know your mother would be the best grandma on earth, and that she'd care for you and that baby in any way you need. But, Ethan?"

I can hear it coming. "Your mom's trying to keep you safe. She's trying to look out for you."

"I know that," I say. "Believe me."

"More important than what your mom thinks, what does *Beth* want?"

"She wants—" I realize that I don't really know. "I mean, when I told her we could raise the baby together, she kind of freaked out a little bit. She said it's not my baby, and that I don't need to make crazy offers like that."

"And then what did you say?"

"I told her it wasn't crazy and that I meant it. I

told her that finding out she was pregnant didn't change how I felt about her."

"Is that true?" Steve looks surprised.

I think about what he's asking, because it feels like something I should check on. But it's still true. "Yes. I mean, would it be easier if it wasn't true? Yes. Would it be simpler if it was my baby? For sure. But Beth was the same person before that she is now. We've all done things that we might not do over, but it doesn't mean we aren't the person we always were."

"What do you like about her?"

"Her parents are awful," I say. "And I think that's made her strong. She's light. She's kind. She's selfless. She's hard working. She's talented. She never asks for things or makes space for herself. She's not greedy or demanding. She's kind, and she makes people around her better, and when she is stuck in a bad situation, she tries to improve it. I was really proud of her when I found out that she refused to follow her parents to Seattle."

"Proud?" Steve asks. "Or just happy she wasn't leaving?"

"Both." I shrug. "She wants to study photography. She applied to UCLA, but Izzy told me she didn't get in. Instead of wallowing, she found a job where she gets paid to take photos. She's saving up money to do what she wants, which is getting better at photography."

"You like her for good reasons," Steve says. "And you have a good heart. But you might have handled things the wrong way with Beth."

"How?" This is what I wanted to get out of my mom. Could Steve really know? "I thought she'd be happy to hear I'd raise it with her. I thought she'd be happy that I wasn't upset, that I still liked her, and that I'd stand by her side. I didn't expect her to get more upset."

"Right now, Beth's standing at a fork in the road," Steve says. "She's got a big decision to make, and having you tell her you'll help her down a particular path. . .well."

Oh.

"It was basically like you told her what path to take."

Shoot. "It would be like someone offering to help me with my college classes—assuming that I would want to go to college and that I'd need help."

Steve points at me. "Exactly. You're still taking community college classes online because your mom insists, but your heart's not in it. That's fine. But if someone last summer had suggested that you let them help you succeed. . .at something you didn't even want? It would feel like they were both insulting you and telling you what to do."

"It would've made me really angry."

"If you cared a great deal about them, you might have just been upset."

"Do you think she wants to. . ." I can't even bring myself to say it.

"I have no idea what she's considering," Steve says. "If she just found out, my guess is that it's all so overwhelming, she doesn't know what she's considering either. Keep in mind that she's living with her aunt, her parents aren't the greatest, her job taking people out fishing is probably about to end as the weather turns, and she's already struggling just to earn enough for photography classes."

"So if you were me, you would tell her that no matter what, you'd support her?"

Steve shrugs. "If that's true. If it's not true, you shouldn't say it."

"Thanks for talking to me," I say. "And for the advice. I think it was pretty good."

"You're welcome."

"I'm surprised," I say. "I thought you'd be like my mom and warn me off."

Steve sits down on a bale of hay. "Our decisions in life define us, but a large factor in that is the people who stand beside us. Some people will support you when things are hard. Others will abandon you. This baby isn't your problem, and it wasn't your fault that she has this big decision to make. But if you care about someone like it sounds like you care about Beth, I'm not going to tell you that anything you do to help her is wrong. Just make sure that whatever you decide, you won't resent her for it later. That wouldn't be good for either of you."

I think about what he said all night. And then I think about it the next day. By the time Beth's off work and willing to meet with me, I've made up my mind.

The corner booth at Brownings isn't exactly the nicest place to talk, but it's a public place, and she's not right around the corner from Steve's anymore, so she can't exactly just pop over to the grove.

"You wanted to see me?" She hasn't even sat down yet. I guess she's not really down for small talk. She glances at my empty table and then back at my face.

"I've been thinking." I point at the chair. I'd walk

around and pull it out for her, but I already know how hard-core she'd roll her eyes.

She sighs heavily, but she does, thankfully, sit. "What?"

"Have you told the father yet?"

Her lips are a flat line. "He denies it's even possible."

I frown. "He—what?"

"He says that it can't be his, and I'm either faking being pregnant to get him to come see me, or that I'm doing this to get money."

I can't help tightening my hands into fists. "What's his name?"

She rolls her eyes. "Ethan, why do you think I hadn't told you that?"

"I hate that guy."

"If he'd been excited and wanted to come date me, would you like him?"

That sets my teeth on edge. "No."

"Well."

I can't help my exhale. "Look, this is what I decided, okay?"

"What did you need to decide?" She shakes her head. "I really don't even know why you wanted to meet me again."

I reach across the table and take her hand. "You don't know why I wanted to meet you?" I squeeze her hand, because it's trembling. "I love you, Beth. That wasn't some line. And pregnant or not, it's still true."

She yanks her hand back, her voice a hiss. "I'm pregnant with someone else's kid, Ethan. My dad has done everything he can to make you hate my entire family—"

"And none of that worked." I cross my arms.

"You're an idiot."

I lean forward, bracing my hands on the table. "You're finally getting it."

She freezes, her face shocked.

And then she laughs. Loudly.

"There." I smile, too. "That's what I've been trying to do for a very long time. I love you, Beth Ellingson. You're my Juliet. And do you know what Romeo's and Juliet's problem was?"

"Their families?" She smirks. "I'm not a genius, but I remember the play."

I shake my head. "No, not their families. Their real problem was that, when push came to shove, they were too stupid to live. Literally."

She laughs again, and this time, she kind of snort-laughs at the end. She claps a hand over her mouth.

"We aren't that dumb," I say. "Don't take the poison. Take my hand instead. Don't let our families, or our friends, or anyone at all pull us apart. No matter what you decide you want to do, I'm here. I'll help with everything you need. I'll punch that loser, or I'll rub your feet. I'll help put together a crib, or help you look over adoption applications. I'll change diapers, or I'll help you decide if you want siblings for him or her or an only child family. Just, whatever you do, don't give up on *me*. On us. Not yet."

Beth looks at me for a long time. Then she finally speaks. "I need to think about things. Can I do that?"

"Of course," I say. "For as long as you want."

22

BETH

Having piles of crocheted stuff occupy every corner of your house is crazy. Spending all your time and money caring for plants is nearly as bad. I'm aware that both things are true, and yet, I keep coming back here. Dolores Jenkins is really nice, and I think she likes the company.

"You're absolutely awful at this." She laughs.

I mean, she's not wrong. What was supposed to be a tiny stuffed lion looks an awful lot like a melting blob of butter with orange strings puking out of it. "I can't keep the stitch count straight. Can you show me again?"

"I thought anyone could learn," she says. "I know I told you that, but it might not have been true."

"Wow," I say. "One little setback and you give up?"

"It's been two weeks," Dolores says. "And so far, you've failed to make a hat, mittens, a scarf, socks, and this lion."

"Rude," I say. "Do you know what all those have in common?"

"You?" Dolores' lip is twitching.

"And my *teacher*," I say. "Geez."

"I think you're having trouble focusing."

"I'm plenty focused." I narrow my eyes and look at the golden yarn. "So here goes nothing."

Dolores puts her hand on mine. "Didn't you say you have a baby shower to go to?" She glances at the clock. "I really don't think this lion is going to be ready in time, even if you miraculously figure things out."

I swallow.

"I mean, far be it from me to shoo you off when I never have company, but I'd hate to think you were avoiding going because you can't decide what to tell a certain someone who will be there."

Even the thought of Ethan makes me nervous.

"You like him." Dolores looks so dang smug. "An awful lot."

"But—"

"No. Even I'm tired of hearing you say that he's too good for you. Just go to the shower and tell him you'd like to date."

"He'll want to know what I'm doing about the baby, and I don't know yet."

I've made my mind up a dozen times.

I've decided to keep it. And then the next morning, I'll wake up in a cold sweat, terrified. Then I decide I should probably put it up for adoption. That feels right. It feels smart. It feels safer. And then before I go to bed, I'll think about whether it's a boy or girl, and I'll wonder, and I'll think about how tiny his or her hands will be, and I'll decide I need to keep it.

Lather.

Rinse.

Repeat.

Repeat.

Repeat.

I have no idea what to tell Ethan that I want to do, so I have no idea what to say at all. Which means that I've continued to avoid talking to him. I do look at his photo every night and wish that this baby would have his eyes. Or his smile. Or his hair. Or his mouth.

It's strange that I care so much about someone I've never even dated. He's the only person who knows I'm pregnant, except Dolores.

"I think he said he'd stand by your side no matter what you decided," Dolores says. "Didn't he?"

I nod.

"Then you don't need to know what you're doing with the baby. You just need to know what you want to do with him."

The 'do with him' part sounds almost. . .naughty. And it makes me think thoughts I should not be thinking, which makes me blush, which makes Dolores smile.

"Go to the baby shower," she says. "Because we both know what you want to tell him." She leans closer. "Just do it. You've tried telling him to stay away, and it never worked. For once, believe what he's saying. It's not about what *you* think about you. It's what *he* thinks about you that matters."

I realize that she's right.

All this time, I've been thinking that somehow I tricked him. That one day he'll wake up and realize I'm a disaster, and then I'll be more wrecked because I've come to rely on him. But I can't live my life not doing things because I'm afraid. If I have a baby of my own, I'd tell them to do the opposite of what I've been doing.

"Okay." I stand up. "I'll let you know how it goes."

"If you're busy after tomorrow, too busy to come by, I'll understand." I've gotten to know her well enough to know that's true, but I also know she'd be sad. It was a strange twist of fate that brought Dolores Jenkins into my life. Frankly, meeting Ethan was weird too. On that first day we met, it was literally so that my aunt could spy on them and my dad could steal from them. And yet, here we are.

I met Ethan at my family's worst, and he loves me.

I met Dolores at my personal low point, and now she's a dear friend. A bizarre friend, but a friend nonetheless.

"Ooh, wait," she says. "Take this with you." She presses another baby blanket into my hands. It's a soft blue with white fluffy clouds and tiny gold stars.

"You already gave me several blankets," I say.

"Those were my nicest ones," Dolores says, "so I figured you might want to keep them if, you know, well." Her face is almost embarrassed. "But you need something for the baby shower, don't you?"

The shower that's for the guy I like's *mother*? For, well, maybe for my future brother-in-law? Ohmygosh. That baby could be my brother-in-law, and if Ethan and I got married, our babies would be almost the same age. It's so weird. "Um, yes. I need something amazing."

Dolores spins around and grabs something else.

"What's that?"

She shrugs. "Something amazing?" She sets the tiniest blue booties and hat that match the blanket right on top of it, and then she grabs some teensy mittens, too. All three things are the same color as the blue of the blanket, but they're made of a yarn so fine that it almost looks like they're a store-bought knit and not hand crocheted at all. It's all so cute, it makes my insides hurt.

"But will a baby that small really need mittens? I doubt they'll take it outside in the snow."

Dolores' smile is a little self-satisfied. "They're to keep the baby from scratching its face."

Babies scratch their own faces? Why? "Oh."

"Trust me," she says. "It's a decent gift."

"Thank you," I say. "I really appreciate it. Truly."

"I hope tomorrow goes really well for you." I can tell she means it, and I feel at peace for the first time in two weeks.

I wish I could hold on to that feeling, because the next morning, I'm a ball of anxiety. I put on pants and a shirt. Then I take that off and try a dress. But I feel like I can see a bulge. I chuck it in the corner. But I'm wasting too much time. I throw my sweats back on and do my makeup as carefully as I can.

I can't wear too much, or I'll look like a clown. Or worse, a prostitute.

I've never been this nervous while getting ready for anything.

Why?

It's not Ethan. He seems to like me any which way.

It's his mother.

I'm going to see him at her big event. The event where the entire town, it feels, is welcoming her new *baby*. You know, the thing that's growing inside of me that no one knows about? The thing that I shouldn't have, seeing as I'm eighteen, single, and barely able to pay my bills while sponging off my aunt?

Ugh.

I change three more times, and I'm sweating like a pig from all the anxiety and the clothing changes, but finally I settle on a blue and white sundress. It's one my mom bought for herself, but it was a bit too small for her, which means it came to me. It didn't really fit me either, but my boobs are bigger now, thank you baby, and it looks just right.

I hear a lot of talking going on outside, so I figure they're probably almost ready to leave. When I crack my door, I hear a lot of laughter. "What's going on?" I peek around the corner.

Aiden, Will, and Donna's faces all swivel toward mine.

"Do you think this will work?" I smooth my dress down as I step out into the open. I'm nervous even asking them. It's not something I usually do, solicit feedback on my clothing, and I can't think the last time I wore a dress. It's not like I wear one to run a tour on a fishing boat where I'm snapping photos of men holding fish. Because of the wind, I never wear anything but pants or shorts.

"Whoa," Will says. "Who are you trying to impress?"

Oh, no. He's going to figure it out. And if sweet but clueless Will has figured it out. . . "Shut up." I duck back into my room. Do I change? I could wear the—*no, Beth, no*—I grab the gift bag and force myself back outside. I picked this dress for a reason. Today is an important day, and everyone will be dressed their best. Probably.

"What's that about?" Aunt Donna asks on the other side of the door.

"She clearly likes someone," Will says. "No way a teenager takes that much time to get ready unless she's after a guy."

I need to distract them. Maybe a joke. "Or a girl."

"Except you're not gay," Aunt Donna says.

Okay, I just need to get moving before I decide to skip the whole shower entirely. Dolores is right, though. I may not know what to say exactly, but I need to give Ethan some kind of answer. I'm not being fair to him. I hold my gift bag in front of me like a shield. "I'm not."

Unfortunately, it attracts too much attention. "What's that?" Aunt Donna's looking at me like I'm a chubby mouse and she's a starved barn cat.

I decide to hide it behind my dress, because there's no good way for me to explain how I got this blanket. "It's a baby shower. I have to take a gift."

"I know."

Why did my simple statement make Aunt Donna look like an advertisement for people who need Prozac? She's grinning so much she looks entirely bonkers.

"You can have our gift," Aiden says, "to keep for yourself, if we can put our name on yours."

Their gift? What's he talking about? Why would they want to put their name on my gift? And if they do, I have to tell them what it is, and then I have to answer questions about how I got it.

Ugh.

"Yes, what he said," Aunt Donna says. "Look how *cute* our gift is. Will said it looked like a baby Tasmanian devil." She does some weird thing with her hands that might be a reference to a really old movie or something? Once I stop trying to figure out what she's doing, I notice what she's holding.

I can't tell what it is, exactly, but it's not cute. "What in the world is that?" I lean closer, hoping I can figure out what it is, but now that I'm closer, the face is even uglier. It's creepier than the weird dolls my grandma collects. Its face freaks me out and without thinking, I flick it away. The bizarre blue blob somersaults across the table and lands right in front of the trash can. "Quick. Someone shove it in there and tie the bag." Then maybe I'll still be able to go to sleep tonight.

"If we feed it after midnight, we'll all be in trouble," Will says. "Or if it gets wet, right?"

"Shut up," Aunt Donna says. "What did you get that's so much better, anyway?"

"Literally anything would be better than that," I say. But that feels kind of mean. Seriously, though, what was she thinking? She's usually so competent. "I can't believe you bought a little stuffed animal."

"It's not the only thing I bought, but it's the only thing that arrived."

"Still, what were you thinking?" I can't help shaking my head.

"The ad for it confused me," Aunt Donna says. "The kids playing with it were having so much fun."

"With *that*?" I can't even imagine anyone playing with it. What do you do with it? Chuck it at other kids' heads?

"It didn't look like that in the ad," Aunt Donna says. "But stop changing the subject. What's your gift?"

Oh, no. We're back on that? I thought we'd successfully changed gears. "No way."

"Those crooks on Amazon charged me thirty dollars for that monstrosity," Aunt Donna says, circling toward me like a cheetah.

"Oh, man," Will says. "I can't believe you paid thirty bucks for that." He's not being weird, at least. He sits down on the sofa and crosses his arms. "If we don't have a gift, then I'm not going either."

"I also bought a box of diapers." Aunt Donna points at a relatively small pack of diapers. "But I don't see you with anything, so don't blame this all on me."

"I'm a guy. It's a given that my date's going to pick out a gift for us both. If you want cash, I'm always happy to contribute."

I see my window and try to take it. I have a car. I don't have to go with them. I slide back quietly, and I'm about to duck into my room when. . .

"Where are you going, Beth?" Stupid Aiden and his big mouth.

"She's trying to hide." Aunt Donna takes another step in my direction. "Just tell us what's in the bag, Beth." She starts moving faster.

I do what anyone would do. I move away from

the person who's almost chasing me now. "What are you going to do about it?"

My aunt calls in the big guns. "Will."

He hops up like a well-trained golden retriever, and pretty soon they're all chasing me like I'm the last iPad at Target on Black Friday. I can *not* explain why I don't want to cut them in. Aunt Donna's being a total lunatic, but my heart's racing so fast I can't think. Aiden's acting like we're on an Easter egg hunt, and Will looks like he'd be happy to take any exit off this freeway to Crazy Town.

"Just show me," Aunt Donna finally wheezes. "Holding it up is stupid. It's basically eye level for Will, right?"

Will sees his chance and shifts to his tiptoes immediately, eyeing my bag from which all the tissue has jumped ship. "It's a blanket!"

For some reason Aunt Donna looks even more agitated. "But you can't knit!"

"It's definitely a blanket," Will says. "And a cute one, too. Blue clouds with little gold stars in between them."

She starts gesturing at me like she's playing Pictionary. Or she's trying to communicate with apes at the zoo. "Where'd you get that?"

"You know that rose lady?" If I say her name, they'll *really* think it's odd.

"Dolores Jenkins?"

Will's eyes widen. "But she hates everyone."

"She likes Amanda." I remember her saying Amanda Brooks was too good for Eddy Dutton. I thought it was weird, since most people think the opposite. "And she likes me."

"No way she made you a blanket," Will says.

"She loves to crochet, not knit," I can't help explaining. Oh, no. Now they're really looking at me strangely. Time to make up a story. "Um. So, last year, I helped her cover her roses before the first freeze. She said she owed me one." There, that seems believable. You have to cover roses, right?

"It's mine," Aunt Donna shouts, like she's been possessed by the spirit of her weird blue frog devil. "You're going down, you little freeloader."

The only way out is through. Someone said that once, so when I get close this time, I break for the door.

Aunt Donna doesn't chase me, thankfully. It would have been nice to show up at the shower in some kind of pack so I might have a chance of blending in, but I really can't have Aunt Donna poking around for more details about Dolores Jenkins or why she'd make me a blanket. It's not fair to Dolores, and we're not at the stage of our friendship yet where I know how well she stands up to torture, so. . . It's just better all around to avoid any interrogation.

The whole way there, I think about what I'm going to say when I see Ethan. I'm not totally sure exactly how things will go, but I have the basics of a little speech all strung together when I pull in and park, and then I see a line of ponies in rainbow-colored blankets prancing past my car, and every thought in my head shoots out my window.

Where am I?

I actually pull the invite out of my purse to check. I thought it said the Gorge, but maybe I misread it somehow. But no, the invitation is clear. I'm correct on the time and the location, so why is there—an elephant thunders past me, his enormous feet slamming into the ground like the strike of timpani drums.

What on earth is going on?

But then I see something even more amazing than the ponies, than an elephant, than dancing dogs. I see Ethan, who must have seen my car, nearly jogging toward me, grinning the biggest grin I've ever seen. He's so beautiful, and seeing him brings me so much joy that I practically leap out of my car.

And I realize that's my answer. Isn't it? I spent an hour picking an outfit because I wanted his mother to like me. His face lights up my world like the Fourth of July. Even if this crashes and burns spectacularly, I have to at least try.

So what if our timing has never been right?

So what if no one else understands?

So what if I'm literally pregnant with someone else's kid?

If he doesn't mind, I should stop minding on his behalf. I fling my door open and jump out. Before he can say anything, I gush about the animals and the circus and the crazy, insane display of celebration that is apparently the norm for his family. And then Ethan gets closer and I can't help myself. I open my mouth to speak.

But he cuts me off. "I know what I said before was a lot." He looks so intense. "I always come on a little too strong, but my mom pointed out that we've never really dated, and I want to. Maybe it'll help you decide what to do with. . ." He looks around. "The situation. Or maybe not. But either way, I want to date you. I want to hold your hand. I want to hug you every day."

I look at my tall, sweet, handsome, charming, kind, generous friend Ethan, with his broad shoulders and his wide open heart, and I say, "You can. Let's do it."

His eyes widen, and then he blinks slowly, like a computer rebooting.

So I open my arms and I wrap them around him, and I hug him tightly. I don't ever want to let go, but there are people *everywhere*, and so finally, I do.

"I still can't believe this is a baby shower," I whisper.

"My Aunt Helen's something else," Ethan says.

"Your whole family is spectacular," I say. "So I guess I shouldn't be surprised."

"Yeah, but she's next level," he says.

"I think she fits right in." Unlike me.

Ethan strolls toward the entrance right next to me, until, right before we reach the sign, he slides his hand around and takes mine. My heart does a somersault that would make that little blue frog devil proud. It feels like I've been waiting my whole life for this moment.

"Can we talk for a second before we go inside?" His fingers, laced through mine, pull back gently. "It's going to be loud in there."

"Okay," I say. "Did you change your mind?" Because I might die if he did. But he doesn't *look* upset or stressed.

"Not at all." He bites his lip in a deliciously boyish way. "I just wanted to say something."

"Go ahead."

He tugs us around a corner and to the side of the main tent. There are people streaming past, but we're sheltered from their view and hearing. "At first,

I waited every minute, every hour, and every day to hear from you. But the more time that passed from when I told you I wanted to date you and when I promised I'd stand by your side, the more likely a negative response seemed."

"I'm sorry, but—"

He presses one finger to my mouth, and a little thrill runs up my spine. I'd almost forgotten the feeling entirely. I kind of want to nip at his finger, but it feels. . .inappropriate somehow, so I don't.

"In anticipation of being turned down again, I came up with a little speech. And now that you haven't turned me down, I guess I don't want it to go to waste."

"I like your speeches." I can't help my smile.

"Well, then prepare to be dazzled." Ethan looks down at his feet, embarrassed? Is he?

"I'm not teasing," I say. "I really do like them."

He looks up. "I learned something on the day my dad died." He coughs. "That doesn't sound like I thought it would. It sounds, I don't know, kind of dire or something. But that was probably one of my darkest days, and I was dreading going into that building. I was scared, and I was lonely. It felt like no one else in the world would ever understand me like my dad did. And I was really broken. It felt like I'd never be whole or happy again."

I hug him, then, pressing my face against his chest. I breathe him in, and I hope he can tell how sorry I am that he went through all of that.

"Beth."

I back up enough to look at his face, but he keeps me close. "My mom held my hand that day, and she hugged me, and she smiled through her tears. I learned that no matter how scary the thing that you're facing is, no matter how sad, no matter how hard, it's better if you're facing it with someone you love and trust."

Oh.

"I know that your future has some big question marks, and I know that you'll make the very best decisions that you can. No one can predict the future, and I can't promise anything except that I will stand by your side and make the scary things less lonely as long as I possibly can."

I'm not sure how long I hug him after that. It's not hot. It's not passionate. It's comforting, and that's exactly what I need. As we walk into the big striped tent, ready to celebrate someone who's having a baby they want, a baby they're going to keep, a baby who is half the mother and half the father's DNA, I think about how profoundly the Brooks families have affected Manila in the last two years. They came in like a whirlwind, but they settled in like the support beams we didn't know we needed.

Ever since I got the positive pregnancy test, I've hovered somewhere between wet-your-pants and heart-stops-dead levels of fear. But for the first time since that afternoon, I feel calm. I feel safe. I feel. . .ready to face an uncertain future. Because I'm not alone, and I trust that Ethan will stay by my side till the end, no matter what ending we write together.

And when life hits you with a surprise, that makes all the difference.

. . .

*** I hope you enjoyed The Surprise as much as I enjoyed writing it. It began as an idea for a novella, and then as I plotted, I realized that it HAD to come before The Setback, and that it HAD to be read—and it definitely didn't stay novella length. Whoops! I hope it's a happy surprise!

And don't worry. The parts of the story that feel a touch unresolved (for me) will be addressed in the The Setback! The plots started to overlap! I'm off to work on it right now. And if you haven't grabbed it yet, you'll want to go get The Setback now.

But what if you've already preordered the last book in The Birch Creek Ranch Series and you want to know what to read next? Have you checked out my Finding Home Series (a complete, 9 book series) starting with Finding Grace? If not, check that out now.

But if you have already, can I recommend you try Seed Money next? It's the first book in my new Scarsdale Fosters series, a standalone romantic women's fiction series that will follow the family of foster kids that the couple in Seed Money raise as their own.

ACKNOWLEDGMENTS

To my readers, THANK YOU. You guys are my heart and soul and the reason I do this at all. I'm sorry for the pain I inflict on your favorite characters.

Actually, I'm not really sorry.

But I *wish* I was sorry. I feel like I should get credit for that. I really do love interacting with you all in the FB group and on my page. The extrovert at my core appreciates that most of all. Thank you for loving my stories almost as much as I do.

Thank you to my husband. He's patient. He's long-suffering (even when I say for the 907th time, "this book is no good!" he pats my head and says, "you say that every time, and they're always solidly mediocre. Don't worry. This one will be, too.") I love you. Thank you for inspiring all the amazing men I write, so I can keep writing romance people want to read.

Thank you to my mother. She's unfailingly supportive in both writing and on the home front.

There's no one else I would ever choose but you as a mother, an example, or a friend.

Thank you to my mass of children for inspiring the kids in the Birch Creek Ranch. You help me keep them all straight, because I shamelessly copied your personalities. And you're all so supportive of my writing, including reading and cheering for the people I make up, especially the ones who resemble you. Your excitement means a lot.

And thanks to my palomino darling, Leo, for missing out on several rides with me while I wrote this frantically as a surprise for my fans. You and I are both fatter as a result of it, but people will read it for years to come. I think it was worth it.

ABOUT THE AUTHOR

I have animals coming out of my ears. Seven horses. Three dogs, three cats, thirty-ish chickens. I'm always doctoring or playing with an animal... and I wouldn't want it any other way. But Leo (my palomino) is still my very favorite.

When I'm not with animals, or even if I am, I'm likely to have at least one of my five kids in tow, two of which I'm currently homeschooling.

My hubby is the reason all this glorious madness is possible. He's the best parts of all the amazing men I write (although he's bald and his six pack sometimes goes into hiding because of cookies.)

I also love to bake, like to cook, and feel amazing when I find time to kickbox, lift weights, or rollerblade. Oh yeah, and I'm a lawyer, but I try to forget that whenever I can.

I adore my husband, and I love my God.

The rest is just details.

PS— I'm active on social media and have a face-book group I comment in often. (My husband even gets on there sometimes, but his sense of humor is strange. You've been warned.) Please feel free to join me here: https://www.facebook.com/groups/750807222376182

ALSO BY B. E. BAKER

Yuck! What's for Dinner?

**I also write contemporary fantasy and end of the
world books under Bridget E. Baker.**

The Russian Witch's Curse:

My Queendom for a Horse

My Dark Horse Prince

My High Horse Czar

The Magical Misfits Series:

Mates: Minerva (1)

Mates: Xander (2)

The Birthright Series:

Displaced (1)

unForgiven (2)

Disillusioned (3)

misUnderstood (4)

Disavowed (5)

unRepentant (6)

Destroyed (7)

The Birthright Series Collection, Books 1-3

The Anchored Series:

Anchored (1)

Adrift (2)

Awoken (3)

Capsized (4)

The Sins of Our Ancestors Series:

Marked (1)

Suppressed (2)

Redeemed (3)

Renounced (4)

Reclaimed (5) a novella!

A stand alone YA romantic suspense:

Already Gone

Made in United States
Troutdale, OR
12/09/2023

15492720R00192